DOWN TO A SCIENCE

CONTENT WARNING:

This book contains graphic sexual content and
on-page depictions of anxiety, as well as minor
homophobia from a parent, a tense/toxic mother-
daughter relationship, a parent in a non-fatal car
accident, alcohol consumption, and references to past
emotional abuse by a romantic partner

Down to a Science

A NOVEL

KAT PAIGE

First Paperback edition February 2025

ISBN 979-8-9901182-2-5
ISBN 979-8-9901182-3-2 (ebook)

For my aunt, who didn't get to witness how much the world has grown. Though there is still so much growing to be done, I hope this book can be a healthy seed in a forest of love, acceptance, and pride.

Down to a Science

CHAPTER ONE
Rachel

Swimming across the Atlantic Ocean isn't difficult, right? Because that's the only way I can afford to go home.

I moved to Edinburgh, Scotland about a week ago, but as of today I am officially living alone in a foreign country. During that initial week, my best friend and brother were with me. Now, they're not. Though they left right on schedule, their departure was sudden because I failed to factor in how much faster time moves when you'd rather it stay completely still.

My fingers drum on my stomach as I mentally go through the list of what I need to do before the start of my doctoral program at Heriot-Watt University, where I hope to earn my Ph.D. in Marine Biodiversity. This task list is growing by the second, but I believe everything will have to wait until I obtain that important little thing called *motivation*. Motivation is an abstract concept, so I remain where I am: splayed across the floor of my brand-new apartment staring at a popcorn ceiling.

One, two, three…

I force myself to stop counting the ceiling bumps at fifty-two.

My task list rushes back to the front of my mind. Number one:

tables. I don't own a single table. I recognize my personal need for tables and I possess the ability to acquire multiple types of tables, and yet, not one. No kitchen table, coffee table, or even a nightstand. Beyond fixing my distinct lack of tables, I have to finish unpacking, go to the grocery store, and buy pens. I own no pens. Like seven notebooks, but no pens. Or pencils. Not a writing utensil in sight. I guess I figured I wouldn't use them because I have no tables and a flat surface is needed to write.

Though, I will have a flat surface in the lab. I wonder if they have extra pens there?

No, I should buy my own pens.

My stomach growls loudly, rumbling inside of me. *Damn it.* I force myself upward, slouching over my bent knees. My body immediately screams to once again be vertical. I *need* to go to the grocery store. There is no food in my fridge and, in this time of existence, food is a necessary part of survival.

I get my feet under me and place my hands flat on my lower back to bend and stretch, creaking and cracking like a woman in her late twenties who spent the last hour lying on the floor. I find my sneakers discarded by the front door and slip them on. Then, I grab my gray ball cap to hide my mess of hair and am out the door.

As I walk the uneven sidewalks, I blow out a rush of air, hoping my swirling thoughts will rush out as well. When I applied for this program last year, it was a dream—that's all. I didn't think I would choose Heriot-Watt as my school, but a gut feeling got to me. This was a chance I needed to jump at.

It's like my best friend Piper keeps saying: "Scotland!" But she's not beside me to say "Scotland!" anymore so now it's just "Scotland." No, no. It's still at least "*Scotland*" even if it's not "Scotland!"

Now, my guts are all over the place. I need to learn to stop trusting my gut. The gut feeling I had when I chose Heriot-Watt has faded, and now here I am—gutless. Or rather, gut-*feeling*-less.

Okay. "Gut" no longer sounds like a word.

Once I arrive at the store, I amble through the fluorescent aisles, hunting for food I like. I didn't make a list. I want to learn what types of food this store stocks so I can plan recipes based on that. Standard items in the U.S. are not always standard items in the U.K. Like, why is peanut butter so hard to find and ranch non-existent? I need to ask Piper to start sending me ranch as gifts. There is this restaurant back in St. Louis called Twisted Ranch that has incorporated ranch dressing into everything on their menu, and they have twenty different types of ranch for dipping sauces and more, and I miss them. When will I be able to go again? I don't think I considered how much I would miss ranch when I chose to move here.

I readjust my hands on the shopping cart to mimic the readjustment of my spiraling brain. I'm fine. I'm okay here. I only wish my start date was sooner. That's all. My program doesn't begin for another week and until I have my research to focus on, all I can focus on is the absence of what I have always known.

As I'm picking through the apples, trying to find one without a single blemish, a laugh pricks my ears. A familiar laugh.

Oh no.

Isla. That was Isla's laugh.

Isla and I met on my first day in Edinburgh. It was a wonderful day. Until it wasn't. I didn't think I would ever see her again.

My eyes dart around the produce section, searching for curly black hair until I find her handling a melon and chatting with an employee. *Flirting* with an employee, I should say. The words, "You do seem to be a melon expert," exit her mouth.

"Crap." I tug my cart with me as I duck to the ground, hiding behind the apple display. This is not good. Why is this happening? Why is she everywhere? *Oh my god.* I'm hiding. This is *not* good. Why am I hiding? I should be running.

Before I can force myself to move, a throat clears behind me. I pop up so quickly that I knock the lip of my hat against the basket handle, making me stumble down before I straighten. I adjust my hat with a grumble and say, "Isla. Hi."

She's wearing the same burgundy lipstick she wore when I met her. I wish I didn't remember, but that lipstick was smeared on my skin by the night's end. I'll remember that color for the rest of my life.

"You alright?"

I look at her blankly, my brain taking too long to compute. "Are you asking if I'm alright because I bumped my head or in the hey-how-are-you way?"

The corner of her mouth perks in her standard crooked smile. "Both, I suppose."

I don't smile back. "Fine to both, then." I assess her cautiously. "This is a city of five hundred thousand people. The number of times I've unexpectedly run into you is highly improbable."

Edinburgh feels incredibly small. Claustrophobic.

Isla reaches across me to snatch an apple, and a heavy whiff of cinnamon hits my nostrils. *Shit.*

"If you're asking if I'm stalking you, the answer is no. I'm just lucky." She tosses the apple in the air, catching it in her hand before taking a bite.

I narrow my eyes. "Don't you have to pay for that?"

Her throat moves as she swallows. "I will." She studies my face slowly, then unexpectedly reaches for me. I flinch away. Her hand drops as she explains with a gesture toward my cheek, "Eyelash."

"Oh." I swipe at my face and, thankfully, manage to rid myself of the rogue eyelash.

"You need to learn to keep those eyelashes in check," she says, her voice low and dark eyes focused heavily on me.

"You need to learn to stop reaching for strangers' faces," I say flatly. Her expression drops and my gut twists, but I try not to dwell on that feeling as I raise my chin. "I have to go. See you around, I guess."

"See you!" she calls after me as I sprint into another aisle.

I skid my cart to a stop when I'm out of sight, groaning as silently as I can manage. That ridiculous eyelash thing. That ridiculous, adorable eyelash thing. I *do* need to keep my eyelashes in check. I am trying to move on. I'm trying to forget, but I can't seem to avoid her. Unwanted random run-ins need to be factored into each of my days.

When I last saw Isla, she explained her side of what happened between us that night as though it would make it better. It made it worse. Before, I still hoped to fix this. Now, it's clear that we do not know each other, and I am no longer interested in changing that. All of the leftover hurt trickles through me, here in the bread aisle. I force those feelings away.

I push my cart slowly until I am between two endcaps, peeking both ways before I exit and turn into a new aisle.

Hey! Pens! I grab a pack to finish up my shopping.

I don't see Isla again.

When I arrive home, I unpack my groceries, cook myself dinner, and spend the rest of the evening alone. As I do all of this, I do not think about the beautiful Scottish woman who managed to turn my world upside down over the course of one day.

CHAPTER TWO
One Week Ago
Rachel

I'm smiling too widely. The corners of my mouth move downward and stretch outward. Okay—now I look constipated. I turn away from the bathroom mirror to shake my entire body out, wiggling from head to toe before doing a spinning jump back to the mirror, throwing out a smile. There. That one looks natural.

Though, that little jig may come across as strange. I groan and drop forward with my forehead pressed against the mirror. This is useless. The way I smile at my school orientation will not make or break my career. Hopefully. I pick my head back up and use a tissue to wipe away the imprint of makeup I left behind.

I don't even know why I'm wearing makeup. I usually don't, beyond simple mascara (my eyelashes are a translucent blonde). It's not that I have anything against makeup, it's that I feel like a child in face paint whenever I attempt to wear it. I don't know why I thought I needed makeup to make a good first impression, but here we are. The insecurity struck, so the makeup is on. The desire to wash my face and start from scratch nips at me, but I decide against it. I don't have time.

I had a plan this morning: wake up early, take a nice long shower, and go over my research proposal.

However, I did not wake up early. I woke up at 8 a.m., an hour and a half after I planned. I took a quick shower, forgoing the washing of my hair. Any time left to go over my research plans was wasted by my smile practicing.

Piper would tell me that I do not need to practice my smile and that any smile I give will be perfect. I hear her words in my head and try to believe them. I wish she were here with me this morning to talk me down.

It's okay that she's not. She and my brother Nick are out having what I hope will be a great day on the Jacobite train, traveling from Fort William to Mallaig.

I check my watch. If I leave right now, I'll have time to stop for a tea before I catch my bus to Heriot-Watt University.

I exit the bathroom, snatch my bag and blazer from where I'd tossed them on the couch, and am out the door. We are staying in a ground-floor rental flat until I get my hands on the keys to my new semi-permanent flat in a few days. The hallway is dark and concrete, covered in miscellaneous building materials like wooden planks and paint cans that I carefully step around. I push open the crooked front door and out into the tepid morning.

We are staying in the Haymarket area of Edinburgh, which I like. It is close to where my apartment will be, so I'm trying to learn the neighborhood. Right now, I'm headed to a café I spotted yesterday when we got off the tram from the airport. My phone is clutched in my hand, and I have a map pulled up as I attempt to navigate the streets of my home for the next three years.

As I halt at a crosswalk, my stomach churns. Hunger and nausea consume me, but I don't know if the nausea is from lack of food or nervousness. Perhaps both.

Once I can cross, I merge onto a more populated road.

School responsibilities weren't supposed to start yet. I was supposed to have two whole weeks before any kind of anything related to my program. But now, here I am, on my way to an orientation after being in this country for less than twenty-four hours. I am ready to chicken out.

Once I make it to the café, I order an English breakfast tea with milk and sugar, take it from the barista at the end of the wooden bar, turn to leave—and nearly slam into the woman entering.

"Oh my god," I say, clutching the tea to my chest, thankful that only a splash exited the small hole at the top of the cup. "I'm so sorry."

"No bother, love." She throws me half a smile, and I can't take my eyes away.

She is very pretty, standing a couple of inches taller than me with light brown skin and gorgeous dark brown eyes. Her black hair is curly, one half pinned back to expose an ear lined in silver hoops. Dark burgundy paints her lips, matching the burgundy eyeliner shooting sharply from her eye.

She attempts to walk away but I can't stop myself from asking, "I didn't spill anything on you?"

She looks at me full-on and says, "No. I'm perfectly dry." Her eyes narrow as she takes a step forward, reaching toward my face. Eyes wide, I flinch away from her outstretched hand. She explains mildly, "You've an eyelash on your cheek." I tense as she plucks it off and displays the lash on her close-cut, manicured finger. It's bumpy, coated in brown mascara.

"Thanks," I say, eyeing the lash. "I suppose I need to make a wish now?"

"Hmm?"

My face burns as I avoid her eye. I'm making this interaction weird, aren't I? I'm always doing that. "Is wishing on eyelashes not a thing here?"

She smiles easily. "No, no. We do that here." My eyelash is perfectly balanced on her finger as she brings it closer to my lips. A hint of a tattoo is peeking out the sleeve of her black, oversized button-down and I feel the wild temptation to roll that sleeve up to examine it. "Give us a blow."

My face is on fire. I'm sure I resemble a tomato. My tongue skims my bottom lip before I gently purse my mouth, closing my eyes and thinking to myself, *I wish for a reason to call this place home.* I blow.

When I open my eyes, the woman is watching me. "Wish for something nice?"

"I hope so." I stare back at her for a beat too long before I jerk myself out of it. I'm going to be late. "Uh." I laugh awkwardly. "Thanks. I have to get leaving. Get going. Um, bye."

She chuckles and lifts a hand in a lazy wave. "Bye."

I run out of the café. *Oh my god.* She is so pretty. My face is still flaming. People on the street probably think I'm coming off of a marathon based on how I am literally heaving.

Should I have asked for her number? Or at least her name?

I am so bad at this. But then again, of course I am. I'm a bisexual twenty-seven-year-old woman who has never even kissed a woman, so what the hell do I know about anything?

I shake my head, shaking myself out of it, leaving no time to dwell on another item to add to my list of missed opportunities. I need to find my bus.

...

I walk the ten minutes from where the bus dropped me off to a collection of monotone academic buildings. I'm searching for the

William Perkin Building where I am to meet my supervisor in their office on the second floor. When the buildings start to thin, I realize I have made a slight wrong turn. My watch warns me that I'm cutting it close, but I'll be fine to do a quick loop. I take a left up a hill in between two buildings, then another left. That's when I spot the blue sign marking the building. After cutting through a parking lot, I thrust open the glass front doors and find a staircase to the second floor.

I don't see Dr. Andonov's office. I do another loop, stopping in front of every door to make sure I don't see them inside. They are nowhere to be found. I check my watch again. Now I *am* late.

I scramble for my phone so I can email my advisor. **HELP**, I first type, then think better of it. I start over.

> **TO:** Naila Zgheib
> **FROM:** Rachel Moreau
> **SUBJECT:** Re: Orientation with Dr. Andonov
>
> Hi Professor Zgheib,
>
> I'm having trouble locating Dr. Andonov's office. I am in the William Perkin Building on the second floor, but cannot find it. I am sure I'm missing it, but could you please let me know which side of the building it's on?
>
> Thanks!
> Rachel Moreau

I anxiously pace while I await her reply. Five minutes pass.

> **TO:** Rachel Moreau
> **FROM:** Naila Zgheib
> **SUBJECT:** Re: Orientation with Dr. Andonov
>
> I believe you're on the wrong floor. 2nd floor in the UK is equivalent to the 3rd floor in the US. Go up a flight.
>
> -Z

"That makes no sense," I mutter aloud, running for the stairs.

I sprint around the second floor, which is actually the third floor, of the building and skid to a stop in front of Dr. Andonov's office. A lean person wearing a light-weight black sweater is behind the desk, typing furiously on a keyboard.

"I am so sorry I'm late," I heave, my face surely the color of a tomato…again. I attempt to give a normal smile—and fail stupendously.

Dr. Andonov looks up from their computer, blue eyes hard. "Ah, yes, you are, aren't you? It's fine. Please sit."

I take a seat in a black plastic chair in front of their desk and let my orientation begin.

Dr. Andonov starts with a rather difficult question. "So, Miss Moreau, why Heriot-Watt?"

I swallow. My brain says, *Um, Scotland?* but I know that is not the correct answer. I am an academic. I picked Heriot-Watt for reasons beyond the country it is located in. Like the fact that it's new and different and I will learn so much here.

"The proximity to all the different bodies of water was a huge decision maker," I end up saying. "The variety of locations to gather samples for my initial attempts to hone in my research will be useful. Along with the high quality of the program and the standard the university holds its students to."

Dr. Andonov smiles. I gave the right answer. "Ah, yes. I agree. So, your focus is on the effects of microplastics on marine organisms. Do you know if you are going to stay broad or focus on a more specific group, say microorganisms or mammals?"

"That's a good question. I do find the effects of microplastics on microorganisms especially interesting because of their role in marine ecosystems," I answer. My head calms as I begin to explain additional reasons why I chose Heriot-Watt and the preferred direction of my research.

Dr. Andonov asks me several more questions and then explains their research and how it aligns with my plans. They then take me on a tour of the building. Dr. Andonov's office is on the second-actually-third floor, but the labs where I'll be spending most of my time are in the basement (or "lower level," to make it sound less dingy). My pace is set at 1.5 speed to keep up with their long strides.

"Are there many students here over the summer?" I ask, scanning the empty halls as we hasten past darkened labs and meeting rooms. The rooms that have windows only have small rectangular windows stationed near the ceiling.

"This year, not any in this department. You're bound to find some in other departments, but you're going to be on your own in these labs until September, I'm afraid."

That's actually how I prefer it. "That'll be fine. However, I'm excited to meet fellow students in September. Grow my community and all that."

We pause in front of the elevator and Dr. Andonov gives me a long look. "Community is important in both an academic setting and in one's personal life. I must ask, Miss Moreau, do you know anyone in Edinburgh?"

"Yes," I answer automatically.

They smile kindly. "Beyond myself and Professor Zgheib."

"Oh, then, no." I am going to be completely alone. I like being alone, but there is a fine line between being alone and being lonely. But I've done this whole new school, new people thing before. I can do it again. "I've been here for about a day, though, so give me time."

Dr. Andonov's eyebrows shoot up. "A day?"

"My flight got in at noon yesterday."

"Oh my goodness. Zgheib did not mention you had only just arrived. I must apologize for not giving you time to settle."

I shake my head. "It's fine. I'm happy to jump right in."

"Well, I do think I should give you time to get over your jet lag, at the very least. I think I've covered all I need to." They check their watch as the elevator dings and the doors open. "I've held you hostage for long enough. Enjoy the rest of your day, or get some rest. I'll be gone for the next month on a research trip, but Zgheib will be here to welcome you on your first day."

They bid me a final farewell as we reach the ground floor, so I thank them and am on my way.

Before heading back to the rental flat, I give myself a solo tour of campus that doesn't amount to much. A lot of the buildings are closed. Afterward, I find the bus to Haymarket, feeling both pleased with the success of my orientation and terrified of the looming solitude that will overtake me once Nick and Piper head back to the States.

CHAPTER THREE
Isla

The sun is an infrequent patron of Edinburgh, so I am always happy to see her. The bright rays warm my skin as I hop off the tram at Princes Street, overly caffeinated and perpetually knackered. To last my day, I need to push through the exhaustion and lean on the caffeine.

I'm a tour guide with Scotland Expeditions where I lead various tours around the city of Edinburgh. As I walk to Edinburgh Castle, the starting point for my 11 a.m. tour, I check my lipstick in my phone camera. Looks perfect, as per usual. I love this stuff. To date, the only thing that can smear it is someone else's mouth.

My sleep schedule is never one to marvel at, but I don't think I slept beyond two hours last night. No reason why beyond the constant to-do list chipping away at my brain. The lack of sleep made for a rough wake-up before my 9 a.m. tour.

I switch from my phone camera to the notes app to peek at said to-do list.

- Pick up guitar??
- Call Frank

- o   Snag a 3 p.m. tour
- o   Loan application

Okay. Well, I know one thing that isn't going to receive a tickmark today—the loan application. I should not fill that out when I am not fully rested. As I pause for a car before crossing the street, my eyes fall closed with a small sigh. Maybe I should wait even longer on the application. My brother could get a fire under his arse and agree to go in on this with me.

No, no. I am done waiting for my brother to make up his damn mind about something that affects both our futures. Opening a café was my idea, so I can take full custody of the dream.

A yawn escapes me as I keep walking. Maybe two things won't get done. I'm not sure I can manage another tour. If I'm this fatigued now, I'll be doubly tired by this afternoon. I can operate on very little sleep, but this feels like a trailing-off-in-the-middle-of-a-sentence kind of sleepiness.

The inclined path to the castle seems more steep than usual as I trudge up it with a grumble. I need to get any inkling of a grumpy mood out before I see my tour group. The coffee I gulped down earlier gave me less energy than the flirt with that cute American girl did—though pretty girls always are an energy booster. I will never pass up the opportunity for a flirt.

When I reach the meeting spot, I hold up my little orange flag to signal who I am to my group. It's summer, so the stands are set up on the castle's esplanade for the yearly concert series. The concerts don't start until July, so the stage is not yet built, which gives us still a nice view of the castle.

People slowly start to gather around me. Once the whole roster is accounted for, I do my introductions. My group is small today, five people, and they're quiet. I hate a quiet group. They don't all need to be chatty, but one in the bunch is nice.

"Edinburgh Castle was built in 1103 AD," I say, gesturing to the massive brown, stone structure behind me. "This castle is also one of the most besieged places in all of Europe. Can anyone guess how many times it has been sieged over these past nine hundred years?"

No one says a thing so I answer for them. "Twenty-three times. I know we as a group probably don't have a lot of experience with sieging, but I can assure you that is a lot."

We next descend the hill, and I continue us along the brown, tan, and gray stones decorating the Royal Mile with the spire of St Giles' Cathedral guiding our way. The street is already crowding over for the day, tourists weaving in and out of the endless row of identical souvenir shops and missing all of Old Town's hidden gems. They'll tread over the Heart of Midlothian without a proper spit or get stuck on a set of stairs they could manage to avoid.

Before we make it to St Giles', I tell my group, "The Royal Mile connects the two royal residences of the city—the castle where we were, of course, and Holyrood Palace. And, I'll let you in on a secret, it's more than a mile between the two. It's approximately 1.13 miles long. That would be 1.81 kilometers. It's what we call a Scots mile."

I keep talking and walking until the hour is up.

After I find some lunch, and another cup of coffee, I figure it's as good a time as any to try my luck at retrieving my guitar from the music shop.

There's been no message informing me she's ready, but I have hope and a desperate need to get my hands back on my baby. When I was playing her a few days ago, one of the capstans broke off, snapping the D string with it. I tried to fix it myself but, after much frustration, determined a new capstan was needed. The guitar is old—I found her in a resale shop when I was seventeen—so I wasn't shocked, but bloody annoyed. For my set at a local pub the night before last, I had to borrow an acoustic guitar from a mate of mine. I cocked up a few times because it didn't feel right in my hands. It's smaller than mine and too light. The bigger and heavier the guitar, the better. I'm hoping to secure a last-minute gig tonight for some extra pocket money and having my guitar on hand would be a great assistance to that.

I catch a bus in the direction of the shop. At my stop, I trudge down the steps of the bus and onto the pavement. The shop is to my right; however, my eyes are drawn left toward golden hair shining in the sunlight. A blonde woman looks up and down anxiously at her phone and spins in slow circles. As I draw a little closer, I realize I recognize her. It's that sweet woman I saw in the coffee shop earlier. If possible, she's even more harried than she was this morning.

"Hiya," I say, causing her to jump and spin around to face me with those big brown eyes.

"Hi," she says. Then, recognition takes over and she says again, "Hi," before adding an unnecessary but delightfully cute, "Hello."

I grin. "Hi." I point to where her mobile is clutched tightly in her hand. "You lost?"

Her face burns bright red. "A little. I thought…I thought I had gotten off at the correct bus stop but I started walking one way then realized I didn't recognize anything. And my phone was working this morning, but now it's not. Like, the international plan has stopped functioning and nothing is loading, and I know it would be better to get on a plan over here because I'll be here for so long but I don't know how to do that, because I'm a grown woman but I'm still on my parents' phone plan. I don't even pay them for it. They pay. But they say it's fine because I'm a student and…and…" She trails off, her face somehow deepening to a greater red. It's alarmingly adorable. "Sorry," she mutters, eyes trained on the ground. "I normally am not a big talker, but I talk a lot when I'm nervous or anxious and I am both."

"It's fine, love," I say with a tone that will hopefully put her at ease. "Where're you trying to go? I'll help you find your way."

She peeks back up at me shyly. "Oh, um, my rental flat? It's around here somewhere." She reads off the address.

I make an affirmative sound. "I'll walk you."

She shakes her head quickly. "Oh, no. That's okay. If you point me in the right direction, I'm sure I can get myself there. I don't want to inconvenience you."

"No bother," I say, pivoting and setting off, glancing back once to make sure she's following me. She is. Curious, yet cautious.

As we stop at a junction, waiting for a long queue of cars to pass, I stick my hand out. "Isla, by the way."

She shakes my hand with a surprisingly firm handshake. "Rachel."

We start to walk again. "You said you'll be here for a while, Rachel? How long, then? A few weeks?"

"Oh, no. Three years. At least."

My eyebrows shoot up. "Three years?"

"Yeah," she says. "I'm a Ph.D. candidate at Heriot-Watt. For Marine Biodiversity. My program starts in two weeks, but I had this last-minute orientation today. I was really stressed about getting there, then I got confused because floors are different here? Like the third is the second, and the second is the first? I don't know. Maybe that's obvious."

"No, I can see how that would be confusing. That's impressive, though," I say genuinely. "About your Ph.D. How long have you been in the city?"

She checks her watch. "About twenty-six hours."

I blow out a puff of air. No wonder she's so flustered. "You here alone?"

"No. Not yet. My brother and best friend are with me for the week. Right now, they're on the Jacobite train."

"That's nice."

"In theory. They don't exactly have a history of getting along, so I'm afraid Piper is going to kick Nick out of the car and leave him somewhere in the Highlands."

"Let's hope not," I say with a cackle.

We take the turn onto her street. She spots the door of her rental and says, "Here it is." She looks back at me. "Thanks for your help."

I brush away her sincere tone. "You won't find me coming up with an excuse to not walk a pretty girl home." Her cheeks pinken, sending a thrill through me. "Maybe we'll run into one another again?"

"Yeah, hopefully." She digs out her keys and shoves them into the lock, throwing one more glance in my direction before she goes inside and I decide it's safe to walk away.

I should have asked for her number, I suppose, but the lass has been in this country for just over one day. I'm not going to hound her. I'm sure if I get the inclination, I can find her on social media and slide into her DMs. I am what we'll call a professional DM slider.

I turn around and head back toward the music shop. That detour was ten minutes in the wrong direction, but I doubt Josie will fault me considering she prefers it when I don't show up on my days off. I work part-time at Josie's Music Shop, equally to give my legs a break and to increase my income.

I push through the purple, wooden door of the music shop, the bell above head announcing my entrance. The shop is cluttered in the best way, every wall covered with a mixture of varied instruments on display and posters of bands and musicians. The floor is littered with instruments that can't be hung on walls, like pianos and drum sets. There are stacks of sheet music and rows of records, CDs, and even cassettes and 24s in the back of the shop.

With a furrowed brow, Josie studies me from behind the counter set up in the smack center of the floor. "Why are you strutting through my door? You're not working today."

I have known Josie since childhood because she and my mother grew up as good mates. As I've grown into adulthood, they've grown apart, but Josie and I are still close. To be truthful, I don't understand how they ever were mates because she is so much cooler than my mum. She always wears these long, flowing dresses with colorful waistcoats or jumpers, depending on the weather, and scarves in her graying brunette hair. Today, she is wearing an ankle-length denim dress and a furry orange jumper, with a matching orange scarf in her hair. She looks fantastic.

"Picking up my baby?" I say hopefully, fingers lightly tracing over a red electric guitar hanging on the wall beside the door. "What else?"

"She's not ready yet."

My shoulders sag as I approach the counter. "What do you mean she's not ready?"

"I mean, she's not ready. It's not a matter of just popping the capstan back into place. I'm replacing all of your tuners, but none I have on hand fit. I had to order more in." She sighs distastefully.

"I'm getting a bit tired of fixing that guitar of yours. Might be high time to buy a new one."

I gasp in disbelief. "*Never*," I emphasize. "I'll still be playing her on my deathbed."

"Right, pet. Well, come back in a few days. I'm sure I'll have her done."

"You can't have her done by the end of today? No other tuners work?"

"No."

I press my lips together. "Fine, then. I don't have a scheduled gig on the books. I was gonna call Frank or Bonnie about a last-minute one tonight, but I guess I won't." With no luck picking up my guitar, that's a solid nothing done on my to-do list. *Damn.* I was counting on that gig. "I know I'm not working today, but do you need a hand with anything?"

Her eyes lift to the sky because she knows she won't easily be rid of me. "I'll give you a tenner if you organize my new orders by letter. Then you need to leave."

Aye, success. "That'll do."

I take my time putting the orders in order, but the task still only takes ten minutes. With a groan, I plop down on the purple velvet couch in the back room and let my eyes fall closed. A nap won't hurt me. After twenty minutes of something akin to sleep, I go back up front with Josie. "Orders are in order. Also, I had a nap." I steal a sip of the tea she has resting beside her. It needs more sugar. "Anything else you need from me? I can gather the orders and pack 'em up."

"No, no. You loitering around here is not going to fix your guitar any faster. Off you pop." She takes out her wallet and thrusts a tenner at me.

I resist the urge to stamp my foot in protest as I take the bill and slide it into the pocket of my loose jean shorts. "Fine. See you tomorrow?"

She shoos me out. "Aye. Off with you."

I exit, swerving around a few entering customers as I do so. In front of the shop, I pause and shove my hands in my pockets. Despite the nap, my eyes are heavy. I know I should go home, but my lack of productivity for the day has guilt clawing in my chest. Going home feels like giving up. But I have nothing else to do but wander or go sit in a pub somewhere. I wouldn't mind taking up residence on a stool but I won't provide myself with very good company today. Och, I guess I'll go home and take another nap. Or, I'll be honest with myself, doom scroll until I need to eat.

I trudge about a block in the direction of my flat and…well, who do I see once again? Rachel. Previously nonexistent energy courses through me. She's walking slowly down the street like she's trying to take everything in. Or like she's trying to memorize her path so she can find her way home again. I wish I had breadcrumbs to offer her.

She's changed into a midi-length black thin strapped dress layered over a white T-shirt. She spots me and smiles cautiously.

With a hand over my eyes acting like a visor, I chuckle to myself as I approach her. "You following me?"

Her face burns that lovely tomato red again and she shakes her head viciously. "No. Of course not."

My mouth perks. "I was joking. We seem to be having a lucky day of run-ins, you and I."

"Right," she says, returning my smile. "I'm usually much better at picking up sarcasm. I think my jet-lagged brain is making me, well, lag."

"That's fine. You'll catch up eventually."

"I hope."

"So, what're you up to now? Is your phone working?"

"Ah, no. Not quite. I'm just walking around, learning the city." She swings her wee leather backpack off one shoulder and to her front so she can dig through it. She pulls out a glossy, folded paper. "My rental has maps of the city so I'm doing this the old-fashioned way."

I nod in approval. "The best way to learn a new city is to get lost in it. I've done that a time or two thousand."

She puts the map back in her pack. "Are you not from Edinburgh?"

The way her brown eyes meet mine so intently sends a prickle down my spine and through to my toes. My voice feels thick as I answer her. "Not originally, no. I grew up in Newtonmore. I moved here for uni and never left. University of Edinburgh."

Nap be damned, I'd be happy to spend the rest of the day getting to know this pretty bundle of nerves. And I wouldn't mind getting to know a different bundle of nerves tonight.

I point ahead. "I'll wander with you, if you'd like. But don't be afraid to tell me to bog off."

"No, please. I'd like that. My sense of direction isn't as good as I'd like to think." Then she quietly adds, "Also, you seem like pretty good company."

Heat builds in my neck. "I'm famously good company." With my hands in my pockets, I look around, trying to decide which way to take us. In my opinion, visiting local establishments is the best way to find one's place in a new city so I'd like to find a path that offers several options. I indicate my head to the right, up a hill. "This way."

We set off.

She offers, "I'm from St. Louis, Missouri. In America." Her

nose wrinkles. "Sorry, that was silly to say. I figure that's obvious from the everything about me."

She's not wrong. "Now, which one is Missouri? One in the middle?"

"Yeah. The Midwest. St. Louis is about five hours south of Chicago, if that helps."

"It does. Never been there myself, but my brother traveled all over the States for a year or so after uni. He hit Chicago at one point."

"Are you and your brother close?"

I click my tongue. "It varies. We get along if that's what you're asking. He still lives in Newtonmore. He'll visit me often enough. I don't much go out to visit him."

"Why not?"

"Edinburgh is better than home."

She doesn't pry, even though I can tell she wants to. All she says is, "Right." That is perfectly enough.

She says, "I'm close with my brother. We're less than a year apart so it always felt like we were twins." She picks at her fingernails and adds, "I feel bad about leaving him. To move over here. You know?"

I nudge her lightly as we pause before a zebra crossing. "That's not something to feel bad about. Doing things for yourself is not a bad thing."

"Then why do I feel guilty?" she asks softly.

I stop us in the middle of the street with a hand on her arm. "Is he making you feel guilty?"

She goes stiff under my hand so I decide to remove it.

"No. No, not at all. Nick is being great and supportive, like he always is, but I can tell he's sad. Honestly, I'm a little afraid he's going to try to follow me over here. Which wouldn't be a bad thing, but it also would be because then Piper would be alone. Piper is my best friend and, I mean, she doesn't *want* Nick to be there for her, but she also does, I think? I don't know but—" She cuts herself off with a hand over her face. "Oh my god. I'm rambling again. Please shut me up."

"Never shut up," I say seriously. "Want my opinion?" She nods. "The two of them are sad because they'll miss you. That's nothing to feel any guilt over. You'll miss them too, right?"

"Right." She sighs. "Thanks. I needed to hear that."

We start walking again. She needs a reason to call this city home. I'm not saying *I'm* going to be the reason, but I am determined to help her find whatever that reason is.

CHAPTER FOUR
Rachel

I'm having trouble focusing my gaze ahead and not at Isla as we walk. Thankfully, she's spouting off facts about the city so I'm not staring unprompted, but, god. Those eyes. That *mouth*. How can I not stare?

Once the angle of the road declines, colorful shops sprout up around us. My eyes catch on one.

"Armchair Books," I say aloud, pausing to peek at the window display of books set up behind the green storefront. "I've heard of this place."

"It's great," Isla muses. "Want to have a look?"

Even though I would like that, I find myself saying, "We don't have to."

"Naw, let's go in."

She opens the front door and gestures me inside. The carpeted floor creaks beneath my feet as I take cautious steps into a store crowded with both books and people. Isla is close behind, mimicking my creaks. The space is magical, lined floor to ceiling with wooden shelves stuffed to capacity. Though far from true, it feels like every book ever printed exists in this store.

A man comes around the corner, arms weighed down by books and a lanyard around his throat. He spots Isla and says, "Isla, you alright?"

She gives a charming smile. "Fine, fine. And yourself?"

The man holds the books up in a gesture. "Wasting the day away, as per usual. Anything I can assist you with? I still owe you for your help driving my nan across town."

"We're just here for a look," she says, steering me away. "Tell your nan I say hello."

We tread deeper into the shop. "Friend of yours?" I ask as I pick up a book bound in navy blue leather, gold foil stamped on the spine. My fingers trace carefully over the textured material.

"Somewhat," she says casually. "I know him from around. Friend of a friend of a friend. I know a lot of people like that." She changes the subject. "You like books?"

"Oh, yeah. Huge reader. Both for school and pleasure." I slide the book I'm holding back onto the shelf. "Though, I mostly read e-books. I love physical books, but they take up so much space." I don't add that I left behind an entire bookshelf at my parents' house. Can't take all your books with you when you move halfway across the world. It's better this way. Fewer possessions means less to hold me down. Less to hold me back. My fingers graze the crammed shelves. "There is something so peaceful about being surrounded by books. They're warm. Welcoming. Ideally, I'd line my apartment with books."

Isla strokes the spine of a book with two fingers. "They are a comfort item, I agree. Not a huge reader myself, but I always meant to be." We keep wandering together through the shelves. "What genre takes your fancy?"

"Anything," I answer honestly. "I love romance, but I also get really into fantasy. I like the odd thriller. Literary fiction as well.

Hard to like only one thing."

We peruse until I've had my fill and then both leave the store empty-handed. Though, I have plans for another visit.

We set back down the road with no specific destination until Isla gestures at a pub across the street.

"Stop for a pint? You'll need to find a local haunt if you're with us for three years. This is one of my favorites."

"Sure," I say, glancing around the corner of the pub toward a nice view of Edinburgh Castle. I'm not sure I'll ever get used to the commonality of castles here. I follow her through the black-painted wooden doors, the bartender greeting Isla by name as we enter.

She sits us down at a dark wooden table near the back, the smell of beer less prominent. There's a sprinkling of people in the pub, making the casual setting oddly intimate. She stands back up almost immediately. "First one's on me. A welcome to the city drink. Do you know what you want?"

"You can get me what you're having. Unless it's really dark. I don't do really dark beers."

"Naw. You'll like this lager. It's a national favorite."

As she runs up to the bar, I take the chance to check my hair in my phone camera.

Once I made it back to the rental today, I scrubbed my face raw to remove the makeup. With that mess off my face, a change of clothes, and the relief of my orientation going well, I might be looking forward to starting in a couple of weeks. Finally. I'm still wary, but I expect to get past it. Dr. Andonov is extremely passionate about their work, to the level I hope to be. That's a good sign. A great one. A sign I needed.

It was late enough in the day that my mom was awake back home, so I called to check in with her while I had WiFi, which made me feel better. I expressed some of my varied concerns and she told me to make a list of every good thing I've experienced today. Even if it's not a long list, she said, something is better than nothing. So, I did just that. Except I made a PowerPoint. I love a good PowerPoint. Pictures, bullet points, graphs. Perfection. It was five slides long.

I hope that when I get back to the flat, I'll be able to add Isla as one more slide. I'm thrilled at the prospect of making a friend. A friend whose mouth I can't stop staring at.

Isla comes back to the table, an amber pint in each hand. As she sets one down in front of me, a splash of foam slips over the side. I catch it with my finger, sliding it up the glass, then pop the tip of that finger into my mouth, licking off the foam. When Isla's jaw flexes, I realize what that simple action has done for me, accidental or not. I hypothesize that Isla has been successfully seduced and am thrilled at the prospect of gathering evidence to support this hypothesis.

She crosses her legs and leans closer. "Come on then, first sip." She picks up her glass and I follow suit. We tap the pints together and I sense her focus lock on my mouth when I take my first taste. I draw it out for as long as I can before my eyes light up in delight, the flavor crisp and refreshing.

"Ooo. That's good!"

"Told you, you'd like it." She takes a sip of her own. "So, I could ask why Marine Biology, but I think that's obvious: Mermaids."

"Duh," I play along. I avoid correcting her to tell her that it's Marine Biodiversity because the semantics don't matter.

"But what I will ask is: why Edinburgh? Hell, why Scotland? Aren't there better programs in places like Australia or Hawaii?"

I sip my beer. "Possibly. I applied to other programs. My heart was set on one in Wellington, New Zealand, but I didn't get in. And that's fine. Disappointing, but fine. I did get offered one in Maine, actually, that I was interested in but…I don't know. Something about Heriot-Watt felt *right*. When I was accepted into the program, it felt right." I try and fail not to grimace.

"What was that?"

"It's just….it doesn't feel *right* anymore. But it doesn't feel wrong either. I don't know. I'm having complicated feelings."

Her foot hits mine under the table. "Well, give it a week, maybe? And hey, now you've met me, so that's got to make this place ten times better."

I blush furiously, scolding myself as I refuse to meet her eye. *So* embarrassing. I manage to get out, "Yeah. Definitely a plus," without completely going up in flames. I take another sip, hoping to cool my face. "Something feels off. I'm sure it's just nerves."

"Well, you can always change your mind and head back to the States," Isla offers, though she looks like she would be disappointed if I did.

"That's what my brother said."

"Smart bloke."

"He has his moments."

Once we finish the lagers, Isla runs up to the bar to order us another round before I can even open my mouth to offer. She's wonderful. Like, so fun to talk to and really, really pretty. Gorgeous, in fact.

Isla is exactly what I need today. Even though I'm an awkward mess around her, she is doing a pretty decent job of making me feel comfortable. That's all I require in social settings—to feel comfortable around someone. Sometimes it never happens and I continue to prove that I don't have a firm grasp on how humans interact with one another, but when I find those people who I can relax around, it's great. I can see her being one of those people. Even if she ends up only an acquaintance, at least I'll know someone in the city beyond Professor Zgheib and Dr. Andonov.

Isla returns with two pints in tow. She sets one down before me.

"Let me pay for these," I say, reaching for my wallet to pull out a few bills.

She waves away my money. "No need. You can pick up the tab another time."

"Alright." I put my wallet back.

I take another drink. The lager *is* really good. Even if the colloquial nickname for it is the "big juicy."

"So, you know what I do. Water life science. What do you do?"

Her face twists, but she tries to cover it up with a flash of her teeth. "Tour guide, shop worker, occasional dog walker. Other things."

"That's fun," I say genuinely. "Especially the tour guiding. I bet you know so much about the city."

"Eh." Her lips curl. "You don't have to lie, love. It's not the dream." She leans back in her chair and takes a long sip, looking out the window behind me, toward the castle.

"Then what is?"

"Och, there's always different ones. Once upon a time, I thought I was going to be a famous musician. Or work in the music industry. As a producer or something."

"That would be so cool. You don't want to try to pursue that?"

"Not anymore. I still like to play music, just not forever. It would be a guaranteed way to stay in debt for the rest of my life is what it would be." She shrugs. "I have a good life. A decent one, at least. I have room for more dreams."

We continue chatting as we finish our second round. I let her lead the conversation, otherwise I might start grilling her in an attempt to learn everything I can. Instead of telling me more about her dreams, Isla is giving me a list of every pub or bar where she knows the bartender and can get me a free drink, including the three she used to work at. If I were fuller of myself, I would say she's trying to impress me. Not that I need a single extra thing to be impressed by, beyond her. Like the way her dark eyes glint when she gives a smart comment or the crooked smile she gives when she makes a joke.

"I haven't asked," Isla starts after downing the last swallow of her drink, "have you been to Edinburgh before? I'm assuming yes."

I try to hide my cringe. "Will you think I'm crazy if I say no? If I tell you I decided to pack up my entire life and move here sight unseen?"

"Crazy? Naw. Adventurous? Yes." She leans back in her stool, her head visibly moving up and down to scan me. "Wow, so you haven't seen anything but the campus, the bookshop, and the streets around here then?"

"No, haven't had the chance yet. I mean, I did a loop around the city in a car yesterday, but I was so focused on the road and other cars that I didn't actually see anything."

Her eyes glint mischievously. "Well, then let me show you one of the best parts." She stands, shoving her stool back with a scrape. "Come along." She is out the door without waiting for me to say yes.

I swallow the rest of my drink in one gulp and hop up to follow, jogging after her.

"Where are we going?" I ask when I catch up.

"It's a surprise. I'd blindfold you if I trusted myself to keep you from tripping."

"I'd trust you," I say without thinking. My cheeks flush for the seven thousandth time today. Sigh. I need to just accept my permanently flaming cheeks in her presence.

Isla nudges me. "Well, that makes one of us. I don't have a blindfold on me, do I? You'll have to be very unobservant until we get there."

We walk through the streets with a purpose, past colorful shops, pubs, and cafes. I smile to myself as we pass a red phone booth because that is just *so* British. We turn on Cowgate and traverse through a somewhat gritty area.

While we're on Cowgate, we cross under a weatherworn bridge and I can't help but ask, "Is this one of those places that would have been overrun with human waste in the olden days?"

I immediately regret the question.

Isla snorts, putting me at ease. "I wasn't going to bring it up, but aye. Because we're at the bottom of a hill, all of that would travel down here from the Royal Mile." She points back at the exposed archway of the bridge. "Those were built so people wouldn't have to trudge through it."

We turn left on Blair Street. There are more hills in Edinburgh than I expected. Like, I knew on some level it wasn't completely flat, but this sucker is steep! My feet are starting to whine and my thighs are threatening mutiny, but I hold back my complaints because I know wherever we're headed will be worth it.

After crossing the bridge over Waverley Train Station, we eventually arrive at a set of stairs. Isla leads me up them, then we start to make our way up a hill before coming to a second set of stairs. This set is taller and steeper than the last.

Death by stairs was not my anticipated end.

My legs are burning as we reach the second half of the stairs and my breath is labored, but I try to contain it so Isla doesn't think I am immensely out of shape. It doesn't help that Isla is running up the stairs like she climbs them every day. Hey, maybe she does. I wonder if this is one of the places her tour goes? She's giddy about whatever she's planning to show me.

Once we get up the stairs and start on the next steep hill, I recognize a structure from my many Google searches (and the copious links Piper sent me). I cannot tell you what it's called (that's what Piper is for) but it's a stone tower with a cross set atop it. Once we get to the top of the hill, to my left is a large monument with twelve tall pillars topped with a flat layer of stone.

Isla takes a sharp left, reaching back to grab my hand to pull me along beside her. I tell myself not to stiffen under her touch. It's not that I don't want her touching me, I just have never been super comfortable with physical touch. It took me basically a lifetime of Piper to get used to her because she is a very touchy person. I'm comfortable with Piper, but with people beyond my best friend, even my brother, a little touch can be too much. I'm trying not to be that way with Isla. She takes my hand so casually that I don't want to pull away. I *want* to hold her hand, so I hold tight, hoping she won't let go. She doesn't.

"This is Calton Hill," she says.

"Seems…historic," I observe. With my free hand, I point to the monument we are approaching. "Is Dugald Stewart a friend of yours?"

"He's only an acquaintance."

We stop in front of the monument and I glance up at the pillar-built, round structure. They like their pillars here.

Isla squeezes my hand. "Right. You said you trust me, so let's put that to the test. Close your eyes. I'll guide you."

I do as she says. She grabs my other hand and walks backward as we ascend a dirt hill. The wind slaps me in the face, whipping my hair around my head in hopefully an attractive way and not a rat's nest way (doubtful), as we climb higher. Isla's grip on my hands grows tight. When we reach more solid terrain, I trip.

"Sorry," she says, "uneven ground. High steps."

I pick my feet up higher, feeling ridiculous, but find that I don't care as much as I normally would.

"Alright," she says, stopping us. She releases my hands and moves to grip my shoulders. I involuntarily flinch at the surprise switch in contact and hope she doesn't notice. She doesn't seem to. "Keep your eyes closed a bit longer." She spins me slowly counterclockwise, then back clockwise a fraction. "Trying to find the best spot," she murmurs, warm breath reaching my ear, causing a shiver along my spine.

She stops me and switches her two-handed grip on my shoulders to one arm around both of them. My breath hitches and I try not to stiffen. I relax into her touch, inhaling her cinnamon scent as she stands beside me.

"Open your eyes," she whispers, prompting another shiver.

I slowly do as she says and suck in a gasp. We are so much higher than I realized. I gawp at the city and the water beyond, shining blue in the sunlight. A clocktower in what is designated as Old Town is in the distance below us. Behind it, Edinburgh Castle. We can see a 360-degree view of Edinburgh from here, every shade of brown, tan, and taupe imaginable. It's warm, inviting, magical, magnificent.

She says, "Best view in the city. Some might argue for Arthur's Seat, but I prefer this."

I jump unnecessarily. It's not that I forgot she was here—trust me, I am very aware of her presence—I just became so distracted by the view that the world grew quiet and her voice brought me out of that trance.

"It's wonderful," I breathe. I face her, my eyes big, growing from trying to take in the view to trying to take in her. "Thank you."

I could stay up here forever. I'm tempted to. It's rather blissful, this wonderful view with this delightful woman by my side. I really like her. I know I hardly know her, but I have never clicked so instantly with someone before.

Her eyes lose mine at the genuine thankfulness in my voice. "I'm sure you would have made it up here on your own."

"Yeah, but thank you for taking me here today. Thank you for today in general. It's exactly what I needed." It is. It's giving me hope.

"Well, it's not over yet." She takes a few steps away from me. "Shall we keep exploring?"

"Yeah," I say, itching to grab her hand again, but holding back, unsure if we are on the same page.

We get a closer look at the giant pillar structure (which Isla explains is the National Monument of Scotland), and she goads me into climbing up it. A lot of people are climbing it, so I'm not alone, but I am boosting myself onto the ledge in the most ungraceful way, fully aware of her eyes on me. She climbs up with me, a lot more elegantly, that crooked smile back on her face.

"I love climbing shit," she says.

I'm tempted to comment on how she can climb me whenever she wants, but I realize that that attempt at a flirtatious remark probably won't make any sense. She's taller than me, for one.

We hop back down, her first so she can help me. She puts her hands on my waist and I swear to god I nearly swoon. After that, we catch a few more grand views of the antique buildings of the city, then make our way back down the hills and stairs, neither knowing what is in store for us next.

CHAPTER FIVE
Isla

As we reach the bottom steps from Calton Hill and continue down the street, I'm rattling on about Edinburgh's free ghost tours. I used to lead one but decided to stop because those mainly pay in tips and I needed something more substantial.

I trail off when I spot a familiar mane of ginger hair up ahead. "Corrine!" I call before I think better of it.

Her arms are exposed to show off her two sleeves of colorful tattoos, appearing as vibrant as always against her pale skin. Full-length black pants cover her legs, but I know full well those are equally as covered and stunning as her arms.

"Isla. Hey." She narrows her eyes and says accusingly, "You haven't set up that appointment yet."

I cringe. "I know. I know. I have the money saved up, just haven't gotten around to making the call."

"You always keep me waiting. Guess I'm used to it." She playfully tisks.

Rachel shifts uncomfortably, obviously wondering what we are discussing but not wanting to seem intrusive. I catch her confusion with a sheepish grin.

"Sorry, love. Being rude. This is Corrine. My tattoo artists and a…friend." The hesitation before the word friend makes it clear that we have previously been more than friends. Och, that was not intentional.

Rachel lifts her chin in an adorable show of dominance and sticks out a hand. "Rachel. A new friend."

Corrine looks back and forth between us with a raised eyebrow, immediately clocking my mouth's urgent desire to get between Rachel's thighs.

"Ah." She shakes Rachel's outstretched hand. "Well, nice to meet you." She turns back to me. "If you're not busy, I have space now."

I check the time, contemplating. "The studio isn't closed?"

Corrine shrugs. "It's my studio." To Rachel, she offers, "I can give you something too." She considers her. "Not sure if you're a tattoo person? I don't want to pressure you into your first one."

"Oh," Rachel says, surprised. "It wouldn't be my first tattoo, but I don't have anything in mind."

Tattoos, huh? My eyes drag over her in pursuit, but I find no evidence of ink. I am very interested in locating said tattoos later.

"You can have a look at the book. Decide on something there," Corrine suggests.

I turn to Rachel with a glint in my eyes. "What do you think? Fun intro to the city. You know, tattoo artists have been making a name here since the late 1800s."

She toys with a loose strand of her hair, contemplating. "That's very cool. Okay. When in Edinburgh, I guess."

I let Corrine lead the way, making sure my steps are in line with Rachel's.

If we're counting things in my favor versus things out of my favor, we're three to one. In my favor, Rachel liked the bookshop, the pub, and Calton Hill. Out of my favor, we're on our way to spend time with an ex of mine.

I'm itching to seize Rachel's hand again, but I don't want it to seem like I'm showing off for Corrine. Or, god forbid, like I'm trying to make Corrine jealous. We were never serious, Corrine and me. It was always just sex and that ended the moment she found a serious girlfriend. We really are friends. It's not out of the ordinary to spend time with her, but I hope us having a history does not deter Rachel from enjoying herself.

Corrine takes us to the glass-paned shopfront that has served as her studio for the past two years. She unlocks the front door and pushes it open with a jingle, flipping on the lights to reveal a clean, black-and-white studio lined with greenery.

"Rachel, there's a book on the counter. Or if there's anything simple you have in mind, I can sketch a quick piece for you."

"I'll check it out." Rachel approaches the glass front counter, her hands wringing together.

Is taking a girl I met today to get a tattoo odd? Sure. But hey, what a memorable first date. City exploration, romantic views, and now: tattoo. Her willingness to go on these adventures with me is invigorating.

Rachel pulls the faux leather binder toward herself and starts to slowly flip through the laminated pages, examining each image thoroughly. As Corrine disappears to the back to fetch supplies, I step up beside her and say, "You don't have to get anything if you don't want to. You don't even have to stay if you don't want to. Neither of us do. We can go do something else."

She flips another page. "I'm not expected anywhere. Nick and Piper aren't going to be back for a bit, so I'm totally free." She closes the book. "What are you getting?"

I pull out my phone to show her the sketch of Corrine's. She sketched out three options for me about a month back and this is the one I landed on. It's a guitar with Forget-Me-Not flowers in the strings, which, yes, for someone who plays guitar is rather predictable. But it combines two of my loves: those flowers and music. I wish I had a more significant reason for my love of Forget-Me-Nots, but my passion is fueled solely by their lovely blue color (even if the tattoo itself will only be black outlines). It'll go in an empty spot on the side of my right arm below the shoulder.

"That's beautiful. I love the flowers," Rachel says, admiring the picture. "It'll look great on you."

"Yeah. I think so." The tattoo will remind me of something I love and something I want to keep in my life. Sometimes, music is my life. Or, it used to be. I used to write songs all the time but one day the words were gone and all I had left was the music. That's all I've been able to string together lately, music without words. I pocket my phone. "It'll finish up the sleeve."

I drop one side of my button-up shirt off, leaving me in just my tank, to show her my arm. It's decorated in a combination of Forget-Me-Nots, vines, and random musical things, all outlined in black ink. Some of the vines and flowers make their way past my shoulder, lightly kissing my chest. I show her a few specific images in the sleeve, like the one on the back of my arm, just above the elbow. It's a set of over-the-ear headphones and a cord that curls and wraps around to the front of my arm, mixing artfully with one of the vines from the flowers. There's another one on my wrist that looks like a play button on a music app. I also have a vinyl record under my elbow crease, a cassette tape on the inside of my upper arm, and musical notes scattered in there. Lastly, I have a wee Venus planet on my left arm, under the elbow crease. It's the lone tattoo on that arm. "There's another on my hip, but I can show you that when we're alone."

Her eyes flash at the suggestion. "I'd like that."

My tongue skims my bottom lip, ready to propose we forget the tattoo parlor and head back to mine. No, no. I don't want to rush things. I like to take my time. A slow build to the climax of our day, so to speak. "I'd like you to show me a bit of yourself as well." I pause as the blush builds in her cheeks before I let her off with, "You said you have a tattoo already?"

She nods quickly and clears her throat. "Two." She leans against the counter and lifts a leg so she can show me the one on her ankle. When I catch sight of the creamy white flesh of her thigh, I have trouble focusing on the tattoo. "I have this one, which is a little nerdy. But pretty, I think."

When I pull my eyes to it, I agree. The tattoo is a beaker with a floral arrangement stuck in it like a vase. It's really nice and very her, from what I've learnt about her already.

She drops her leg. "The other is on my ribs. Let me see if I can…"

I open my mouth to tell her not to go through the trouble, but she has already pulled down the cotton of her dress under the armpit and lifted the shirt she has layered under the dress to expose the tattoo.

"Here we go. This guy. To remind me to make use of every second I have, even if I'm using that second to take a breath."

The tattoo is an hourglass with sand pooling at the bottom and a sprout emerging from the sand. I'm looking at the tattoo, I am, but I am also distracted by the desire to sink my teeth into the soft skin exposed under her breast. *Och*, I'm a horny mess.

"I love them," I say genuinely, swallowing my lustful thoughts. There is a time and a place, and my ex's tattoo studio is not one of them.

"Thanks." She shrugs nonchalantly as she fixes her clothing. "I might get a mountain range on my arm if Corrine has time. It's one I've thought about. Just an outline."

My eyebrows perk in interest. "Mountain range. How come?"

"It's a symbol of courage. I may often regret my courageous choices as soon as I make them, but I make them. I think I should feel proud of that."

"You should," I agree. I reach for her right arm, taking it gently to inspect the blank canvas. "Where would you get it exactly?" I brush my thumb over the smooth skin just above the crook of her elbow. "Here?"

She visibly swallows at the trailing contact. "Yeah." Her eyes are trained on my hand.

I guide my thumb over the spot again. "It would look sexy here."

I'm not sure I've spent too much time thinking about this part of the arm before. I'd say I'm not really an arm person, so to speak. More of a leg person, if I were to pick a limb, but picturing this tattoo on Rachel's arm, imagining my tongue running over it, has me thigh-squeezing-ly hot and bothered.

Corrine comes back out with gloves and her ink gun. "Ready?" she asks, causing Rachel to jolt out of my grasp.

I attribute that reaction to the sudden interruption as I throw Rachel a quick flash of my eyes before spinning toward Corrine. "Ready," I say, dropping off the other arm of my shirt and tossing it over the counter. I settle in the chair.

I catch Rachel having a glance at my braless chest and quickly diverting her gaze. I smirk and pat the open stool next to the chair. "Have a seat. I'll need someone to hold my hand."

Corrine's eyes lift to the sky, but Rachel does not notice. She takes a seat beside me and grasps my hand tightly as the prick of the needle hits my skin.

...

Corrine applies the clear plastic seal over my tattoo and says, "Alright, there we are." She asks Rachel, "Did you decide if you want anything?"

Rachel's eyes widen. "I don't know…I don't want to take up your time."

"If there's something you want, I can do it for you."

I squeeze her hand encouragingly before releasing it.

"Well, I was wondering if you could do a mountain range? On my inner arm. Above the elbow. About this big." She holds her thumb and forefinger to her arm. "Just like a black outline."

"Aye, I can do that. Easy. Let me sketch something."

Corrine grabs a tablet and pen to draw a quick sketch. She rotates the tablet toward Rachel when she is finished. "Like this?"

Rachel lights up. "Yes! Could you add a little shading?"

Corrine turns the screen back to herself and adds a few quick lines. "Like this?"

Rachel nods vigorously. "Yes, perfect. Literally what was in my head."

"I'm in everyone's head"—Corrine winks—"and I certainly don't mind being in yours."

I clear my throat and both of them turn to look at me. "Sorry," I say casually. "Something in my throat." Corrine rolls her eyes at me again. I swing my legs off the chair, swapping spots with Rachel.

She sits down and settles in as Corrine readies the stencil. Corrine presses the design to Rachel's forearm, leaving a purple outline where the tattoo will be. She grabs a mirror and holds it up to Rachel. "That spot correct?"

"Yes, that's perfect."

Corrine dips her gun in the black ink and holds the needle over Rachel's arm. Rachel quickly snatches my hand, flinching when the needle touches her skin. I lay my other hand over the one that holds hers, clasping it tightly.

She looks at me but doesn't say anything. She offers a small smile that causes my heart to lurch in my chest. I smile back, locking in on her gaze. Despite the lack of comfort this chair brings, I could stay in this exact position for the rest of my days. The comfort in her eyes is enough.

Listen, I'm good at making friends. I'm relaxed around strangers. I have no trouble putting myself out in the world. However, even with all of that in mind, I have never felt *this* at ease with another person.

By the time Corrine finishes up and applies the clear seal to Rachel's tattoo as she did mine, I'm ready to have her all to myself again. Rachel draws her gaze away from mine and toward the tattoo, beaming. "It looks amazing. Wow. Thanks, Corrine."

"You're welcome." She pulls off her gloves and stands up, leading us to the counter to settle the bill. "What does the rest of your evening look like?" she inquires as she writes up a written receipt for each of us.

I shove my hands in my pockets. "If Rachel will let me keep dragging her about the city, I was thinking that."

Corrine nods and looks to Rachel. "This one'll drag you about all night if you don't stop her," she warns. "Sleep and she are not friendly."

"My sleep schedule is off anyway. I don't mind," she says.

Corrine hands Rachel a receipt. "Welcome to our city, Rachel. You've already met the most popular person in it, so I say you'll fair pretty well."

I try to take the compliment at its word, but it comes off as somewhat of a jab. I'm sure Corrine didn't mean it that way. However, it's a good time to move along.

"I'll see you later, Cor?"

"Later," she responds.

Rachel and I leave the studio, walking a few paces before pausing outside of it. I gently grab her arm for a better peep at the tattoo. "It looks great. Are you pleased with it?"

She smiles hugely. "Yes, very much so. You happy with yours?"

"Yeah," I say, lifting my collar to glance at the red, inked skin. "Can always trust Corrine."

"She's very talented." Her eyes move downward as she asks timidly, "So, you and Corrine. Are you…or, I mean, have you… or you know what? None of my business."

I incline my head to the right, urging us to keep moving as we stroll away from the shop and up a brick-paved road. "We never dated, but we did have a bit of a thing. It's long over. We're just mates now."

She nods, leaning into me. "Okay. Good."

I raise my eyebrows, a sparkle surely in my eye. "Good?"

"Yeah, good. Good to know." She clears her throat. "So, where to now, tour guide? You've gotten beer and a tattoo into me, what's next?"

I laugh as we find a more populated street. "Don't forget the view!"

"Never." She stops walking and pulls me over to the side of the pavement so we can be face-to-face out of the way of pedestrian traffic. "Take me somewhere special to you."

"Like where?"

"Dealer's choice," she says. "There has to be somewhere that isn't a pub or bar you know the owner of or a tourist attraction or the tattoo studio of an ex-thing that means something to you. The street corner where you had a perfect kiss, say, or a bus stop where Paul McCartney asked you for directions, or the store you were in when you got the job offer as a tour guide. I don't know. Something like that."

I press my lips together as I contemplate. Somewhere special, huh? Well, there is no street corner where I've had a perfect kiss. There are plenty of places where I've had great kisses, don't get me wrong, but none were perfect. Definitely have never had Paul McCartney, or anyone of note, stop and ask me for directions. The moment when I received the job offer to be a tour guide was not special. I have no clue where I was on that day.

However, I do have an idea. I take her by the hand and feel her relax into my grasp. "Come on, then."

It's a decent walk through Old Town, but Rachel doesn't seem to mind. After the initial hill, it's fairly flat ground. I point out the National Museum of Scotland as we pass it, and I make her stop to say hello to Greyfriars Bobby. I also indicate which pubs, cafés, restaurants, and shops I like when we pass by. Finally, we halt in front of a light blue shopfront in between an antique store and an ice cream shop.

The space is as vacant as it has been for the past two years, the glass front door covered in brown paper on the inside and the windows in desperate need of a clean. Yet, I think it is perfect.

"Here we are."

Rachel squints at it then looks back at me, confused. "An empty store?"

"An empty café," I correct.

She edges closer to me. "So, what's the story with it?"

"My brother and I have been talking about opening a café for years and this is where it will be." I step forward, pulling her with me, and press my face to the window. Rachel hesitates for a tick before following suit. Our breath fogs the glass.

I push my finger against the window to point at the back corner. "Back there is where the counter will be. It'll be filled with pastries and baked goods—made by my brother, not me. Can't bake to save my life. And over there"—I move my finger slightly—"is where the coffee machine will be. I *can* make a good latte. I used to be a barista." I move my finger again. "Then there will be tables set up along the walls and in the middle. The kitchen is hiding down that back hallway. I would love to also have a shelf with used books to sell, or maybe art from local artists, but that might be too ambitious."

Rachel pulls her face off the glass to look at me with bright eyes. "That's so great! Why a café?"

This answer is easy. "I like to talk to people. If I own a café, I can be behind the counter and meet new people every day. I can become a safe hub for residents and travelers alike. I can cement my place in this city."

"I think you've already done pretty well to cement your place here. From what I've heard, you're like Edinburgh's star resident. Meaning, there's no doubt in my mind your café will be successful. When are you going to open it?"

"No idea. Ben doesn't live here and I need him to afford this. I'm all in but he keeps hesitating and I don't know why. This place has been vacant for years though, so logically something must be wrong with it. However, I'd like to think it's holding out for us."

Her focus turns back inside. "Maybe it's haunted."

"In this city, that's a plus." I glance at the antique shop next door. "*That* place is haunted." I refocus on the café. "Since Ben won't stop dragging his feet, I've been considering doing it on my own. I'd have to hire a baker, but I could do it. I have a mostly complete business plan and the small business loan application on my computer ready to be filled out, but I haven't done it yet. I have to fill it out with or without Ben, but with Ben I wouldn't need as big of a loan." I sigh. "It'd be easier to open it with him than without, and the dream was for us to do it together. I could do it by myself, but I'd be sad about it."

"Well, I believe it'll happen for you. And soon." She angles her head toward me, leaning against the window. "Thanks for showing me this."

I mimic her lean. We're hardly a breath apart, near enough that I can count the freckles on her cheeks. It would be so easy to lean in and kiss her. When she glances briefly to my lips, I sense she would be happy if I did. I lean forward a fraction…and she pushes off the window, taking a few steps away. I mentally take a step back, wondering if I misread the signals. That's fine. Like I said, I'd like to take my time with her. Follow her pace, instead of mine.

"I've had a great day," I admit, shoving my hands in my pockets.

"Me too. Even though my feet are killing me from all the walking." She shifts on her feet to ease her pain. "I don't want this day to end," she says, crossing her arms over herself and gazing up at the sky. "It's still light out! How can we stop now?"

"Your people aren't missing you?"

She gnaws her lip as she checks the time on her phone. "Nick and Piper should be back by now. Piper is probably freaking out because I'm not home. If today didn't go well, Piper will kill me if I leave her alone with Nick for even longer."

"What about your brother?"

"Oh, even if they fought the entire day…hell, even if Piper abandoned him in the Highlands, Nick probably had the best day of his life. He's desperately in love with her."

I narrow my eyes. "I thought you said they don't get along?"

"They don't, but he's still in love with her. And she…well, I honestly think she's a bit in love with him too. So, they've either come home even more separate than before or…" She smirks.

I finish for her. "Or they'll have finally admitted their feelings for one another. Impressive." I weigh my head. "Well, I'd say there is no harm in us grabbing supper and letting them be alone a bit longer. When was the last time you ate?"

Her eyes light up. "I picked up a sandwich for lunch, but nothing since then. I'm starving."

CHAPTER SIX
Rachel

I drop my napkin on the table and place a hand on my pleasantly stuffed stomach. "That was so good. I want to keep eating it forever."

We're at a small table shoved against the wall of a dimly lit restaurant, empty plates and a battery-powered plastic candle between us. Isla took me to her favorite Indian restaurant and after the meal I just ate, it's mine as well. That butter chicken was the best I have ever had. Pure bliss is the only true comparison.

Isla dabs at the corner of her mouth with her own napkin before dropping it on the table beside mine. "Add it to the list of places you'll need to revisit."

"This place will be dangerous," I moan. "I'll want to come back every night."

She laughs out, "Then I'll come with you."

I check the time mainly to make sure it isn't passing too quickly. When this day ends, the bubble I've submerged myself in with Isla will pop. No future day will be as great as today.

I stare at the SOS symbol in the service bar on my phone. Oh, how I wish my phone was working. It only works when connected to WiFi.

"Do you think this place has internet? If I wait any longer to respond to whatever texts sent by Piper, she'll think the worst. She's probably already thinking the worst." My gut tweaks in guilt. I hope she had a great day, but if not, she'll be very upset. It's so late now and she can't get in contact with me. *Oh god.* I am a horrible friend. My eyes are downcast as I mumble, "I should have made a better effort to check in."

Isla waves that away. "I'm sure it's fine. If she's angry, she'll get over it."

Ha, she doesn't know Piper.

She holds out her hand for my phone. "I know the WiFi password. Give 'er here." I unlock my phone and do so. She types in the password then hands it back.

I cock my head at the screen. Weird. I only have two texts. One is from my mom confirming the time the boxes full of all my earthly possessions are supposed to arrive. The other is from Nick, not Piper. Not a single text from Piper? No, **SAVE ME**, or anything? Fascinating. Is she okay? If she wasn't with Nick, I'd be worried. The text from Nick came a few hours ago.

> Hope you had a good day. Pip and I are having dinner in Fort William before heading home, fyi

I bite the corner of my lip as I reread the text. He called her *Pip*. He hasn't called her that in years. They had a good day.

I check their location but only see Nick's. Maybe Piper's phone died or she too does not have service? Oh, wow. They're still on their way home, paused at a rest stop two or so hours out. Meaning I have more uninterrupted time with Isla. Since they had a good day, they won't mind if I keep enjoying mine. I relay this to Isla.

"You don't need to keep entertaining me, though," I add quickly.

She chuckles. "If you think I don't want that, you're cracked, love. I'd be happy if this day never ended." She stands, her chair scraping against the floor. "Come on. Next stop: a bar where I obviously know the bartender."

Once we're back on the street, after every server in the restaurant wishes Isla farewell by name, she leads me to two skinny, wooden doors marked with golden owls. Beside the doors is a red wooden sign with golden lettering. HOOT THE REDEEMER PSYCHIC PALM READINGS CRYSTAL BALL READERS WAITING FOR YOU INSIDE.

"This is a bar?" I ask, eyeing the sign suspiciously.

"A not-so-secret secret bar, yeah. Cheesy, but nice. Come on."

She grabs me by the hand. I'm getting used to her doing that. I'm starting to crave it, in fact. It is overwhelming how quickly she has wormed her way into being someone I feel this comfortable with. I've known her for…what? Approximately twelve hours? How is she doing this? This has never happened before. Not with my one and only boyfriend. Not with the guy I had a situationship with. Not with that one-night stand guy. Never. She grabs my hand, just my goddamn hand, and I can hardly breathe—but in a way that makes me desperate to receive all of my air from her. This need is frightening and so terribly exciting.

With her hand in mine, she leads me down a set of stairs under a neon angel sign. She pushes through a door behind a fake psychic woman with a crystal ball and into a dark bar lined with walls of tarot card paintings as well as paintings of 1950s-style people holding ice cream and drinks. On a wall near the bar, there's a vending machine for boozy ice cream, and in the back corner, there is a claw machine with different mystery drink flavors. There is also a wall of red stadium seats settled under a painting of a three-breasted woman.

"Cool," I exhale, surveying the room with a ridiculous expression.

Isla pulls me up to the bar and makes me pop a squat on a stool next to her. She waves at the approaching bartender, a tall Black man in his late twenties wearing a tan T-shirt and dark jeans.

"Rachel, this is David. David, Rachel." She hops back up. "We're doing mystery flavors," she declares, pivoting away before immediately pivoting back. "You're not allergic to anything, are you?"

I shake my head. "Not a thing."

"Brilliant." She runs away to the vending machine.

I turn my attention back to the bartender—David—with a smile. "May I have a glass of water?"

"Sure thing," he says and my ears perk up at the sound of an American accent. He hands me the water and asks, "How do you know Isla?"

"Met her this morning. I'm new in town and she's been taking me around."

A strange look crosses his face—only for a moment before it's gone, but it is enough to alarm me.

I glance back to make sure Isla is still at the vending machine, then lean in close. "Tell me, is this something she does a lot? Meet random women and spend an entire day with them?"

He chuckles. "Not that I know of. Isla's great. I actually don't know if she's spent this much time one-on-one with anyone in a while. She works herself ragged, from what I hear." He gathers a few empty glasses from the end of the bar. "But what do I know? Honestly, I don't know her well. I know her through her brother.

He's the best guy I know."

My chest softens at that. Maybe the power of this thing between us isn't in my head. She feels it too.

Isla runs back with four plastic balls gathered in her hands. She drops them down on the bar and David raises an eyebrow. "Oh, don't look at me like that. Two for each of us." She slides onto the stool next to mine. "Mix and match as you feel best."

"You got it," David says, popping open the balls one by one to find the slips of paper with flavors hidden inside.

I try to get a peek at the flavors, but Isla gently turns my head toward her with two fingers on my cheek. "It's a surprise."

"Fine," I sigh.

Moments later, David sets a blue drink before me. "Blueberry, elderflower, and gin for you." He sets a purple drink in front of Isla. "Blackberry mint mojito for you."

My mouth opens in delight. "Ah, fun! Thank you." I say to Isla, "These are on me. You paid earlier."

David cuts in, "Actually, they're on me." He turns away to take care of another patron.

I laugh. "You weren't lying about the free drinks."

"Never do lie." She holds up her drink. "A cheers and a welcome to the city."

I tap her glass with mine and then take a sip, the blueberry flavor exploding in my mouth. I lick my lips. "Yum." Isla's eyes swoop downward to my lips and instead of leaning in like I want to, I sweep my head around the bar again. "This is such a cool place."

"You should see the toilets."

"Spend a lot of time in the toilets?" I ask in a sultry way that I immediately realize is really weird. I was trying to be flirty. Like please-join-me-in-the-bathroom-for-sexy-things flirty, but wow was that not the question to accomplish that.

I cover my burning face. "Forget I asked that. Oh my god." This on top of bringing up the abundance of human waste in the olden days earlier, Isla probably thinks I have some weird obsession.

Isla is cackling though. "Enough to see the walls. They're papered in torn pages from *Fifty Shades of Gray*."

"That's fun," I say from behind my hand.

She draws that hand away from my face, leaning in close and murmuring, "Don't cover that blush."

In response, I blush harder. "Sometimes I feel like every word that comes out of my mouth is wrong," I admit.

Her thumb strokes over the hand she is still holding. "I disagree. Everything you've said today has been exactly right." Her eyes go to my lips again and again I divert it by taking a sip. She leans back, taking her hand with her, accepting the message I wish I didn't give. I am *so* bad at this.

Our night rushes on as we finish those drinks and another set that I finally get to pay for before I bother to check the time. When I do, I'm startled. "It's 1 a.m.?"

We've spent the last two and a half hours talking, as we have all day. I feel like I know everything about her, but also like there is still so much to learn.

"Shutting this place down," Isla comments.

I take my final sip before sliding the glass back to David with as sober of a smile as I can manage. I'm tipsy—but the good kind of tipsy. Pleasantly tipsy. We wave goodbye to David as Isla stands and pulls me up with her, keeping hold of my hand as we exit the bar.

I lean into her as we walk, feeling loose and playful. A feeling I have been chasing all day. A feeling I love to have with her by my side.

"I had a great day." Keeping hold of her hand, I spin in the street like she's twirling me in a dance.

She laughs, squeezing my hand as I settle back into her side. "Me too. I'll walk you home. Don't want you losing your way this late."

We set off in the direction of my rental flat, taking a shortcut down a cobblestone pathway. I stumble, and Isla steadies me by placing both hands on my shoulders. "Easy now, love."

Before she can pull away, I catch her wrists. I have a split second to decide whether or not to do this.

I kiss her. She lets out a happy moan at the contact and I take that as permission to open my mouth on hers, tasting blackberries and mint on her velvet lips. I let go of her wrists so I can swing my arms around her neck and lace my fingers in her thick hair, pulling her as close to me as she can get. She takes the cue and backs me into the stone wall behind us, pressing her full body into mine. Her hands snake down my waist before settling on my hips, grasping tightly, balling the fabric of my dress in her fists.

Now this better be the spot of her perfect kiss because it most certainly will be mine. It's sloppy, both of us moving urgently as if aware we should have been doing this all day so we are now trying to make up for lost time. It is so, so perfect. My body is alight with a mixture of pure desire and desperate elation.

I dig my fingers into her scalp, hoping I'm not hurting her. Her tongue traces the inside of my mouth, tangling with mine, as one hand slides to cup my ass against the wall. A car drives by but I don't even care. Let the whole world see me getting kissed—ravished really—by this amazing woman. The world needs to learn what a perfect kiss looks like.

When I pull away for air, her burgundy-painted fingers catch my face, tracing gently along my jawline. "Rachel," she says breathlessly, "do you want to head back to mine instead?"

"Yes," I say, because wow do I really, really want to go back to her place. "I need to tell you something, though. I haven't done this before."

She kisses my neck. Into my skin, she asks, "What? Had sex?"

"No," I pant. Her mouth is now on the soft spot above my collarbone and I lose my train of thought. Once I find my way back, I expand, "No, I've had sex before. I just haven't with another woman before. I actually haven't ever kissed another woman before. But you can take care of me. You seem…you're perfect."

That wasn't the intended end of my sentence. What I was going to say was, *you seem like the kind of person I could hold on to for the rest of my life*, but I stop myself before my tipsy brain word vomits how connected to her I feel, how much I like her, how I have never met someone like her, how I want to spend every day for all of eternity with her. We met *today*. I need to be cool about this.

But as her hands drop from me, I don't feel cool. I feel cold.

"Wait, really?" She steps back, no longer touching me. Why is she not touching me? Why is her not touching me equivalent to being shoved into a tub of ice?

I take a step forward, trying to close the gap, but she backs up again. I freeze. "Yeah? What's wrong?"

Her nose crinkles. "Nothing, nothing. I just didn't realize that's what this was."

"What *what* was?"

"I didn't realize you were experimenting."

I open my mouth to say something, but nothing comes out. My brain is having trouble computing what she just said.

Experimenting? Who said anything about experimenting? This seems a rather uncontrolled environment to be conducting any reputable experiments in. I've no need to experiment. The conclusion of what and who I like has long been reached.

She continues, "I thought…never mind what I thought." She scans me up and down, evaluating me in a way she hasn't all day. I feel shamefully naked under this unfamiliar gaze. She shakes her head. "I should have guessed. Listen, I've got to go. You can get yourself back alright?"

She quickly walks away without waiting for my answer.

"I…" I start, not knowing how I plan to end that sentence. *What?* I don't understand what's happening. Am I truly this drunk or does this not make any sense? By the time my brain catches up to my situation, I say aloud, "I'm not experimenting," even though she is too far to hear. "I'm bisexual!" I shout. Then add more quietly, "I'm just bad at it."

A voice from above shouts, "Congrats, lass! Now shut it!"

Isla doesn't turn back.

What just happened?

CHAPTER SEVEN
Isla

Shit. *Shit.* I need to turn around. I can't catch my breath. I need to go back to her. My heart is pounding out of my chest. That was…not good. That was bad. That was not the correct way to react. Why are my hands trembling like this?

Her words repeat in my head. *You can take care of me. You're perfect.*

Perfect for the night but not forever.

"Fuck."

I find a wall to lean back against, fist clenched against my chest as I try to regulate my rapidly thumping heart, now only seeing spots before me. I blink hard to clear my vision. I don't even know why these old feelings came back tonight. I put something on her that I shouldn't have. Rachel is not Kenna. She is not my ex and she is not every woman who used me in the past. I gasp for the air that refuses to enter my lungs. I can't *fucking* breathe. In for seven. Out for seven. In. Out. In. Out.

People have always gravitated toward me. I've been out since I was a teenager and pretty confident about it. I will flirt with anything that moves. I'm aware of all of this. But because of that, women who want to explore their sexuality feel more comfortable doing so with me—which if they are truly trying to understand themselves is perfectly fine. It's when they're just looking for a bit of fun that it makes me feel bad. Something to tell their mates about later. Or maybe something they'll never admit to anyone. A lot of times, they're just looking for a bit of fun.

The phase of my life where I let people use me is over, but when I was younger, I didn't have enough self-respect to care. Now, I care. Now, I don't want to be used.

But that is not what Rachel was doing. I *know* this.

I bump my head against the stone wall behind me, feeling my breath start to ease out more naturally, my vision clearing with it. I need to go back. Rachel is nice. She is *so* nice and sweet and smart and…and she'll understand if I explain. If I apologize.

I push off the wall and rake my hands through my hair, gathering it behind me before letting it drop back behind my shoulders, the bulk of it driving me wild.

I jog back with the expectation that Rachel will still be where I left her, staring after the mad woman who stormed away after an absolutely perfect snog for no good reason. She is not. Of course she's not. She's nowhere to be seen. She's probably gone back to her rental flat.

God, I hope she's not lost. I left her to walk back alone at one in the morning without a fully functioning phone in an unfamiliar city. Well, I've got something else to add to my to-do list for tomorrow: learn how to not be a terrible person.

Without bothering to think, I take off in the direction of her rental. I remember where it is. I walk the ten minutes there and pause outside the doorway, finger poised to ring the buzzer.

I don't press down. Instead, I draw my hand back in a fist.

Her rental flat is on the ground floor and I assume the big

window next to the door looks into it. I peek into the window and see someone at the other end of the flat. A woman with blonde hair pulled into a haphazard bun has her head resting on a small table. Rachel.

She's not crying—I would be if the woman I fancied ditched me like that—but she does not look happy. She picks her head up and drags a hand down her face before pushing herself to her feet. I duck away before I see anything else. I go again to ring her flat, but hold back. What if I explain and she doesn't understand? Sure, I fancy this woman and I spent an entire day with her but that does not mean I know her. Know how she'd respond to anything I'd say. Will she understand or will she think I overreacted? Well, I did overreact. But will she understand why? I don't know. I'm not sure I can sufficiently explain.

I shove my hands in my pockets and walk away. I don't want to risk it. Not tonight when we're both still tipsy and emotions are high. My chance will come. I'm confident the universe will bring us back together soon enough.

...

I spend the next two days thinking about Rachel and seeing her everywhere, but never actually seeing her. I work the days at the music shop, give tours in the morning and evenings before and after the shop opens and closes. Every time the bell rings over the door of the music shop, I hope it's her entering. Every time I meet with a tour group, I hope she will be in it. Every time someone passes me on the street, I hope it's her. It never is.

On the third day, I am leading one of my more active tour groups. Part of this tour involves climbing Arthur's Seat, a more difficult trek than people give it credit for. I love this tour, especially because I am reasonably allowed to wear leggings. I have on my favorite pair, plus a tank that shows off my arms (now that I can let the new tattoo out in the open air), and my hair is pulled into a thick ponytail. I have a water bottle in my hand and my bag strapped across my chest.

My group is struggling and heaving behind me, but I'm enjoying myself. The fresh air is doing well to clear my head. I dodge other tourists as we get to a stretch of flat, earthy land and I spin around to address my group.

Once everyone reaches me, I say, "We can stop here, if you want, or you can come to the top with me. If you're done, thank you for spending part of your day with me. I'll give you one last fun fact before you go. Arthur's Seat is often thought of as one of the possible locations of Camelot, King Arthur's castle and court. I'd like to think that theory correct." I receive collective nods and smiles from my group. I end it here for those I am parting ways with. "Those of you coming to the top with me, you get one more fun fact." I turn around and usher them all onward behind me. I lose a few, but most come with me. They usually do. They like to prove they can make it to the top.

We complete the rocky ascent, the wind being as aggressive and overdramatic as it always is. Over the wind, I shout, "Final fun fact! We are standing on a sleeping dragon! That's how the legend goes, at least. Long ago, it is said a dragon would soar through these skies, wreaking havoc upon the land and snacking on every little lamb and coo in sight. Belly full of all that lovely livestock, our dear dragon needed a nap. So, here he lay and here he has stayed for centuries. You never know when he may awake." I throw my group a wink. "And that concludes our tour! Cheers to you all. I'll leave you up here to climb down at your leisure. Have a great day and if you're visiting, enjoy your holiday." They're all visiting, but I know some tourists appreciate it when I don't assume they're tourists.

Before I leave the top, I take my time to catch my breath and stare out at the city below. It's a clear day, so the view extends far, all the way to the water on one side and the hills in the opposite direction. I prefer the view from Calton Hill, but this isn't bad.

After a while, when most of my group has long gone on, I start my descent. I reach the initial rocks and turn the corner at the large section of flat land. That's when I spot her.

Rachel, here, at the moment I stopped thinking about her. The universe is having a laugh at my expense, isn't she? I just see the back of her (that perfect little arse in fitted leggings) but I know it's her. And, *damn,* I have approximately one second before she turns around and sees me. This is the chance I have been hoping for but I am not prepared for it. I seriously consider jumping and rolling down the hill as a tactic to avoid her, but it is too late. She sees me. She mouths my name as her eyes go wide.

She isn't alone. A taller woman with brunette hair layered over an icy blonde grabs the hand of a blond man as she leans into Rachel and whispers something in her ear. She pulls the man along with her and past me, giving me a glare and leaving Rachel behind. Her best friend, who understandably hates me, and her brother, who seems oblivious.

I can't stop walking. I can't jump off the cliff. I need to do this. *Oh god.*

She is standing there, frozen, staring at me. I approach her, stopping a few feet away, and say the only thing I can come up with: "Hello."

"Hi," she says back, finally blinking and losing eye contact.

"Hi. I'm happy to see you." I tighten my fists like I'm powering up. "Rachel, I'm so sorry about the other night. I shouldn't have…what I said wasn't…I mean…" I cover my face. Why is this so hard? I inhale deeply and remove my hands to find her looking at me, jaw clenched and body still. Waiting. "I shouldn't have rejected you like that. It was purely a me thing and had nothing to do with you."

I cautiously grab her by the arm, moving us out of the walking path and taking a bold step closer to her. She jerks from my grasp and takes a step back. It hurts, but I deserve it. "Listen, I want to be honest with you. When I was younger, I had a lot of people use me for an experience, nothing meaningful, only to leave me behind at the end of the night or the next morning. Then I had this ex…she doesn't matter. Forget her. In the moment, I assumed you were using me like all those others had. As soon as I walked away, I realized you weren't but…but I reacted out of a place of fear and…and no, I think just fear. We were having a lovely day. I got too in my head and I was given an opportunity to react based on that fear, so I did."

She crosses her arms. "You weren't, though."

"What?"

"You weren't *given* an opportunity. You *took* an opportunity. You *took* an opportunity based on something vulnerable I shared with you. Something that after a day spent with you, I assumed you would act kindly toward." She frowns and peers in the direction of Arthur's Seat. "I appreciate the explanation and understand how that prompted your reaction. I am sorry that you went through that. You should not have been used, and it is horrible that you were. However, it hurts that you thought that I was doing that. I don't understand why you thought *I* was trying to use you. After our day…I don't understand."

I purse my lips. "Because you said I could 'take care' of you." I use finger quotes with the words "take care" to make clear the implications.

Her mouth gaps, aghast. "I meant *take care* of me." She places both hands over her heart and her meaning clicks. I misunderstood. "I meant *be kind* to me. Help guide me through this new, scary, exciting thing we were going to do together." She exhales as her hands drop from her heart. "The thing is, you literally made a huge fear of mine come to life. I have been afraid for years at this point that I would share my lack of experience and whomever I was sharing it with would react negatively, such as you did. You made it a big deal when all I wanted was for it to be a general fact about myself. A simple detail offered before something meaningful."

"I'm sorry," I whisper.

She clicks her tongue and glances down at the tattoo on her arm, still covered with the protective plastic. "It's on me for assuming I knew anything about you. I really liked you. Even after how that night ended, I was desperate to see you again, but I was still overcome by the high of you. We knew each other for one day and I think that day is all we're going to get." She starts to walk away but immediately turns back. "I'm bisexual, by the way. Proudly. I have been out since freshman year of college."

"I'm sorry I assumed otherwise," I say desperately.

Her jaw clenches. "I should catch up to Nick and Piper. Thank you for your apology."

I plead, "Rachel," and reach for her again. This time she avoids me as though my touch will burn.

"I don't like to be touched by strangers," she says firmly.

I stand there gobsmacked as I watch her leave. I don't think I truly considered how poorly my reaction affected her. If I didn't already feel terrible, I do now. Her anger and hurt is justified.

I continue my descent down the mountain, knowing I need to do everything in my power to make it up to her.

CHAPTER EIGHT
Isla

"Now, can anyone guess who Victoria Street was named after?"

I stand before my group with the famous street behind me. They're silent, likely full of people who *think* they know the answer but are too afraid to venture a guess.

"That would be Queen Victoria. The street itself was designed by architect Thomas Hamilton, who is best known for his neo-classical influence on the city. He also designed the Martyrs' and Burns Monuments on Calton Hill. The latter of which was based on the Choragic Monument of Lysicrates in Athens. Hamilton's influence is all over this charming city, so keep an eye out for him as you continue to explore. And make sure to stop by Calton Hill if you haven't been as it is my absolute favorite place in Edinburgh." I give a minuscule bow, because I can't help it. "So concludes our tour. I'll let you go off and enjoy your suppers, but if anyone has any remaining questions, I will stick around to answer them."

Thankfully, this tour group is not heavy on the questions. I've been held here for over an hour answering questions before—often questions I already answered during the tour or some that are in no relation whatsoever to the content of the tour, or Edinburgh itself. This time, I receive tips (from most of them) ranging between one and ten pounds, then they set off to have their whisky and haggis, or whatever Scottish cuisine they find necessary to sample whilst here.

I better start working on a meal for myself as well. There must be something for me to scourge up at home…but I *could* head to a pub and chat with whoever is behind the bar. With option number two, I leave myself open to another chance run-in with Rachel.

It's unbelievable that I happened upon her again the other day in the supermarket. I mean, she said it, in a city of five hundred thousand, the likelihood of us crossing paths this many times is preposterous, yet here we are. Each time, I have a glimmer of hope until I'm reminded how I mucked it all up.

She wore a heather-gray cap over her hair in a low ponytail, and her freckled cheeks were as adorable as always. But she didn't blush. That first day we met, I made her blush so many times.

She wants nothing to do with me.

I push my way into the first pub I pass and wave at the middle-aged man behind the bar.

"Isla," he says when he sees me. "What'll you have? A Tennent's? Or I know you fancy the Belhaven's."

"Naw, Craig, I'm not having a drink tonight. Just a steak and ale pie, if you've got it."

"'Course we've got it. Coming right up."

I slide onto a stool at the end of the bar and pull out my phone, figuring I can get some work done. My business plan is on the cloud, so I pull it up. I read over it for a second, but I can't handle this in the quiet. I pop a wireless headphone in one ear and cue up some music. Oh, well, a great song is playing, so I can't do anything *now*. This song requires all of my attention. Then the next song plays and as it does, I pick at my nails, drum my fingers, balance my stool on the two back legs, and aimlessly scroll through social media. Then Craig brings out my pie. Now it's too late—I can't eat *and* work on the business plan.

It's a silly dream anyhow.

...

The next morning, the sun streams in through my window, waking me up. I don't have a tour this morning and Josie told me to come in at 11 a.m., so I roll on my back to scroll through a few of the group chats I'm in, checking for anything that pertains to me.

Then I hear something—the opening and closing of a cupboard door. There's someone in my kitchen. I sit up quickly. *Aileen?* I check my flatmate's location on the app. No. She's at work. Okay, so either it's her boyfriend with a key that I don't know about, or a burglar.

I shove my glasses on my face, then slide out of bed as quietly as possible, snatching my trousers from the back of my desk chair so I am not confronting a potential criminal in my pants.

I creak open the door and tip-toe out. As I move closer to the living room, I survey the hallway but I don't see anyone. When I clear the hallway, I turn my head slowly to see someone lounging barefoot and shirtless on the couch.

"Och, Ben! Why are you naked?" I chuck a blanket at my brother from where it was resting over a chair.

He seizes the blanket and drapes it over his shoulders like a cape, even bothering to tie the two ends in front at the base of his neck. "I'm not naked. I spilled coffee on my shirt. You have a washer so I'm using it."

I chuck one of his discarded socks at him next. "How did you get in?"

"Aileen let me in."

"Aileen was here?" Ever since Aileen started dating her boyfriend, it's like I live alone. I don't mind. I'd live alone if I could, but having a flatmate saves money that can be put toward the café.

"She let me in on her way out. Said she was stopping by to grab a blouse for work. She and I both agree I should have a key. Though, she was a tad irritated by my presence."

"Everyone is irritated by your presence. Why didn't you text me? You can't just show up here."

"I didn't see you when I was in town a week ago and I felt guilty."

He made the drive two times in that short of a timeframe? That's odd. "You were in town a week ago? Decided to harass David, then?"

"Why are you being such a grump? It's exasperating."

My eyes lift to the ceiling. "I wasn't expecting you to show up unannounced and naked this morning. Why are you here, besides to wash your shirt?"

He relaxes back on the couch. "I've been having a bit of a week. Thought I'd come see you."

"Why were you here a week ago?"

"My minging week started about two weeks ago. I wanted to see David. Also, I was hoping to run into this couple I met the other day."

I raise an eyebrow. "You're into couples now?"

"I'm not not into couples. I would thrive in a throuple; we both know this. But no, they were stranded outside the café, buggered off without a word mind you, but the woman left behind a necklace. I was hoping to return it to her. Her fingers never left it as she spoke to me, probably how it got yanked off. Seemed important."

God, always trying to do nice things, he is. "How do you expect to find her? This is a big city."

"Already did. Ran into them on the way to David's that night. Necklace returned like the good Samaritan I am."

"Jesus," I say. "How the hell did you run into them?"

His shoulders lift. "Not mine to question the universe. Works in mysterious ways."

I sit down in the chair across from him, pulling my legs up in front of myself and leaning my chin on my knees. "Do you think the universe can help me go back in time?"

His eyes soften. "Likely not. Why? What'd you do?"

I shift so my forehead is now pressed to my knees and I don't have to look at him. With my voice muffled, I explain what happened with Rachel.

"She hates me now," I finish.

I don't know if I expected kind words or something along those lines, but that is not what I get. Ben throws a pillow at me and says, "Damn. Way to let past trauma halt a blossoming relationship."

I pick up my head and glare. "Go home."

"Listen, it doesn't sound like she cares about you enough to hate you."

"I honestly can't tell if you're trying to be helpful or not. I need you to leave."

"I'm just saying, move past it. Sounds like she has." He laces his hands behind his head. "I'll leave when my shirt's dry."

…

Ben does not leave when his shirt dries. In fact, he mucks about my flat as I get ready for work, exchanging my glasses for contacts and braiding my hair, then he comes to the shop with me. Josie is thrilled to see him, but he spends my entire shift poorly playing instruments and un-organizing things I just organized.

Josie informs me that my guitar still isn't ready, which does not help my piss poor mood. Apparently, the tuners haven't come in yet.

Following my shift, Ben makes me get a meal with him. After, he finally takes his leave, giving me an uncharacteristically tight hug before he departs. "If you truly think Rachel is someone for you, don't give up. Unless she tells you to leave her alone. Try to get in her good graces. Be nice. Be her mate. Be a kind face she can look forward to seeing. Though, I'm not sure why anyone would look forward to seeing your face."

"Och!" I push out of his embrace. "Arsehole."

He pats me on the head and then climbs into his car to drive off.

I trudge back to my flat intending to finally fill out the loan application. I brought up the café to Ben this evening, but he sidestepped the question like he always does. Told me it wasn't time yet. It's time for me. I'll do it alone.

But again, I'm lying to myself. I sit down in front of my laptop and manage to get nothing done.

CHAPTER NINE
Rachel

I spend the solitary days before the start of my program searching for the finishing touches on my apartment. A picture for a glaringly empty spot on the wall, a few more utensils for the kitchen, a toilet brush. And, yes, a table. Well, a nightstand. Other tables will have to wait. I have to maintain some sort of a budget considering I have no income.

My phone started working again after that first day and has been working fine since, so I can traverse the city without the fear of getting lost. Well, without the fear of not being able to get myself *un*-lost. I get lost a lot. I force myself out of my flat at least once a day. It's not that I'm unmotivated to leave, I just don't know where to go or what to do, besides shop for my apartment. Once those last few finishing touches are applied, the thought of spending another pound on anything other than food makes me want to bury myself in cement to keep my hand away from my wallet.

On this particular day, my outing is to a new coffee shop. While I'm waiting for my tea, I spot someone familiar at a corner table, but I can't place him. He's a tall, Black man with short hair, about my age, with his head buried in a laptop, holding coffee to his lips but not taking a sip.

I have to stop analyzing my subject when my tea is set on the counter. I fetch it, popping off the lid so I can dump in a packet of sugar. I grab a wooden stirrer and swirl the liquid around before turning back for one more good stare at the man. He's wearing a bright orange, short-sleeved button-down shirt with neon-colored geometric shapes and black pants.

This time, he looks up and catches my eye. My instinct is to dart out of the coffee shop because he caught me staring, but before my body can catch up to that instinct, he says, "Hey."

His voice sparks the memory of how I know him. He's the bartender from Hoot the Redeemer. The bar Isla took me to.

"Hi," I say back, forcing myself out of my head. "Sorry—I was totally staring."

He chuckles. "No, you're good. You're Isla's friend, right?"

I smile, appreciating that he recognizes me too. "Friend might be too strong of a word." Certainly, too strong of a word.

His chin tips up in understanding, though I think his understanding infers that I got some that night. Which I did not. "Ah, I see." He sticks a hand out and I step closer to his table to take it. "I'm David," he reminds me.

"Right. Rachel," I say back. "It's nice to meet you…again."

"You too." He closes his laptop, abandoning whatever had so raptly caught his attention. He gestures to the chair across from him. "Want to sit?"

I consider the chair for a moment. What else do I have to do? "Sure." I slide into the seat and take a sip of my scalding tea, letting it burn the roof of my mouth. I cringe, but try to act like that didn't happen. "So," I start, eyes on the verge of watering, "you're American. Or Canadian, I guess. Can I ask what you're doing in Scotland?"

"The accent gave me away, huh?" He weighs his head. "American in theory, Scottish in practice. My dad is Nigerian, actually, and my mom is American, but they met here in Edinburgh. I was born here, but we moved to Massachusetts when I was ten, so I picked up the accent pretty easily. Decided to come back for uni and have not left."

I nod, impressed. "So, you like it here, then?"

He cocks his head. "Do you not?"

I shake my head quickly. "No, no. Not what I'm saying. I guess I haven't settled yet." I wrap both hands around my burning cup of tea, letting it rest on the table. "I guess what I'm asking is, how long did it take you to find your place here?"

His head weighs from side to side. "I'd say it took me a month or so to feel established here. I was at uni and having trouble figuring out who I wanted to be. Honestly, it was Isla's brother, Ben, who helped me find my place. Invited me to have lunch with him after class one day, and that was that. He's been one of my best friends ever since."

I smile. "That's nice."

"It is. But hell, maybe if I wasn't in school my entire time here, I wouldn't feel as in place as I do. I'm getting my Ph.D. in Mathematical and Computer Sciences."

My eyes light up as my mouth drops in delight. "Really? Where?"

"Heriot-Watt."

I release the tea to clasp my hands under my chin, giving him what I'm sure is a ridiculous grin. "I'm getting *my* Ph.D. at Heriot-Watt! That's why I'm here. For Marine Biodiversity. My focus is on the effects of microplastics on marine organisms. I'll end up getting more specific, but I'm going to let myself start my research before I narrow it down, though I'm leaning toward a focus on microorganisms."

His eyes light up as well. "No way. Well, welcome. I know we're in different departments but I'm in my second year, so I'm happy to answer any questions you have." He sips his coffee. "When did you get here?"

"Just under two weeks ago."

He squints. "Well, Rachel, I'm starting to think that may be why you don't feel settled yet. And hell, I know you said friend was too strong of a word, but you've managed to meet Isla already, so that's something."

I must make a discernable face, because he asks, "What?"

"Just, with Isla…" and everything that happened between us spills out. I start with our meeting, then the view from Calton Hill, the tattoos, the bar, the kiss, what happened after the kiss, Arthur's seat, and end with the grocery store. He nods along intently, eyes soft. When I'm finished, I cover my mouth. "Oh my god," I say into my hand. "I am so sorry. You did not need to know all of that."

"It's fine. Really. My fault for making you comfortable. I think it just means we're meant to be friends." He scratches behind his ear. "I am sorry that happened to you. I know this won't mean much, but I know Isla. Her apology was genuine. I'm sure she feels bad about laying that assumption on you. However, your refusal to accept her apology is also reasonable and valid. Putting yourself first is okay."

I didn't know how much I needed to hear that. I didn't know how much I needed to *tell* someone everything. I do that, though. I hold things in until I know the exact right thing to say. But if I wait too long, I explode and dump everything on the first person within earshot.

Though, it's not like I've been completely keeping this to myself. I did tell Piper what happened with Isla that night after Arthur's Seat. We were in my bedroom at my new flat, sharing the bed while Nick slept out on the couch, and I told her every detail in a whisper. Then she pulled me in and hugged me tightly, telling me it would be okay. I felt better after that because sometimes you just need to talk to your best friend. Even if nothing is fixed, knowing they're by your side, physically or emotionally, makes everything better.

However, since I'm giving her and Nick space to do things I don't ever want to know about, I haven't told her about running into Isla again. They deserve a bit of after-vacation, first-couple-of-weeks-in-love bliss. Before they left, Nick and Piper confessed their love for one another and made out in public like lovesick, horny teenagers.

It's silly, but sometimes validation from someone who doesn't love you unconditionally is necessary, so to David, I quietly say, "Thank you."

"Of course," he says. He leans forward, almost conspiratorially. "Do you want to get lunch?"

...

"Daily FaceTimes my ass," Piper scolds as she answers my call. Her hair is done in the half-up, half-down style she prefers so she can show off her dual-toned hair. I'm cooking dinner, chopping up vegetables so she can't see but the very top of my head on the screen.

"I've been busy!" I argue. I also have nothing to talk about. "And you've been getting busy, I assume." I scrunch my nose tightly. "Ew, ignore I made that joke. That was gross."

She cackles, phone moving away from her face as her head tips back. "Yes, we have. In a lot of different places, mind you."

"Ew," I say again. "I do not want to know that about my brother."

She rolls her eyes. "Oh my god. It's not like I'm describing the feeling of his dick in my mouth, which, by the way—"

"Piper Greenway, if you finish that sentence, I swear I am hanging up this call and not talking to you for a week."

"Fine," she pouts.

I'm unbelievably happy for her and Nick, but at the same time, selfishly, my heart is breaking for myself. It shouldn't be. This isn't about me. But I feel bad for me. Me is lonely. But I suppose getting less so.

"So, what'd you do today?" Piper asks.

"I made a friend," I answer proudly. "His name is David."

She squeals. "Yay! Is he cute?"

"Very. However, ninety-nine-point-nine percent chance that he is exclusively into men. Also, I'm literally just looking for friends right now. I don't need anything more complicated." Despite being lonely, I do know what is and isn't good for me.

"Nothing wrong with complicated. Nick and I did complicated for a bit."

"You and Nick did complicated for half a day. If that. Your life is a Hallmark movie with X-rated content. There is nothing complicated unless you choose to make it so."

"Good golly, she's sassy this evening."

"Sorry," I sigh. I am. "I just miss you guys."

"But you made a friend today! In less than two weeks in Edinburgh. You'll have us replaced in no time!"

"Impossible."

Piper has been my best friend since I was nine years old. She is completely irreplaceable, and rightfully so.

"So, first day tomorrow. Are you nervous?"

"A bit."

"Gotta give me more, Rach."

I huff. "Of course I'm nervous, but I'm also not. I'm finally getting to a familiar place here. In concept, I mean. Academic settings are my jam. I know exactly what tomorrow will look like for the most part. Since Dr. Andonov, the lead researcher, is away, Professor Zgheib said I'll start by building my research plan. It'll be a lot of reading scientific articles."

"Super fun," Piper says. "You're so smart. I love how smart you are. Everyone is going to be so jealous of your brain."

"Sure."

"Now, don't practice your smile in the mirror too much tomorrow. One, it'll make you late. Two, your smile is perfect."

...

I practice my smile in the mirror for too long. And shocker, I'm running late. Once I arrive on campus, I find my advisor in her office.

Professor Zgheib gives me the same tour Dr. Andonov did on the day of my orientation, but I don't complain. Outside of my head, at least. Then she leaves me alone in a lab. Once Dr. Andonov is back in town, I assume they'll be down here with me occasionally, but until then, I'm alone.

I spend the day as I expected I would—learning the systems of my new university. I secure accounts for all of the scientific journals and databases I'll need and log into my school email. Then, I'm not sure what to do. In order to start my research, I need samples.

Oh, well that's what I should do. I pull up a map to find bodies of water in the area that I can collect samples from. Here's a reason why owning a car will be useful—I can drive myself to more obscure bodies of water as opposed to hitching a ride on a bus and walking whatever distance necessary.

I have a decent savings account going because I took a few years off from school after I got my masters to save up for my Ph.D. However, not decent enough to drop on a vehicle. Not if I want my savings to last the entirety of my program. I'm not allowed to work on my current visa. Though, not to be that person, but I could convince my grandparents and parents to help me put some cash toward a car. As my Christmas gift, maybe? Not important. I'll find my way to the water sans car.

I take my time and make a solid list of sample locations. While typing out my list, an email notification pops up in the top right corner of my computer screen.

It's Dr. Andonov. They sent over a chunk of their research for me to look over. I click into my email to start downloading the papers, but the email below Dr. Andonov's distracts me.

It's from the Victoria University of Wellington in New Zealand. I'm sure it's a random newsletter—which is so fun to receive from a program that rejected me. I swipe my fingers on the trackpad to delete the email but pause before completing the command. The newsletter could include interesting findings I should know about. I click on the email and find that it is not a newsletter.

It's a personalized email addressed to me. I've been put on a waitlist. A waitlist? They rejected me—this must be a mistake. I read the email. Then I read it again. They're referencing the program I applied for, but like I said, it *has* to be a mistake.

Even if it's not, it doesn't matter. I'm in Edinburgh. I chose Heriot-Watt. I'm on the verge of being happy here. Even if they email me again to inform me I have been accepted, I won't go. It's too late. I'm already here. The program I am in is a great program. I am lucky to be here.

I drum my finger on the base of the laptop. But what if I would be happier there?

Nope. No. I delete the email.

Then I go into my trash folder and recover the email. I read it once more. No. Okay. I'm done. This means nothing. I am here in Scotland. I can stay here in Scotland. But, wow, it would be such a great opportunity. I mean, New Zealand!

No, no. Scotland can be Scotland! again. I'll make sure of it.

I delete the email again and for good measure, I delete it from my trash folder. I am not moving to New Zealand.

I go back to Dr. Andonov's research. There's so much of it— it will take me days to get through it all.

Perfect. My ideal way to spend time.

I start with an article about microplastics, which is part of my focus. Microplastics are small pieces of plastic that are under 5mm and can be extremely harmful not only to our water, but all marine life. Since it's a rather recent form of study, not a lot is known about the true effects of microplastics, but Dr. Andonov has made waves in terms of discovery. I hope to do the same. Microplastics don't only come from larger pieces of plastic that have been broken apart, they're also in personal hygiene products that we use on the daily. On purpose. Like, those little scrubby beads that were in facewashes and body washes and even toothpastes. Since they're so small, that's why they can pass so easily into our water system. Dr. Andonov has written four whole papers on the microbeads in facewash and their negative effects on marine life in Scotland. They were at least part of what helped microbeads to be banned in the U.K.

I spend the rest of the day reading. As I'm reading, the hair becomes unbearable on the back of my neck. This happens a lot. I like how my hair looks long, so I keep it long, but if it touches me too much, it bugs the hell out of me and I need to get it up and away as soon as possible. With my eyes still perusing the article, I pull my hair up into a ponytail using the scrunchie kept around my wrist. Instant relief washes over me. My hair is getting too long. I meant to get it cut before I moved, but I ran out of time. Suddenly, I was on a flight to Scotland and about a month overdue at the hairdresser. I need a refresh on my roots as well.

Well, getting my hair done can be something to cement my permanence here—if I find a hairdresser I like, there's another element to make this place my home. Once I finish the article, I start to hunt for hairdressers in the area. I find one with good reviews not too far from where I live and book an appointment.

Perhaps I won't only get a trim. Moving here was a big change, maybe I need a bigger change in my appearance to reflect that. I'm okay with change. I love it, in fact. Can't get enough of it. This may be just what I need.

CHAPTER TEN
Isla

I burst through the door of Josie's shop with my hands folded in prayer. "Please, *please*, tell me my guitar is ready. I have a gig tonight. I don't want to borrow one again."

Josie puts her hands on her hips. Today, she's sporting a fuzzy purple jumper over a long, black skirt. "Have you slept more than three hours this week?" she asks, inspecting me like I've strolled in sporting head-to-toe mud. It takes everything I have to not check my reflection in the window.

"Yes."

Josie keeps her hands on her hips and stares me down.

"I have been sleeping, Josie." Not a lot, but I have been. Enough to function.

Her hands drop. "Of course, your guitar is ready, pet. What do you take me for? I'll grab it so you can gawk at it, but then I expect you to get to work."

She shuffles to the back like the guitar isn't two weeks later than promised and then comes out holding my baby. I take it from her and cradle it in my arms as such. "God bless," I say, opening up my case to place the guitar inside. "Did you give her a polish as well? She's shiny."

"Yes, I gave her a polish. Needed to. When was the last time you did so yourself?"

I cringe. Never, is the answer. I'll wipe away any scuff or mark, but I don't believe I have ever polished her. "Like a month or so ago."

Josie narrows her eyes. "Sure." She goes back behind the counter and starts to reorganize a stack of pins. "Go put that in back. You're late already."

I glance at the clock on the wall. I'm three minutes early, but Josie operates on her own time. Always has. I run my hand through a bin of guitar picks, choosing a clear one with purple marbling before tossing it back in the pile. "Will do. How shall I start my day?"

"By reorganizing the sheet music. People come in and mess with it, you know. They always get out of order. Then work the counter. I have more instruments to repair."

I do as directed, dropping my guitar and bag in the back, then make my way to the sheet music, going through each packet and reorganizing it by letter. Organizing the music doesn't take me more than an hour, even though I take my time. When I complete this task, I head back behind the counter and take the spot Josie was occupying when I walked in. The shop is deserted this afternoon, so I pick at my nails and stare longingly out the window at every person who walks by, hoping they'll enter the store so I have someone to talk to. Eventually, a couple of teenagers wander in, but they're just here to mess with the instruments we let anyone play. One of them clearly knows what they're doing on the piano, but the other is hopeless. They're strumming a guitar so poorly I'm desperate for earplugs. After a while, they wander off and then the store is empty again.

Josie comes out from the back at ten till five and says, "Go home. Dead day. I'm closing early."

I spin toward her. She's holding my bag and my guitar case. "Are you sure there's nothing else you want me to do?" I'm restless without a task or job. My gig isn't until later this evening.

"No, no. Go test out those new tuners. Off with you, lass."

The door jingles and a few people enter. I look back to Josie, hopeful she'll request my help with the patrons now that she can't close. However, she continues to usher me out, using her hands to shoo me.

"Fine," I say, moving out from behind the counter to give her a quick hug goodbye. I retrieve my guitar case from her hands, then go on my way, exiting by way of that jingling door.

I should go home, but instead I head to a park because whenever I wander the streets, I hope to run into the girl the universe keeps bringing me back to. While I hope to see her, I've no plan on how to…what? Win her back? Make her forgive me? I don't know.

My endgame is unspecific but simple. Her. I want her, in whatever form she'll let me.

First step: find Rachel. I'll sort out the other steps as I go.

I take a seat on a bench and pull out my guitar, keeping the case closed so it doesn't look like I'm busking. Not that I am opposed to doing so. I have certainly left my case open before whilst playing on the street and accepted the few pounds dropped in there. Hey, I'll always take an extra quid or two. Today, I'm just tuning and testing out the new strings in the fresh air.

I strum the tight new cords. Unsurprisingly, Josie has it perfectly done. I play a few chords, making sure it feels right on my fingers. It does. Then I play a few more chords and soon enough I'm playing a song. It's a little melody, a go-to one of mine written back at uni. Now, the lyrics are shite, but the melody itself is still pretty good. I always think I should go back and write new lyrics, but I haven't gotten around to it. The words have never been my strong suit, but the music itself makes sense to me. However, I keep hoping to find something, or some*one*, who can bring the words out of me. She's out there somewhere.

I go through it a few times before I decide to cool it and head home. I need to eat something before my gig, anyhow. I pack up my guitar, throw the strap across my chest so the case rests against my back, and go on my way.

I climb the blue carpeted stairs to my flat with heavy feet. When I walk through my door, I jump.

"What the fuck?" I say when I see Ben sat on my couch, drinking a smoothie. "Why are you here again? You were here only three days ago."

His response is an obnoxious sip of the smoothie that, judging by the blender and dirty chopping board, he has concocted using fruit from my pantry. I huff an annoyed sigh. That fruit was going to be this evening's meal. Part of it, at least.

"Would it kill you to be excited to see me?"

With a calming exhale, I place my guitar down in the foyer. I take a seat across from him, leaning forward with my hands resting on my knees. Newtonmore is more than a two-hour drive one way. Too far of a trek for Ben to be taking this regularly. "What are you playing at, Ben?"

"Nothing."

"Bennett."

"Islington."

My eyes go to the sky. I do not need to correct him and tell him that that is not my full name. It is just Isla and he is well aware. I stand up.

"If you don't want to tell me what's the matter, I don't care. I have a gig tonight, so I'm going to fix my hair, find something other than my fruit that you ate for myself, then leave. You are welcome to join in on any of those activities. Especially the hair. Yours is looking a little gray."

"Ha ha," he deadpans. Ben has been graying since his early twenties. Honestly, the streaks look pretty good on him, but as long as he remains himself, I will never tell him that. He runs his fingers through his salt and pepper hair, still leaning heavily on the pepper. "The gray looks hot and you know it. You're jealous that you too don't have hair this interesting." He shifts on the couch so he can flip his head forward to show me a fully silver lock in the back. "I'm just waiting for the entire thing to look like this."

I cross my arms as he lifts his head back up. "You are impossible to insult."

"It's called confidence. You should get some. It's great."

I stomp off to my bedroom so I can attempt to do something to the mane. I keep a pretty decent hair routine, but there are some days when it wants to fight. Today is one of those days. I wish every day was a good hair day. Like the day I met Rachel—my hair looked so good that day. I always attempt to do something nice to it when I have gigs, but the problem is, that task is impossible when it insists on being argumentative. It took me a while to learn how to manage my hair after I hit puberty and it went curly on me.

I add a little dry shampoo to the roots and fluff it up. I rake my fingers through it. No. This cannot remain down. I pull it into a bun, letting a few hairs loose to frame my face. It looks fine. I leave my room.

Ben glances at me from the couch. "I wish I had curly hair," he says longingly.

I roll my eyes. "I'll take your hair gene if you take mine."

He reaches a hand out for me to shake. "Deal." He presses his lids shut before slowly cranking open one eye. He drops my hand and sighs. "Didn't work. Damn."

"Damn," I repeat.

...

I sit down on a wooden stool set up on a raised section of the floor passing as a stage in this pub. A rather full pub, at that. Not that I mind. Never have been one with the whole stage fright thing. I find Ben in the crowd, sat alone at a table sipping a beer, and smile. He beams back before he sets down the pint and claps his hands together obnoxiously, giving a, "Woo!" after it.

"Ah, my one fan," I say into the mic to receive a polite titter from the crowd.

I strum my guitar, starting on a cover of a Mitski song. I go through my set, ending on claps from the crowd. Before I hop off the stage, I offer them a thanks. Then, I drop my guitar at the table with Ben so I can go up to the bar to grab myself a drink. It's on the house, as it usually is.

Ben's friend David is arriving as I return to the table. He seems surprised to see me, which is odd. I figure if Ben asked him here, he would know it was because I was playing.

"Hiya, David," I say, taking a seat. "You missed my set."

He frowns. "Ah, were you playing here tonight? Sorry about that."

I wave him away. "No worries, love."

Huh. That word feels wrong in my mouth. That was a common form of endearment for me—until Rachel. Now it feels like her word. *Och.* I've got it bad, haven't I? I need to get past it. She's past me. I should do her the courtesy of the same.

I incline my head to the bar. "If you mention me, you'll get a free one."

"Good to know. I never get free drinks," he says as he walks to the bar.

Ben leans over to me and stage whispers, "That was a joke. Because he's a bartender."

"Thank you," I loudly whisper back, tone flat. "I didn't get it."

He continues, still whispering, "It was a layered joke because he's also bloody fit, so he gets free drinks from that as well."

I go back to my normal volume. "Aye, you sure you're not in love with your best mate? Wouldn't surprise me the way you always go on about how fit he is."

David rejoins us, drink in hand, and says, "Ben isn't my type."

Ben waggles a finger at him. "In desperate times, you may change your mind."

"So," David says after a sip, "what's wrong, Ben?"

"Nothing."

David and I lock eyes. "Same thing he said to me earlier. I don't believe him."

David's mouth presses into a line, eyeing Ben warily. "Me neither."

Ben's head drops backward in exasperation. "Nothing is *wrong*. I'm just in town. What's the big deal?"

"Not that I'm not happy to see you, but you're more of a once a monther," David says.

"You've turned into a once a weeker," I add.

He says stubbornly, "I'm here as moral support for my sister." He looks to David. "She got her heart broken, you know."

I cringe at Ben's words and David's raised eyebrows. "Broken is too strong of a word. Squeezed tightly to the point of pain is more accurate. And it's my own damn fault."

David asks, "Rachel? Or someone else?"

Ben swiftly turns to him. "How do *you* know Rachel?"

I pipe in, "I took her to Hoot. They met there."

Now David cringes and I don't understand why until he says, "Actually, Rachel's becoming a friend of mine. We ran into one another at a café a couple of days ago. She's getting her Ph.D. at Heriot-Watt as well, so we grabbed lunch that day and a drink last night. She's great." Then he adds unnecessarily, "Sorry."

"Oh," I say. I had forgotten that David too was on a Ph.D. route at the same uni. "I didn't realize. I mean, why would I? I haven't spoken to her since…aye. Well."

"Will it make you feel better or worse if I tell you we talked about you?"

I blow out a puff of air. "I'm assuming she told you what I did?"

"Yeah."

"Then worse. But I'm glad she has someone to talk to about how shitty I was."

"Yeah," he says again. Then he rolls his head like he's contemplating saying the next bit. "Listen, I know I don't know you well, but I do know that just because you did a shitty thing does not mean you are a shitty person."

I give a small smile. "Mind telling her that?"

"I'll mention it if I can. But so we're clear, I refuse to get in the middle of this. I will be transparent with you, as I will be with her. I refuse to pass messages between the two of you or try to convince either of you of the other's worth."

"That's fine," I say quickly. There are already too many people involved in something I wish would have remained between her and me. "I won't ask you to talk me up or arrange a chance meeting or anything odd."

Ben fans his face dramatically. "And he knows how to set healthy boundaries? Hubba, hubba. Maybe I am in love with you?"

David rolls his eyes. "Ben, I must stress again, you are not my type. I usually prefer them, above all else, into dudes."

Ben lifts his chin. "Right, that would be an important factor. The ladies do take my fancy. Platonic love affair it is." He takes a large gulp of his drink. "So, when can we commence operation make-Isla-get-over-the-random-scientist-girl-she-hardly-knows?"

I shove him on the arm, almost knocking him off his stool as David cackles at the beer sloshing from Ben's glass.

"Go fuck yourself, Bennett."

CHAPTER ELEVEN

Rachel

"We spent all day on the beach collecting samples and all day before in the bowels of one of the science buildings combing through the archives of some microscopic life from like ten years ago so we can compare how it has changed and evolved because it was taken from the same water and shore, but it's been ten years, you know? So, the amount of microplastics in the water has likely increased by a terrifying amount. I know the novelty is going to wear off eventually, but right now, I am so excited by every-thing and I want to brag about how cool my life is." I finally take a breath and shrug sheepishly.

Since I met him, David has become subject to my information dumping. I'm at Hoot sitting at the bar and talking at him after another very silent day. Most of my days during these initial three weeks of my program have been pretty silent. There are no other students in the Center for Marine Biodiversity and Biotechnology for the summer, despite plenty of other students being on campus, so the majority of my day is spent with Dr. Andonov. Dr. Andonov is back in town and has driven me to a few different bodies of water to collect samples to help with my research. I really like Dr. Andonov. I already admired them and their work before I started at Heriot-Watt, but now that I know them? They're so cool. I have never met anyone else as interested in microplastics and microorganisms as me. Dr. Andonov is also quite happy being quiet. As am I, but I'm not used to being one of two quiet people. I'm used to one very chatty person (Piper) and then me, so when I see David at the end of the day or for lunch, I explode with the need to hear someone speak, even if that someone is me.

David grins though, leaning forward on his elbows across the bar. Every time I apologize for talking too much, he scolds me, so I don't apologize this time. "That's really great."

I sip my water. "When does your program re-start? You've told me a million times but I am not retaining the information."

"You're refusing to retain the information because you don't like the answer," he lightly reprimands. "September."

My face goes slack. Right. David's also in a three-year program, but unlike my full year-round deal, he has a summer break. Though it's the kind of course where he does have work to complete during the summer, but he doesn't need to be on campus for it. He does most of his work during the day, then bartends in the evenings. He's entering his second year officially in the Fall.

"I like the hair, by the way," David says, gesturing a loose finger toward my head as he clears a glass from the bar.

I run a hand through it. My hair appointment was yesterday. I didn't get too much cut off, just enough to irritate me. It still hits my chest. However, I added an addition of curtain bangs. I really, really like them. Piper says they frame my face perfectly. The biggest change is the color. I went a little darker with the tone, going for honey rather than the platinum I had.

He takes a peek at his watch. "I've got another ten minutes here. You want to head home or go somewhere and get a drink where I don't work?"

"I'm down." I have to go to campus tomorrow, but not too early. And just to sit in the lab to look at microorganisms and zooplankton with a microscope.

A little over ten minutes later, David is guiding me down Rose Street and to a casual pub he likes. We take a seat and David runs to grab a drink for the both of us. I peek over my shoulder to the back of the bar where a stool is set up under a spotlight with a microphone settled in front of it. Oh, they must do live music. That's cool. I love live music in bars and restaurants as long as I can still hear myself having a conversation.

David returns and sets my drink in front of me as he sits. He looks behind me, his eyes going wide. "Goddamn it."

I turn around but don't see anything alarming, so I swivel back to him, my eyebrows scrunched together. "What?"

"I swear I did not do this on purpose. I didn't think…" He inclines his chin behind me and I turn around again, picking my ass up off the seat to see over some taller heads. I still don't…

"Oh."

Isla. Isla, hair loose and curly, framing her face in a goddess-like fashion, is settling herself on the stool behind the microphone, guitar perched on her lap.

"I didn't know she sang."

"We can leave," David offers, already moving to stand and abandon his full pint.

I gesture for him to sit back down. "No, no. Don't be ridiculous. I do not need to avoid a woman I had one bad kind-of-date with." One great kind-of-date, I should say, with a bad ending. "It's fine. We're here. She's here."

I miss whatever Isla says to introduce herself but catch as she begins with a cover of a Noah Kahan song. She has a beautiful voice. Like really beautiful. I can't help but watch her as she sings, eyes closed as she's breathing out the music, mouth pressed closely to the microphone, and fingers expertly strumming the guitar. I gulp. *Oh no.* She is still so very hot. The slight perspiration on her brow from the warm light shining on her, the way her lips move with the song, and those elegant fingers. Oh god. A yearning in my chest flushes downward, making me involuntarily squeeze my thighs together. This is embarrassing. I turn away, feeling my face heat.

If David notices, he doesn't comment, which is one reason I like him. He never pushes me beyond my boundaries. He glances behind me at Isla and extends a tight smile. I don't have to turn around to know she's spotted him. And I don't want to turn around on the off-chance she has not figured out it is me he is sitting with. Though, I'm sure she'll come over to say hello so what am I going to do then? Act like an adult and be polite? Yes, that is exactly what I'm going to do because it's either be nice and distant, be mean and distant, or make it very clear that I desperately want to lick the sweat off her neck and let her touch me with those elegant fingers. *Damn it.* I am weak.

She plays through her set while I attempt to make conversation with David. When she finishes, she thanks the crowd. My body goes rigid with nerves as I wait for her to approach. She doesn't. Five minutes pass and I think I'm in the clear.

I relax. Good. I know I could have managed to be an adult about it but, god, I'd rather not.

"What are you up to tomorrow?" I ask David, feeling like I can finally focus on my friend and no one else.

He starts to go into great detail about this computer program he's working with and I nod along. What he's saying makes sense but he tends to slip into jargon I don't bother to ask for definitions on. I do the same thing and I know if either of us decided to question the other on the jargon we use, we'd never be able to complete a conversation.

David finally takes a pause and glances over my shoulder. His eyes crinkle when he spots someone behind me. I twist around before I can stop myself, expecting to see Isla. I don't, however. I see a tall man with dark, curly, shoulder-length hair smiling back and holding up a hand in a wave. I swivel back to David.

"*Who* is that?"

He chuckles, moving his eyes back to mine. "Remember that guy I told you about? Callum. The one from my uni days? Who showed up at the party we went to last weekend after you left?"

"Oh, the one with the…" I trail off since he knows how that sentence ends. I nod in approval. "Nice." I glance over my shoulder, more discreetly this time. "Are you gonna talk to him?"

"I have his number. I can text him later."

I make a face. "Coward. Go talk to him." He looks like he's going to argue, so I add, "I won't be upset with you for ditching me. I swear. You really like this guy. I think I'd be upset with you for *not* talking to him."

His eyes grow grateful. "Thanks, Rach." He gets up, taking his drink with him. "If we don't leave together, text me when you get home, okay?"

"I'll do it." We won't be leaving together. I figure I'll finish my drink and then head out.

After David walks away, a text from my brother pops up on my phone.

You should start expecting weekly care packages

I laugh to myself as I type my response.

From you?

I'll contribute, but no. Who do you think from?

God she's an aggressive bundle of joy

One of the many reasons I love her. Weekly was our compromise. She would have done daily. I thought monthly was more reasonable

Bi-yearly would be fine

She'd never go for that. These'll be fun. I promise

Yes it'll be like I subscribed to Jam of the Month. But weekly

Damn right. You'll be stocked for life. Use the jam to make friends

I hate that that's not a terrible idea

The second I put my phone down, it blows up again. This time with a spam of texts from Piper.

My god

Isabel from high school came into the library today and had the gall to act like she didn't remember me

I mean, maybe she didn't, but you would think when someone says, "We went to high school together. We had seven classes together. You were my lab partner," they would at least pretend to remember

I'm not bitter or anything, though

I snort, feeling a pang in my chest. I miss her. I wish she was sitting in this pub giving me this rant in person rather than by text.

Lol sure

So not bitter

But honestly Isabel has always lacked the social graces of pretending to remember someone to be polite. I remember introducing myself to her at least five times. She was a part of Nick's group. Dated one of his friends or something. Tony probably

Really?? Nick said he didn't remember her

Is he pretending to make me feel better?

I hate that but also love that

He's probably telling the truth. Tony and her dated for a month at most

Also Nick literally never looked at other girls in high school. No one except you

Ugh. Don't remind me

Attention still on my phone, I chuckle as I type: **Yeah, me too.**

Suddenly, there is a presence next to me and a husky voice says, "Hiya."

I nearly jump out of my skin. Hand over my heart, I turn to see Isla hovering beside me. So close I can feel her breath on my skin.

I tense. "Hi," I say back evenly.

She slides uninvited into an empty chair at my table. "You mind?" she asks after she's settled.

"Um, no?" Mind is too strong of a word. I clear my throat. "I thought you had left after…after your set."

"Och, no. Had to hit the loo then get my complimentary free drink." She raises the glass as proof of said drink. She leans a tad closer to me, not quite in my space, and says in a low voice, "You look gorgeous, if you don't mind me saying. I like the new hair."

I do not look gorgeous. I'm sure I look fine, but after a day spent by the water, my hair is un-brushed and I'm not even wearing my standard mascara so I basically have no eyelashes. I'm just in a cropped, oversized T-shirt and jeans.

"Thanks," I say. My tongue itches to shower her with compliments—the shade of lipstick I am desperate to kiss off, the shirt showing off a collar bone I am equally desperate to get my mouth on, sharp winged eyeliner that I am unnecessarily jealous of. I've never been able to get my eyeliner to look like that. Instead, I say, "Your voice is beautiful. I didn't know you sang. I mean, I figured you played guitar based on…" I gesture to her arm where the tattoo she got the day we met hides under her sleeve.

Her eyes flash. "Ta. It's something I do a lot. Gigs at bars across the city."

This comment sparks a connection in my head. "Ah. That would explain why you know every bartender in Edinburgh."

"Exactly." She sips at her drink and eyes me. "So, your program has started, yeah? How's that going?"

I stare back at her. I can't believe she's sitting there acting like she didn't hurt me. Like she didn't reject me for sharing a basic fact about myself. Like we can have a normal conversation. I don't want to have a normal conversation. All I want is to be at home in bed. I down the rest of my drink.

"Great," I say as I stand. "Speaking of, I have to be up early tomorrow so I'm going to head home."

"Taking the bus?"

"No. I'll walk."

As I turn to leave, she gets up as well. "Let me walk you home," she offers as she follows me, abandoning her drink. "It's a long way."

"No need," I say, exiting the open pub door. On that first day, I told her where I was going to be living. I hate that she remembers.

She matches my pace, adjusting the guitar case strapped to her back. "Come on. I don't want you getting lost."

I keep walking, hoping she'll take the hint and stay behind. She does not. "I know my way."

That's not exactly true. My sense of direction is horrible and I definitely do not know my way around beyond the routes I take daily. I was going to pull out my phone and map my walk home, but I don't want to prove her right. Isla knows this city like the back of her hand, so it'll only serve as a reason for her to continue to walk with me.

"Say I'm walking in the same direction, then." She looks around pointedly as I turn what I know is the correct way on Princes Street. "Aye, this *is* my way."

I don't say anything to that. I just keep walking. If she wants to follow me home, well, then fine. She can. I hate that I don't hate that this is happening. A small part of me actually likes it, which pisses me off.

I don't think Isla is a bad person. She's probably pretty great, but I *can't* with her. Not tonight. Maybe not ever.

I turn on a street and she keeps pace beside me. I turn again, refusing to say a word. I turn again and, "Crap." I stop. I have no idea where I am. I glance around, unsure.

Isla glances with me. "Are we lost, love?"

Ugh, the "love" sounds mildly condescending today. "No," I say. "I just need to get my bearings." I whip my head right and left, decide I turned the wrong way one street back, and march in that direction with Isla still strolling along with me.

I stop again once I arrive at that intersection. No. Damn it. Maybe that *was* the right way. I swing my head back and forth between my options. And…*ugh*. I recognize where we are. This is right around where we kissed that night. I was already annoyed, and now all those feelings, good and bad, are rushing back to me. They're overwhelming enough to increase the rate of my heart.

Isla reaches out but curls her fingers back before she makes contact. Gently, she says, "If you tell me where exactly you live, I can get us there."

"No," I say, stepping away. Even though she didn't touch me, I could feel a brush of heat from her hand. "I don't need your help. Isla, go home. I can do this by myself."

"I'm sure you can. I just figured it might be easier if—"

"It will not be easier," I cut her off. "Listen, I don't know what you want from me. I don't…I don't want this." I motion between the two of us. "You're great, you are, but I honestly am no longer interested. It's not that you're not…" I gesture vaguely in an attempt to communicate that she is the most beautiful woman I have ever had the pleasure of speaking to, "…because you are…I just…" I groan. "We don't know each other. Not really. In the grand scheme of things, I'm sure we could get past what happened. But I don't want to feel judged for not knowing what I'm doing in any aspect of my relationship. I don't have experience dating women, sure, but I don't have much experience with men either. I'm lacking experience in all directions."

I turn away. "I'm going home. By myself. And you will be walking a different way."

"Rachel…" she says softly. Pleadingly. Even though she is not physically pulling me, I feel pulled back to her.

However, I pivot too quickly. My foot slips off the edge of the sidewalk, twisting sharply as it makes contact with the cobblestone street, sending a jagged pain up my leg as I crash to the ground.

CHAPTER TWELVE
Isla

Rachel is crumpled on the ground and I feel fully responsible. I drop to my knees beside her, asking, "You alright, love?" I see tears and ask more gently, "Can you stand?"

She nods wordlessly, jaw tight. I stand with her, wrapping an arm around her waist, and help her back to the pavement. She nods like she's okay, but sucks in a sharp gasp as soon as she puts pressure on her right foot. She squeezes her eyes shut as she picks up the foot and leans all of her weight on me.

"Ow," she squeaks out.

"Does your ankle hurt?" I ask daftly.

She nods again, mouth tightly pursed.

With my arm still around her, I say, "Let's sit down, yeah? Get you off that ankle."

I help lower her to the ground.

"Thanks," she mumbles as she stretches her injured leg onto the empty street, wincing.

I crouch down to inspect her ankle. It's already starting to swell up. She flinches when I touch it, letting out a little squeak.

"Sorry." I look back up at her. "We need to get you to A&E."

I search around nonsensically like I expect help to appear out of nowhere. "I'll call for an ambulance."

"No," she says quickly. "I don't need an ambulance. I can't afford an ambulance."

I furrow my brow. "You don't have to buy it, love."

She furrows her brow back. "Do you not have to pay for ambulances to pick you up here?"

"No? Wait, do you have to pay for ambulances in the States?"

"Yeah." She closes her eyes. "I guess, sure, then. Just…that's so many people."

I purse my lips, not understanding her point, but trying to go along with it anyway. "If you'd rather me drive you, I can. I'm not too far from here. I'll fetch my car."

She looks unsure. "I don't know…"

"It'll take me five minutes." I stand, adjusting the guitar case still strapped to my back. "I'll get my car, you stay here."

She glares in response, and butterflies flutter about my stomach. With one last glance at her, I jog toward my car. After I toss my guitar in the boot, I hop in to drive back to Rachel. I park the car, leaving it running.

"Here we are. Let's get you sorted." I open the rear door. "We're going to have you in the back so you can prop up that foot, okay?"

"Okay," she grunts as I help her stand. She leans on me and hops to avoid putting any pressure on her hurt ankle.

I help her inside the car and wait until she is settled before I close the door behind her. Once I'm in my seat, I glance at her in the mirror. Tears are still streaming down her face, but I can tell she is trying so hard not to cry. I open up my glove box and hand her a pocket pack of tissues without a word.

The drive to A&E is silent until I can't take it—one minute—

and I switch on the radio. I mumble along to songs I half-know, checking the rearview mirror every five seconds. When we reach our destination, I pull into the car park and drive up to the curb, as close to the entrance as I can get.

"You can't make it in by yourself," I state.

"You don't have to come in with me," she says softly.

I laugh because that's ridiculous. I put the hazards on and get out to help her out of the car. "Alright. On my back."

She reels back and stares at me with wide eyes. "What?"

"Climb on my back. We'll get in there easier than with you limping beside me." I turn my back to her. "Up you go."

She hops around to face me. "No. What? No."

I tut. "The longer you spend arguing with me the longer your ankle will hurt. What's the issue? I can carry you." I turn my back to her again and crouch down to give her less of a height to jump. "Hop on."

She grumbles, "That's so much touching." But before I can straighten up and offer to retrieve a wheelchair from inside, she puts her hands on my shoulders and hops onto my back. I catch her by the thighs and she wraps her arms and legs around me like a koala. I grin despite myself as I'm hit with the scent of saltwater from her hair. Every part of us that touches buzzes.

"This is humiliating," she mutters in my ear.

"Naw, not at all," I reassure her with a squeeze of her thigh. She squirms a bit, but I can't tell if that was a good squirm or a bad squirm. To be safe, I'll assume bad and not repeat that action. I walk us through the automatic glass doors and let her hop off me and sit in the pleather-chair-lined waiting room as I run up to the front desk to tell them what happened. The nurse behind the counter assures me they should be able to get to Rachel soon— quiet night. There are only a handful of other people in the waiting room. We'll need to fill out some paperwork and they'll call us back when they're ready.

I bring the clipboard to where she's sat but don't hand it over. I settle next to her under the fluorescent lights and start to fill it out. Illegally parked car be damned.

"You don't have to stay," she says, stretching for the clipboard.

I hold it out of her reach. "I'll leave if you want me gone, but I don't mind staying. I would like to stay."

"Fine," is all she says, settling back. She keeps her eyes glued to the ceiling-mounted TV playing a rerun of *QI*.

I bring the clipboard back to my lap and write, *Rachel*, before I pause and say, "I don't know your surname."

The ghost of a smile hits her lips, but she still does not look at me. "Moreau. M-O-R-E-A-U."

"Birthday?"

She tells me, "November 12th," and the year.

I hoot. "You're kidding! Mine's one day ahead and two years behind."

The smile cracks, growing full. "That's a coincidence. How did we not figure that out before?"

We spent that entire first day talking, yet I'm not sure how much I actually learnt about her. I hope I get to learn more.

After we go through the rest of the questions, I bring the form back up to the nurse. I sit back down beside her. "How ya doin'?"

"Fine," she says with a groan. "In pain." She shifts tensely. "Distract me, please."

I can think of a thousand different ways to distract her, but none of them are appropriate for this environment. "Well, if we're sharing personal information, my surname is Pyeon. P-Y-E-O-N. And now you know my birthday, so I will be expecting a gift. I'll be giving you one." I go on, filling her in on the personal information equal to what she shared with me. I could keep going, willing to share my National Insurance Number with her if she asks. However, the nurse comes out with a wheelchair, calling Rachel's name.

I stand with her and help her to the chair. "I'll be out here," I say.

Rachel nods stiffly.

The nurse cuts in, "Actually, if you want your girlfriend to come see you in the room, she can. We're going to get some x-rays first, but she can meet you afterward."

Rachel blanches at the word "girlfriend," so I answer for her. "Just new acquaintances with sexual tension, but happy to come with, if you'd like?"

I look to Rachel, letting her decide if she wants me in that personal space. "Okay," she says quietly. She must be in too much pain to dispute the sexual tension comment. Or she agrees.

The nurse smiles and says to me, "I'll come get you when she's ready."

She wheels Rachel away and I take the opportunity to move my car. Once it's parked in a legal space, I retake my seat in the waiting room. I pull out my phone and type a quick message to David, letting him know where we are because he's the only mate I know she has in the city. It's been weeks at this point, though, so she could have many more that I don't know about. Why would I? I'm nothing to her. But I'd like to be something, even if just her friend. Who she has sexual tension with.

The nurse comes and fetches me about twenty minutes later and takes me to the wee curtained-off section of a larger area functioning as Rachel's "room." She's reclined in the white bed, foot propped up and wrapped in white bandaging. She smiles shyly at me as I grab a seat and pull it up beside her.

"They think it's a sprain," she tells me. "I'm waiting for the doctor to come and tell me things."

I say, "Glad it's not broken. Hopefully it'll heal quickly. They give you anything for the pain?"

She releases a long exhale. "Hopefully. And yes. Thankfully." She lays her head back on the pillow and stares at the ceiling. "You don't have to stay," she says again.

It's my turn to sigh. "I'll leave if you tell me to, but if you don't, I am not going anywhere."

She nods, not meeting my gaze. I sit back in the chair, propping my booted feet up on her bed and keeping an eye on her out of the corner of mine. Her eyes prickle with unshed tears.

I drop my feet back to the ground and lean close to her. "What's wrong? Are you still in pain?"

She shakes her head. "No, no. It's silly."

"I'll bet you fifty pounds it's not."

She whispers, "I'm scared."

I reach for her hand but pause before taking it, remembering what she said about not liking it when strangers touch her. As much as I don't want to be, I am still a stranger to her and I have already touched her far too much for her liking tonight. I pull my hand back.

"Why?"

Her voice stays quiet. "I don't know how to do this. I don't know how to do it alone."

I get the feeling this is about more than the sprain. "Do what alone?"

"*This*," she emphasizes. "Life. I…God, I am so used to having Piper and Nick by my side that I didn't know what it would be like to not have them." She gulps. "The last time I was in the hospital with an injury, I was eleven. I broke my arm falling out of a tree. Piper and Nick were beside me the entire time, more than my parents. And, Isla, I appreciate so much that you're here, but…but…"

"But I'm not your best friend or your brother. I understand. I'm sorry. I'm sorry they're not here." I place my hand beside hers, offering comfort adjacent to the only way I know how. I swear her fingers inch closer to mine even if they do not touch.

A tear escapes that she quickly wipes away. "It's just, I feel like I can't even be sad about not having them because it's my fault. I left them behind, not the other way around."

I shake my head. "You're allowed to be sad. You're allowed to miss them. You came here to do something for yourself and I am sure they are thrilled for you." She nods. "You are allowed to feel any way you want to feel about not having them in the same country as you."

She sniffles. "You know, Piper always says I'm like her big toe because I keep her balanced. Well, she's like my whole right arm. Sure, I can figure out how to live my life without her by my side, but it's going to be so hard and take a lot of finagling."

"The two of you fancy your similes, huh?"

She laughs, seeming surprised by the sound. "She's a librarian—I picked it up from her." She angles her head toward me. "Thank you. For listening. Talking that out with me. Driving me here. Staying. I could go on."

"Anytime."

…

When they release Rachel, I take her back to my car and drive her to her flat. She sits in the rear again so she can elevate her ankle. I park on the road in front of hers, turning the car off. "I'll help you inside. Which floor are you on?"

"Second," she says, then shakes her head. "First. Sorry. Can't get used to that."

"Got it."

I help her and her new crutches into her building and up the stairs to her door. She unlocks the door and gets herself inside.

My feet stay firmly planted behind the threshold.

"Well, here we are," I say, not knowing what else there is to say. "I'll let you get some sleep." I don't move, waiting for her dismissal.

She looks back. "Do you…Do you want to come in for a cup of tea, or something?" she asks, voice edging on something akin to hopeful.

Or maybe I'm putting my own hope on her. I grin easily. "Sure." I step over the threshold and close the door behind me. Light blue walls greet me, a scattering of colorful pictures in varied gold frames lining the walls. I point to her cream-colored couch adorned with pillows in multiple shades of blue. "You take a seat. I'll prepare it."

She narrows her eyes. "I feel like you don't trust me to make tea."

I urge her toward the couch. "No, no. I just want you off that foot." I step toward her open-facing kitchen but rotate back. "You *do* own a kettle, correct?"

"I don't microwave the water, if that's what you're asking." She takes a seat, settling her crutches up against the side of the couch and bending down to remove the one shoe she still wears. "I've done extensive research into British culture. I know how to make tea. I also have a teapot sitting on the stove, if you want to be fancy about it."

I spy the teapot in question and feel the corner of my mouth twitch. "I trust you. You can show me next time. Elevate your ankle." I go into the kitchen, fill the kettle on the counter with water from the tap, and flip it on. I grab two mugs from where they are hung on a spinning holder beside it, setting them on the counter.

"How do you take your tea?" I call.

"Not super strong. Little bit of sugar, little bit of milk," she calls back.

I find a spoon for the sugar, and milk in the fridge. I pop two tea bags in her teapot, because I do want to be "fancy" about it, then pour the boiling water in. After it's done steeping, I pour tea in each of the mugs, add sugar and milk, then take them into the living room.

I go to set them on a table when I realize she doesn't have one.

She cringes, sensing my momentary confusion as I hover with a mug of tea in each hand. "I haven't bought tables yet. You can use the floor. There are coasters for the hardwood."

I spot four round, light blue coasters stacked up next to one leg of the couch. I set the mugs on the ground for the moment it takes to grab the coasters and slip them under. "There we are."

I gingerly take a seat beside her on the couch, ensuring there is an appropriate amount of space between us. She has her foot propped on a round ottoman with a pillow set atop it. "Is there anything you'd like me to do as long as I'm here? To make your life a little easier?"

She shakes her head. "No need. I…" She trails off, distracted by the buzzing of her phone. Her eyes go to the sky. "She was tracking my location."

"What?"

"Piper. She saw I was at the hospital." She glances at me. "You mind?"

"Not in the slightest."

Rachel answers the FaceTime with, "I'm fine."

Not that I'm trying to spy, but I do see a woman with a mixture of dark and light hair on the screen—the one I saw on Arthur's Seat, now with her hair pulled into a bun atop her head.

Piper shouts, "You were at the hospital! I thought you were dead!"

"I'd be at the morgue if I were dead," Rachel says and I snort involuntarily. She glances at me with a playful glint.

"Rachel Elizabeth Moreau, I do not appreciate that genre of humor from you. Hold on." She angles her head away from the camera and shouts, "Nick, your sister is not dead but is at the risk of getting on my last nerve!"

A male voice shouts back, "That's good. Hi, Rach!"

"Hi, Nick."

The male voice gets closer as he slides into the frame, pressing his face against Piper's. His dark blond hair is short and purposefully messy. "What happened? Why were you at the hospital?"

Rachel purses her lips. "I sprained my ankle. I was walking home and I tripped."

"You sprained your ankle!" Piper shouts. "Oh, Rach. Are you okay? Are you on pain meds? Did they do an x-ray? You're sure it's not broken?"

"Yes, to every question."

Nick grimaces. "Damn, that sucks. Did you go alone or was your friend David able to go with?"

She glances at me out of the corner of her eye. "No, Isla came with me."

Piper scoffs. "Isla? The hot girl who was super biphobic to you?"

I cringe with Rachel.

"I told you, it was a misunderstanding," Rachel says. Not completely a misunderstanding, but I appreciate the mercy she has granted me. Piper opens her mouth to say something else, and Rachel cuts her off with, "And she is sitting beside me on this couch right now, so watch your words, babe."

"Fine," she sighs. "Hi, Isla! Don't hurt my best friend again or I will ensure very bad things happen to you that no one will be able to link me to. Nick will be my alibi."

"Yep," he confirms. "Always."

My face heats. "I believe you. I am very sorry, by the way."

"Uh-huh," Piper says. "So, Rach, how are you getting to campus tomorrow? Can you take the bus with crutches?"

"Of course, I can take the bus with crutches. They're not going to say, 'Nu-uh. Not enough non-injured legs for this bus.'"

They continue to chat as I grab my mug and hand her hers wordlessly. She smiles in thanks. I pull my legs up onto the couch to sit cross-legged, watching her slyly. Rachel will not be taking the bus tomorrow. She just doesn't know it yet.

CHAPTER THIRTEEN

Rachel

A shrill ring fills my apartment as I'm tying my shoe. "I'm coming, I'm coming," I mutter, limping my way to the intercom. I pick up the corded phone hanging on the wall and hold it to my ear. "Hello?"

"Hiya, it's me. I'm driving you to campus."

"Isla? No?"

"Yes? Come on. Let me up. I'll help you back down."

I was planning on taking the bus like I normally do when heading to campus, but I have no reason to say no. It would be a little ridiculous to turn away someone offering me a ride. Not having to walk the ten minutes that would be more like twenty minutes today from the bus stop to my building sounds amazing. She can drop me off right out front.

Also, last night was oddly nice, despite the circumstances. Isla stayed until she finished her tea, and most of that time was spent with me on the phone with Nick and Piper, but I liked having her there. Isla has a good energy and her being beside me through something a little traumatic, such as my first hospital visit in a foreign country, was helpful.

And it was great of her to let David know about it. He texted me last night asking if I needed anything and it made me weirdly emotional to be suddenly presented with solid evidence that he cares about me. I'm not used to that. New people caring about me, that is. For a bit, it felt like I was constantly moving and surrounding myself with new people. I went to Columbia, Missouri for undergrad, then downtown St. Louis for grad school, then back to my parents' house in suburban St. Louis, then off on my own. During all of that, I floated on by without leaving a mark and not allowing anyone to know they'd left a mark on me.

So, all I say to Isla right now is a grumble of, "Fine." I hit the button to unlock the door to the building and then crack my door so she can let herself in while I limp to my bedroom to fetch my backpack.

My front door creaks open and soon Isla's voice shouts, "I brought you tea and a muffin. They're in my car."

This is weird. It's weird that she's here and it's even weirder that I don't mind.

I limp back out and say, "You didn't need to do that." I gesture at her. "You don't need to do *this*."

She grabs my crutches from where they're resting against my counter, bringing them to me and exchanging them for my backpack, which she slings over her shoulder. "Stop telling me what I don't need to be doing. Like I said, everything I'm doing for you is something I want to do. But if you want me to leave you be, I will. You just need to tell me once."

I hold her gaze for a long moment. After last night, I no longer want her to leave me alone. "Okay."

"Okay."

She pivots and marches to my front door, holding it open for me. I close and lock it before she helps me down the stairs, out the front door, and to her car. She lets me sit up front in her green sedan today, but only because she has brought the passenger seat as far back as it can go and put a box under the dash to prop my foot on. She indicates which cup is mine and hands over the blueberry muffin. I store the muffin in my backpack for later, not feeling very hungry right now. The pain meds make me a tad nauseous, so they'll have to wear off before I'm able to eat.

"How's the ankle?" Isla asks, buckling her seat belt.

I shrug. "More swollen and purple than it was yesterday. Which is to be expected at this stage of injury."

"How long did they estimate it would take to heal?"

"They said four to six weeks. I'm hoping for four. I talked to my professor this morning and we decided it's best if I'm contained to the lab until it's healed." I try not to let bitterness invade my tone, but Isla's frown suggests she sees my disappointment.

"Damn," she says.

"It just means I can't physically collect samples at the beach. I have enough samples to occupy my time for now." I toy with the scrunchie around my wrist. "It's temporary so it'll be fine."

"You're allowed to be upset."

My mouth thins. "You're right. It sucks and I am upset about it, but I do know I can still get valuable work done. I have to be in the lab sometimes anyway. *Most* of the time."

"Aye. Good." She glances at my ankle out of the corner of her eye. "Did you bring an icepack? If not, I can run out and get one for you. Have you a freezer to keep it in?"

"Yes, and yes," I say. "There's a freezer in the kitchen on the floor above the labs, and an elevator, so I'll be fine."

Soon enough, Isla takes the turn onto campus and I direct her to the building I'm heading to. She pulls up to the curb and goes to turn the car off, presumably to help me inside, but I say hurriedly, "I can get in by myself."

She sighs, leaning back in her seat. "If you insist." Then she holds out a hand. "Phone, please."

I retrieve my cell from my bag but hold it to my chest. Warily, I ask, "Why?"

"So I can put my number in it. Give 'er here."

I hand her my now unlocked phone and let her type in her number. She sends a text to herself so she has my number as well. After she hands it back, she ignores my previous request and climbs out of the car to help me up. She slips the backpack onto my back before making sure I'm settled with the crutches. "What time are you done? I'll pick you up."

"You don't need to—" She cuts me off with a glare. "Around five o'clock today," I mutter. I can't help but add, "I'm happy to take the bus back."

"I'll see you at five."

I set off with the crutches, still trying to get a hang of them. The crutches they gave me were not the kind I was expecting, not that I am an expert in any style of crutch. These have clasps that go around my forearms rather than padded bars to shove under my armpits. Isla says this style is more common in the U.K. I awkwardly maneuver myself through the front doors and make my way to the labs to find my supervisor waiting for me.

Dr. Andonov frowns at my wrapped foot. "You mucked up that ankle rather badly, didn't you?" They sigh on my behalf, I assume, judging by their next comment of, "No bother. We have collected plenty of samples for you to comb through."

I nod. "We have. I was also thinking that the next time it rains, I could use some of that water as a sample to compare to rainwater closer to different bodies of water."

They make an affirmative sound. "Good thinking. It'll likely rain today." They pull out my chair for me and I take a seat in front of a microscope and a couple of jars of labeled water Dr. Andonov kindly took the time to set out. "I'll leave you here, then. I'll be in my office upstairs, so if there's anything you need, give me a ring."

They pass through the door but twist back to me. "Oh, also, I'm meant to tell you about the gala."

"Gala?" I ask, assuming we're not talking about apples.

"Every year at the beginning of term, the graduate studies program holds a gala to both welcome students for the year and raise money for the school to be gifted back to research programs to better excel studies and research."

"Oh," I say. "That's cool." Dances have never been my thing, so the idea of this is not something I would call thrilling. But I suppose it would be a good opportunity to schmooze with bigger names in the research world.

"Yes, so you get all dressed up and you can bring a date if there's someone you want to bring. Dates are not required, though. It's a great way to meet fellow students, staff, and alumni."

With that, they leave, offering a somewhat dismissive wave, and I am alone in the lab. As I prefer it. Listen, I am all for collaboration, especially as I understand that it often leads to better results, but I find myself better able to focus when working alone.

Gala. What the hell am I going to wear to a gala? I suppose I have a couple of months to figure that out.

•••

Examining and testing the samples we collected takes up most of my day. Just one sample we collected, actually. The others went back in the fridge for me to look at tomorrow or next week. The sample I was examining was so riddled with microplastics, it was horrifying. It was taken from a body of water with an abundance of marine life, so as soon as my leg is better, I plan to go back to collect some more microscopic life.

I only took breaks to use the bathroom, switch out my icepack, and eat lunch. The end of the day comes upon me far too quickly, and I would probably stay later if Isla were not picking me up.

Because, sure enough, Isla shows up at 5 p.m. to fetch me. I exit the building, half expecting her not to be there, only to find her waiting in her car at the curb. She waves through the window and launches herself out of the car to assist me in getting into it.

As she pulls off campus, she asks, "How was your day?"

"Eh. Fine, though I am reminded again about how polluted our water is. Please tell me you drink filtered water."

She makes a face. "I don't drink water."

"Isla, you have to drink water."

"Not a fan of it. I prefer coffee or beer."

I gasp, appalled. She grins and I catch on that she's teasing me. I cross my arms and grumble. "Sorry, I was concerned about the quality of your drinking water."

"I appreciate the concern. Yes, my drinking water is filtered. But I don't drink enough of it. That was true. It doesn't taste very nice, does it?"

"It's water. It tastes like water."

"Exactly."

I click my tongue and drop it. "What'd you do today?"

"Worked at Josie's shop this morning and afternoon. Left a bit early to pick you up." She adds before I can cut in, "Don't you dare tell me I didn't have to. I know. It was a choice and I stand by it." Her hands adjust their grip on the steering wheel. "Then,

I have a tour at six o'clock. Once your leg is better, you should come on one."

"Maybe," I say. I saw enough with the private tour she gave me on my first day. Anyway, I doubt the offer will still be open after my ankle is healed. Her interest in me may pass when I become less interesting.

After she puts her car in park on my street, she helps me up to my apartment then bids me goodbye, promising to do this all over again tomorrow. I try to argue, though I quickly lose to a stern glare.

This is all very nice of her, but I am still extremely confused about *why* it is happening. I text Piper to lament my confusion and she tells me that as long as Isla is making my life easier rather than more difficult, I should let it happen.

Then she threatens to let very bad things happen to her if she hurts me again. Typical Piper.

And surely enough, my buzzer rings the next morning, so we do this all over again.

...

Thankfully, the following day is a Saturday so there is no need for Isla to take me anywhere. I had originally planned on table hunting this weekend for my still table-lacking apartment, but now that walking is a burden, I decide against it.

I'm expecting a quiet day—David has a date with Callum but has promised to come over tomorrow to make me brunch—and I'm looking to enjoy this quiet day by bingeing *Criminal Minds* or something. Ooo or a romcom? I love a good romcom on a rainy day. However, Isla texts me mid-morning.

Are you sick of me or in need of company?

I stare at my phone for a while, then shock even myself with my response.

> Company sounds nice. I was planning a movie day

> I'll be over in the afternoon with snacks

> Maybe I can pick up food from that Indian restaurant? Or is that a bit much for tea?

The Indian restaurant she is referring to is where we ate dinner on the first day we met. I've been craving that butter chicken since we went there the first time, but I completely forgot the name and I have no idea where the restaurant is. I thought I knew and tried to walk by one day but got completely lost. Which I do understand is a habit of mine.

I hate to be reminded of our first day together, but when I glance at the tattoo on my arm, I let the meaning of courage push through. I try to focus on the positive parts of that day, because there were so many, as I finally respond to Isla.

> I'd love that butter chicken again

> It's a plan. See you at yours soon

What am I doing?

I sigh. Whatever. I'm an adult. I can do what I want. Sure, Isla made me angry and hurt my feelings, but despite what my brain argues, I clearly want to and am enjoying spending time with her. These past two days in the car have been nice. I can admit it. We're not five. She apologized for what she did. She seems truly remorseful. I can be an adult and accept that.

It's a dangerous wager, but I think I'll see if she does anything untrustworthy again before I write her off. We're all people. We all make mistakes. I'm not typically one to hold grudges, but I am used to extending cautious feelings. However, with Isla, caution is on the back burner.

For a movie night. Jesus. Wild, I am. I'm being overdramatic. I sigh as I flip on my TV to watch my first movie of the day—a childhood favorite of mine that I do not need to subject Isla to: *Clue: The Movie*. Of course, with all three endings set to play.

The music starts and the thunder crackles as I watch Tim Curry prep the house for the dinner party with the cook and Yvette. And I totally do not check my phone every ten or so minutes to see if Isla has texted to let me know she's on her way. Nope.

The movie ends and I turn off the TV, my eyes heavy. Healing an ankle is rather exhausting. I must fall asleep because I am awoken by my intercom ringing. I struggle off the couch and hop over to answer the phone.

"Hello?"

"It's me!"

I push the button to let Isla up and prop the door open. I limp back to my living room to draw the curtains closed before settling on the couch with my leg propped up on pillows at the other end.

She walks into my lamp-lit flat, calling out, "Hiya!" She kicks off her black boots then jogs into the living room with a brown paper bag and a canvas tote stuffed to the brim. "You are a tiny lass so I do not expect you to eat all of this, but I realized I have no idea what snacks you like, and I'm not sure *you* know what snacks you like in Scotland, so I bought one of everything." She drops to the floor and sits crisscross applesauce as she dumps the large variety of snacks onto the floor. I see Jaffa Cakes, multiple flavors of Walkers, several variations of Digestives, Smarties, Hula Hoops, and more. She really did buy one of everything.

She next opens the Indian food and fishes out my meal. My stomach growls when I smell it. "Yum," I say, taking the warm container from her hands. "Thank you for picking this up."

"Aye, forget it." She pops open her own and scoots so her back is against the couch I am sitting on. "What are we watching?"

"I love a good romcom. One of my favorites is *Imagine Me and You*, despite the whole technically cheating aspect of it, but I'm open to seeing a new one."

"I love that one as well. Might I throw out a suggestion?"

"Shoot."

"*The Decoy Bride*. Have you seen it?"

I shake my head. "Haven't heard of it."

"It's lovely. David Tennant and Kelly Macdonald."

"Kelly Macdonald as in the voice of Merida?" She nods to confirm. "Sure. That sounds good. I love David Tennant."

"Who doesn't?"

I find it on the TV and press play. Isla sits on the floor throughout the movie and while I want to invite her up to the couch, a part of me holds back. As we watch, I can't help but focus on her in the glow of the TV light every time the movie makes me laugh or say, "Aww," to watch her reaction as well. The movie finishes with a kiss, as the best romcoms always do.

I click out of the credits. "That was great. I loved that. I love simple gestures like that."

"A book dedication is a pretty grand gesture."

I weigh my head. "Yeah, but in a more personal way. Like, it's not shouting at the top of your lungs or making a scene. Not for the whole world to see, even if they can. It's private and romantic."

She nods. "Fair. But I love a grand gesture myself. Someone holding a boom box outside my window or standing on a car to shout their love through traffic. They're classics."

"True. But they're a little ridiculous."

"I love a bit of ridiculous in my life." She checks the time on her phone. "I can head off if you're tired. Or we can watch *Imagine Me and You*? My favorite and your favorite?"

"It's a Saturday. Why not?" I pat the couch. "You can join me up here if your butt is numb." *Why* did I bring up her butt? I push past it. "There's room next to my foot."

"Okay. My bum could use a cushion." She climbs up to the couch, settling in beside my propped foot. "Do you need to ice this?"

"Oh, yeah, probably."

She hops back up before I can say anything and grabs the ice pack out of my freezer. She brings it back wrapped in a towel and carefully settles it on my foot. I start the movie and try to ignore the spark that spreads through my body when her fingers brush my skin.

As the movie plays, I am suddenly very uncomfortable. I need to stretch my leg a little straighter. With the position I'm in now, the icepack is resting oddly. I shift and that's better for my leg. But now, it's harder to see the TV. I turn my head and resign to being a little unhappy. Except this is a terror on my neck. I jerk it to the side and crack it. That's a little better. I shift again.

Isla has been watching me. "Are you uncomfortable?"

"Not really."

"That was a lie." She snatches the remote to pause the movie and stands up. "Here. Let's do this." She steals a small, round ottoman from the other side of the room and puts it down in front of the couch. She then takes the pillows my foot is propped on out from under my foot and puts them onto the ottoman. I watch her with my foot hovering in the air, confused before I understand what she wants me to do. I shift so my foot is now propped on the ottoman. That's a better position for my leg.

"Thanks," I say. I lean back and find myself foot-blocking-the-TV-screen too low, so I sit back up and am hovering awkwardly in front of the couch back. The only pillow I have that is not under my foot is the one Isla is using, so this will have to be fine.

She cocks her head to the side. "Stop forcing yourself to be uncomfortable."

"I'm not 'forcing' myself," I argue. "It just happens. A lot. I am never comfortable."

"Well, some would say I am often too comfortable. Let's test that out, shall we?" She settles down on the other side of me, close but not touching. "You can use me as a backrest. Alright?"

No way. Uh-uh. Not going to happen. "Alright," I grumble and lean back into her. This is surprisingly relaxing. And a much better angle. "Thanks." I go to unpause the movie, but before I do, ask, "Are you comfy?"

She wraps her arm around my shoulders, allowing me to settle more securely into her. "This okay?" she gently verifies.

"Yeah," I exhale.

"Then I'm perfect," she says. She takes the remote out of my hands and presses play.

Well, this is certainly cozy. How can one simultaneously be so deeply uncomfortable yet blissfully comfortable?

I can't breathe. I'm sure Isla can tell. I am controlling my breaths so they are coming out so dysfunctionally. I can't focus on the movie. She smells so good. Like what is that scent?

Scottish goddess? *Holy shit.* Actually, it's cinnamon. I love the smell of cinnamon.

We're cuddling right now. That's what this is. It's fine. Piper cuddles me all the time. Often against my will (except not really because I love Piper and don't mind). But I don't do this with the other people I know. Physical touch and I are not friends, but Isla's touch burns me in all the right ways. It's just like the day we met; her touch was almost instantly *right*. While physical touch generally makes me squirm, I crave it from her. It makes no sense. But nothing with her does. I can't help but lean into her, my head against hers. Eventually, I relax and enjoy the movie, my breath slipping back to normal as I cease thinking about it. With her chest moving against my back in the most soothing way, I relax.

When the movie ends, we don't move. Neither of us says a word.

I'm just glad that while we are so close, we're at too awkward of an angle to kiss. Because I have been focusing on kissing her for the last ten minutes. I know, I know. Bad idea, but I'm attracted to her. Obviously. It's basic biology, the attraction I have for her. Pheromones are all over the place with us so close and touching. The intense attraction is rather undeniable therefore I can't get the thought of her lips on mine out of my head. It doesn't help that I have evidence proving our mouths are made to fit together. The memory of her soft skin. The way her hands felt holding me against that wall. The heat growing between us, thick and scorching. Before she shattered it.

I sit up, pulling away from her arm, but I can't quite make it so we are no longer touching. "I love that movie," I comment, just to say something.

"It's a good one," she agrees, pushing herself to a more upright position, breaking our contact.

Without her touch, I'm freezing. *Dammit.* Not again. Why does the lack of her fill my veins with pure ice? How has she, a woman I can hardly claim to know, become my main source of warmth?

I shift, moving my elevated foot to an awkward hover as I sit normally. "I'm getting pretty tired." This night needs to be over. Quickly, before I do something I will surely regret.

She gives me that crooked smile. "I'll take that as my cue. I've an early tour in the morning anyhow. Saturday and Sunday mornings are popular for the Arthur's Seat route." She stands up and gestures to the snacks on the floor. "Please keep these."

"I'll save them for next time." Well, there you go. I have established that I want there to be a next time. It is surprising how often my mouth works quicker than my brain, even if they are on the same page.

She gathers her things and starts to head to the door.

"Isla," I say without knowing what I am even aiming for.

She turns back to me questioningly. I go to stand, but misjudge how to do so only using one foot because I find myself toppling over. Isla rushes forward to catch me before my ass hits the couch. Her arms are wrapped around me tightly, holding me so that our faces are mere inches apart. Her lips are parted, as though she opened them to ask if I'm okay but hasn't gotten the words out yet.

Her *lips*. I'm obsessed with them. I want my fingers in that mouth. God, I want her fingers in *my* mouth. I bite down hard as my hand moves of its own will, thumb tracing along the corner of her burgundy lips.

I keep my hand on her cheek for far too long—sharing her warmth. We stare at one another, neither daring to move. She has the most beautiful deep brown eyes. I could get lost in them.

It appears I already have. I've lost my way and need to retrace my steps before I get so lost, I can never find my way back.

I clear my throat and drop my hand. "Um, your lipstick was smeared. I'll see you Monday?"

She smiles back at me, settling me back on the couch. "See you Monday."

CHAPTER FOURTEEN
Isla

On Monday morning, I wait in my car outside Rachel's flat with a cup of tea and a muffin. Previously, I met her at her door so I could assist her down the stairs; however today she is insisting that she can get down to the car by herself. A part of me thinks she's afraid to let me into her flat—afraid of what she'll do after Saturday night's moment of tension.

As if she doesn't suspect that I am perfectly skilled in places beyond the bedroom, cars included.

Ahem. Not that I think that's what this is, of course. It's not at all what it is. Though, I have a vague hope that one day it might become something. Nothing wrong with hope, just as long as I don't shove my hope down her throat. A friendship is nothing to scoff at and I am perfectly pleased that we are on our way toward friendship. Och, I'm not good for relationships anyhow.

But the hope for *something* persists because when I left her flat, I had to shake out my entire body in an attempt to shake off the massive sexual energy transpiring between us. There had been moments over these past few days where she would look at me a certain way, hinting that the door was not completely shut, but I was convinced I was fooling myself. However, *that*? That was not in my head.

My lipstick does not smear.

And that after ending a night where she spent an entire film in my arms? Come on. There was no reason she couldn't have rejected that. No reason we needed to stay in that position, silent, breathing in sync, for twenty minutes after the film ended.

Twenty. Minutes.

I was happy for the brisk air that accompanied my walk home. It did well to set my head back on straight. Well, not *straight*. Upright, I'll say.

As I wait for her now, I tap my fingers on the steering wheel, a melody strumming through my head. It's the same melody that has been going through my head for weeks. A few words come to me with the melody and I can't help but quietly sing them to myself.

"She's looking at me again. And again, I can't breathe."

I continue to thump my fingers against the steering wheel in the melody, singing the words again. I pull out my phone to type them in the notes app.

But that's all I have. I mentally progress through the cords, holding out impatiently until I can hold my guitar in my hands and hoping more words will come to me, but none do. It's fine. Like I've said, words were never my strong suit.

I shove the melody aside when I spot Rachel carefully making her way out of the building. She pushes open the door with one crutch before finding the ground below with the other one. Her good foot follows the second crutch, then she lets go of the door with the first crutch, allowing it to swing closed behind her. She beams at me through the car window, proud of herself. I can't help but smile back. I also can't help that I get out of the car, darting around to open the passenger side door for her.

"Isla," she groans but accepts the assistance anyway.

"I always open doors for beautiful women," I say, closing it behind her. I run around to my side of the car, hopping back in. "How was your Sunday?"

"Fine," she says, a blush warming her cheeks. There it is. I love that blush. "Hard to explore during my free time like I have been, crutches and cobblestones do not mix, so after David left, I just hung out. How about yours?"

Spent thinking of you is the foolish person's response, so I say, "Arthur's Seat tour in the morning, Josie's shop in the afternoon, walked a few dogs, then an evening landmark tour. Pretty chill evening though—worked on my music until late. Maybe drank one cup of coffee too many." *Did not start my loan application nor tweak my business plan*, I finish in my head.

"Ooo, a landmark tour. That sounds interesting. Is that the one where you go to Calton Hill? I liked Calton Hill."

I smile at the memory of us there, looking out into the bright evening. The tour I gave Rachel that day and her desire to explore more sparks a bright idea.

I chew my lip a second before I throw out, "Well, next weekend, hows about you and I take a drive? I can take you through the city, tour by car, or even out of the city. Anywhere you want to go. Things that can be seen without requiring feet."

Her hands fold under her chin in that adorable way they do when she's excited. Though, her words come out even, "Yeah, why not?"

I groan playfully. "There's the enthusiasm I'm looking for."

She says more evenly, "Woo."

"Better."

"No, but seriously, that sounds like a great idea. Thanks, Isla."

Her lips close tightly. Into her lap, she says, "You know what I want to say next, but I know you're going to yell at me."

"That I don't have to do this? I know, I know. This is the odd thing about being friends with someone: very often, we do things that we don't have to do, but that we *want* to do. Usually because we like the person we're doing them for and want to make them happy."

I wait for her to dispute that we are friends, but she doesn't. Her face goes red and she mutters, "I feel like I owe you something. You've been doing so much for me."

That word. *Owe.* I hate that word. It chips away at me, bit by bit. My voice is serious as I stress, "You owe me nothing. Not even your company. I've said it once and I will say it again, you want me to leave you alone and I will. I am only trying to be your friend. I'm trying to get us to a point where we no longer try. We just are. Okay?"

"Okay."

The rest of the drive is silent. I pull up to the entrance of her building and watch as she gets out of the car, letting her do it herself. Once she's out and steady on her crutches, she twists back to me, dipping her head down to peer through the open window. "I'll see you this afternoon?"

"That you will."

"And, Isla?"

"Yeah?"

"We're past the point of trying. I think we did it. We're friends. Friends who are still getting to know one another, but friends."

...

After I drop my car off somewhat near my flat and start my walk to Josie's shop, I call Ben. He answers on the second ring.

"You busy?"

"Naw," he says. "Group of cyclists just left so the café is empty right now. You alright?"

I adjust my headphones as I ask, "Where would you recommend taking a pretty girl on a day drive?"

"Here, of course. The wonders of Laggan Wolftrax. Can she mountain bike?"

"Her ankle is sprained, so no. Any other suggestions?"

"Damn." He makes a small thinking noise. "So, you have to stay in the car then? Well, best to take a drive through the Highlands. See all that nature shite without leaving the comfort of your vehicle."

I sigh. "Yeah, that's what I was thinking."

"Why do you sound disappointed by that?"

I shove my hands in my pockets as I take a turn one street closer to Josie's. "I don't know. Oh, come to Scotland, see the magnificent Highlands. Sounds basic."

"Stop. Has Rachel—I'm assuming we're talking about Rachel because you're obsessed with the lass—seen the Highlands before?"

He knows me too well. "I don't think so."

"Then she'll be impressed, just like you're hoping she'll be. Done."

"But that's a far drive. It would mean spending the entire day together," I argue.

"And that's a bad thing? I thought lesbians were all over the day-long date thing."

My face falls flat. "Don't stereotype. But of course not. For me. I'm just not sure if she'll agree to that." We're friends. She confirmed it. We are friends. That word alone is enough to make my heart sing and ache simultaneously. Friends is perfectly alright, but are we yet the type who can spend an entire day together?

Ben answers my verbal worry with, "Well, weird suggestion. Maybe ask? And if she says no to the Highlands, take her to Wigtown or something. Come on. Go get that girl to fall in love with you."

I groan, "Fine," and hang up right as I push through the jingling door to the music shop.

...

I pick up Rachel every day this week except for Friday when she says David is driving her. I'm hoping my disappointment doesn't shine too brightly over text. It's only one day without getting to see her. It's fine. I may spend the entire day dwelling about how I'm not getting to see her, but still. There is plenty of work to distract me. I give a few extra tours since I'm not working at the shop, walk a few dogs, and paint a living room for one of Josie's neighbors. That is new for me, but they pay me two hundred pounds for it. The blue paint is a color I think Rachel would take a fancy to.

Thoughts of her haven't completely occupied my mind or anything. Well, that's not true but I would so much rather my thoughts be consumed by her than actual responsibilities. Like, what would you rather think about? Pretty blonde girl who kisses like an angel and smells like clear blue water, or a loan application for a business that will statistically fail?

I took Saturday off from the shop and didn't schedule any gigs in the evening of Friday so I can attempt to get some sleep for the drive. I take a melatonin at 8 p.m. so I do manage to sleep for a decent bit come midnight.

I did not schedule any gigs or tours for Saturday evening as well. In case we get back late. Not for any other reason. I'm not expecting to spend the entire night with her as well. But one can plan for the best-case scenario.

When Saturday arrives, I pick her up bright and early, running up the stairs to her flat before she can tell me not to. She leaves the door open for me and I push my way in.

"Have you any of those snacks from last week? We can bring those with us. If not, we can go buy more."

"I have them," she calls from the bathroom. "In the kitchen on the counter because I was thinking the same thing."

"Perfect," I call as I retrieve them from the kitchen. "I also have a cooler in the backseat stuffed with icepacks for when you need them." I return to see her propped up by her crutches in the living room waiting for me, one white trainer on one foot and the other wrapped and socked. Her hair is curled lightly and she's wearing a red, thin-strap, wide-legged jumpsuit over a white T-shirt. Rachel never wears her hair curled, at least every time I've seen her. And through what I have stalked of both her and Piper's Instagrams (this is a no-judgment zone). Well, unless it's a special occasion. Warmth spreads in my chest. I guess she sees this as a special occasion.

I'm staring. I clear my throat but do not drag my eyes away. "You look…wow. That jumpsuit is…wow."

Her face burns the color of the jumpsuit. "Thanks. Um, it's comfortable. Cotton, wide-legged, stretchy. Since we're going to be sitting in the car all day."

"Smart idea. Off we go." I lead the way out the door and, after she scolds me for trying to help, down the stairs and to the car. I still open the door for her. As I always do.

"Alright, so after you confirmed that you have not been anywhere in this country except the city we are currently in and the closest surrounding beaches, I figured I would let today be a surprise."

"Yes, thank you for verbalizing our text conversation for me.

Do you want to reveal the surprise?"

My eyes flash. "You're welcome. So, today we're going to… drum roll please."

I stare until she clues in, rolls her eyes with a smile, and leans forward to drum her hands on the dash.

"The Highlands!"

"Oh, fun! I've been wanting to go. Thank you."

I crank the car on and look both ways before pulling onto the street. "Don't thank me yet. This could be disastrous."

Her eyes widen. "Don't say that! You'll jinx it."

"Knock on wood," I add as I take a turning off her street and get our day started before she can change her mind. I glance at the GPS on my car's dash. "We're off to Loch Ness."

Her eyes brighten, then darken. "When Piper and Nick went they said there was a steep set of stairs to get down to the water."

"It's fine. I know a spot where we can drive right up to the loch." I halt before a stop light and rotate my full body toward her. "Do you trust me?"

"Yes…" she says suspiciously.

"Then trust that we're going to have a great day. Even if it'll be like eight or nine hours in a car."

She laughs. "I don't mind. That's basically an hour more than it would take to see my grandma back home, and that's one way. I like a drive."

"Good."

The light turns green and I keep going. We soon exit the city and I merge onto the A9. We quietly listen to music for the first half of the drive, not that I mind. Rachel seems to appreciate the silent moments so I'm happy to offer her those. However, I'm surprised when she breaks the silence first.

"When's your next gig? I'd love to go on purpose this time."

I smile. "Not sure yet. They happen spontaneously more than anything. I wish I could say I was on a strict schedule at one pub, but it doesn't work like that for me. I get the itch to sing in front of people, or I go to a pub and they say, 'Hey, you haven't been here in a while. Come tomorrow. We'll pay ya.' That'll usually get a yes out of me."

"Well, I hope you get the itch soon. I liked listening to you sing. Your voice is beautiful."

"Thank you," I say genuinely. I drum my fingers on the steering wheel. "I promise the views will get better the higher we go."

"I trust you."

The song changes and I decide to change the subject with it. "So, tell me about your life, Rachel Moreau."

She snorts. "Meaning?"

I shrug. "Childhood shite. Was it happy?"

She weighs her head back and forth. "Yeah, I'd say it was happy. Nick and I were a team since the day I was born and Piper found us when she and I were nine." She purses her lips. "My parents were…absent is too strong of a word. They were busy. Lawyers. Overworked. Always at the office. The usual, you know? So, it's just weird because I love them and know they love me, and they care about me, but I don't know them that well. I feel like I knew Piper's grandma better than I know my mom. I don't even think I could tell you her favorite ice cream flavor. Hell, honestly, I don't think I've ever seen her eat ice cream." Her face scrunches. "You know what, I think my mom is lactose intolerant. She doesn't eat cheese or yogurt either. Huh."

"I'm sorry," I say.

"I don't think *I'm* lactose intolerant."

I chuckle lightly. "Not about your mum's aversion to dairy.

About you not knowing your parents very well."

She plays with the scrunchie around her wrist. "It sucks, but it's one of those things where they aren't bad parents. If we need them, they're there, but if someone else can come in their place, they're happy to give up their duty. Like, I asked my mom to help me move to Scotland but when I told her I also asked Nick and Piper, she said she would just get in the way. It hurt but I understood where she was coming from. She can never get time off work, so she would have been holed up wherever while Piper, Nick, and I were doing everything moving prep related." She clears her throat. "But yeah, generally happy childhood. What about you?"

I wince. "Decidedly blah in the beginning, verging on unhappy once I got to secondary school. Unfortunately." I sigh. "It's hard to explain. Because, like you, I had my brother and he was the best. Ben is still my best friend. But my parents were…well my mum's the definition of egotistical and my dad supported that. Anything I did, she would always concern herself with how it looked. And every action she took always had a bigger purpose, even if that purpose was just to make others see us exactly how she wanted to be seen. She doesn't do things without conditions. If she does you a favor, you owe her one in return. I felt constantly like no matter what I did, it wasn't good enough. *I* wasn't good enough."

She cuts in. "You are good enough. More than. Please tell me you know that."

"I'm working on it." I swallow and keep going. "And then it was more. They were…let's say, less than supportive when I came out. I first came out to them as bi, because I thought I was, until I actually tried to date a boy and figured out that I am thoroughly unattracted to them. Classic case of compulsory heterosexuality.

But, because I came out as bi, my mum asked why I couldn't just pick a boy. And even though I tried to explain it didn't work like that, she didn't get it."

Out of the corner of my eye, I see her hands wring together. "Isla, that sucks. I am so sorry. She wasn't the first person you came out to, right?"

"No. No. God, no. And thank god. I told Ben first and he was like, 'Yeah, duh. I've seen the way you look at Keira Knightley.'" I laugh and Rachel joins in.

"Ugh, I had the biggest crush on her before I even understood what that was. The number of times I repeatedly watched both *Pirates of the Caribbean* and *Bend it Like Beckham* is actually unbelievable."

"Right? Gorgeous woman. And I maintain the fact that *Bend it Like Beckham* is a sapphic love story. But yeah, after that response from my mum and basically no response from my dad, I didn't tell them I was a lesbian until a couple of years ago. Like five years after I sorted it out. My dad was a lot better about it on the second go, though. Confused but supportive." I chuckle again. "And you know what Ben said when I told him? He said, 'Yeah, duh. I've seen the way you don't look at Orlando Bloom. That man deserves to be lusted after, and there is no lust in you for him.'"

She laughs again. "Is Ben…?"

I shake my head. "Naw, he hasn't labeled himself. Makes a lot of jokes, but claims to be straight. I'm letting him take that journey wherever it takes him."

Rachel glances out the window. "The hills are growing," she comments.

I hum in agreement. The hills surround us as we climb higher, the road disappearing in the distance making it seem like we are driving straight into the clouds. The land beside the road is not nearly as tall and green as it will be on our route home, but I won't spoil the surprise. With a glance at the GPS, I confirm we're driving through the outer edge of Cairngorms National Park. "We're about an hour out."

"Cool." She yawns as she reaches into the back for an icepack. "Ignore that. Cars make me sleepy." She secures the icepack around her ankle. "I'm having a wonderful time."

I bite the corner of my mouth. "I'm having a wonderful time as well."

We continue to make chit-chat as I drive, moving away from the deep stuff. She tells me a little bit about what she's working on—microplastics, water, the works—but can tell I don't understand a word of it so she stops.

"You're teaching me things," I argue as an urge to keep her going. "I won't learn if you don't talk about it. I've been on the environmental conservation side of the internet since we started driving together."

"God, that's my fault. Your phone is listening to me talk about it too much. It's okay."

"It's your life. Nothing wrong with talking about things important to you." I glance at her out of the corner of my eye. "I'm willing to listen to you talk about anything."

"Well, okay, because I did learn something interesting about zooplankton the other day."

I grin as she tells me about that. We go around a loop, finally taking a right on General Wade's Military Road. When I spy the spot where the guard rails disappear and the land meets the water in a kiss, I pull over. Rachel's eyes are already wide and giddy and she hasn't even seen the best part.

She turns to me. "I want to touch the water."

"Of course." I scramble out of the car and run to her side to open the door. I help her out and go for her crutches, but she shakes her head.

"The ground is too soft; they'll sink in. Can I hold on to you and just hop?"

"That'll do."

I wrap my arm around her waist and she wraps her arm around my shoulders like we're about to engage in a three-legged race. The distance to the water is far from long so it only takes a few hops to get us to the edge. Though, I realize she'll need to kneel to touch the water.

"Can you balance for a second?"

"Yeah."

I run back to the car to grab a beach towel that lives in the boot. I bring it back and lay it on the muddy ground. I help her get to her knees and kneel beside her. She stretches forward and reaches a hand in.

"Wow," she breathes. She scoops the water up, letting it escape through her fingers. "Can you imagine how much microscopic life was in the water I just touched?"

I snort, because that is not at all what I thought she would say. "I've got to say, I cannot."

Then she frowns. "Or how much microplastic?"

"There's microplastic in Loch Ness?"

"Of course there is. There's microplastic in drinking water. There's microplastic in rain. There's microplastic in the snow on top of Mount Everest. It's everywhere."

I shiver. "Hate that. I'm glad there are people out there like you who want to learn more about it all."

She smiles sheepishly. "Would you make fun of me if I collected a few samples while we're here? I brought my stuff, on the chance you took me somewhere with water. I mean, Scotland is covered in it. Loch Ness is freshwater so it would be so cool to compare it with the salt water samples I've already collected to measure if there is a different rate of microbes and the different types and…" she trails off, freckled cheeks turning pink.

Every cell of my being wants to kiss those freckled cheeks. Instead, I say, "I am begging you to *please* take some samples."

"Thanks," she says, relieved.

I run to grab her bag from the car. When I return, she pulls out her materials, taking samples of the water, the dirt, and the grass touching it. She packs everything back in her bag, then moves so she can sit down on the towel. I follow her positioning.

"This is absolutely beautiful."

I nod in agreement, reveling in the natural musty scent of the lake. It's been a while since I've been here and each time I have, the shimmering of the water and the vastness of the world in what can be considered a very wee pocket of it, is magnificent. The hills grow taller the higher you go up the loch, but these here are special in their own way, climbing and falling only slightly on the other side of the gray water. Waves wash weakly onto our private shore, not daring to invade our personal space.

Rachel sits silently beside me, staring at the water and I try my best to not stare at her. I think Rachel is someone who constantly seeks more, but can be stopped in her tracks by peace and beauty. This spot has done that for her.

We sit for a while longer taking in that peace before Rachel tells me she's ready to go when I am. We still have a ways to drive since I'm going to take her the long way back, down past Glencoe and eventually through the Glasgow area. I'm going to ensure we get the most out of our day.

We climb back in the car and take off.

•••

Rachel's jaw drops when we drive into the deep valleys and witness the mountains sprout around us, green and lush and magnificent. Water sparkles alongside the road from the bright sun forcing its way through gray clouds. In the distance, I spot hikers making their way along pathways, appearing as little dots to us on the road below. I've seen these lands so many times, but witnessing Rachel experience them for the first time helps me view them through her eyes. Grand, magical, and all-consuming, making us humans in our tiny car feel incredibly small in the most important way. Nature is meant to consume us in its magnificence, not the other way around.

Still staring out the window, Rachel asks, "So, you and Corrine had a thing. Anyone else significant?"

This question catches me off guard, but I like that she's asking because I can let her know there is no one she needs to be wary of. I haven't even eye-flirted with the barista at my favorite coffee shop since I met Rachel.

"Ha, yeah. Corrine and I had a very, very casual thing. We were best mates before our thing, just okay mates now. Erm, I dated this woman named Micky for about three months in between the thing with Corrine. Like had the thing with Corrine, broke it off when I met Micky, stopped talking to Corrine, broke up with Micky when it got a little too serious, and restarted things with Corrine. She now lives in Glasgow. Micky. And before her there was Imala. Casually dated Imala for like six months, maybe? In my early twenties. But besides Micky and Imala, everything else was pretty short-lived. I also had an ex back at uni who things ended less than amicably with." Kenna. I don't want to talk about her. "But yeah, that's about it. You?"

She weighs her head. "A couple of guys, I guess. A boyfriend I dated for less than a year in college. A short-lived situationship type thing in grad school. And then one one-night stand. I don't have much experience with dating and all that."

I hold back my offer to give her the experience. "We all move at our own pace."

"True."

As we near Glencoe, I say, "When your ankle is better, I'll need to take you back here. Too deep in the woods for us to trek today, but there's this bridge you'd love. The Fairy Bridge of Glen Creran."

"Fairy Bridge?" she questions.

"Aye. It's rather gorgeous and certainly magical. The wee folk like to party 'round this bridge. They say, if you cross over it the fairies will offer you a blessing of good fortune." I glance at her wrapped ankle. "They also say the water flowing under the bridge has medicinal properties. Maybe we should venture out there today. Brave the midges with you riding on my back."

She laughs. "I think I'll stick to modern medicine in this case, though I would love to see the bridge. It sounds really cool. You can take me some other time?"

"It's a plan."

We keep driving, having to stop for fuel once. Two hours later, we're back in the city. I pull up in front of her flat and put the car in park.

"Thank you for spending the day with me," I say. If I could repeat this day over and over for the rest of my life, I would.

"I like spending my days with you," she says, rotating her full body toward me.

She pauses for a second, hesitant, so it startles me when she launches forward and wraps her arms around me, squeezing tight. I chuckle and pat her on the back, squeezing her equally tight. She backs up a fraction before surprising me again when she pushes forward, pressing a quick kiss to my cheek. She pulls away just as swiftly, maneuvering herself out of the car and bidding me farewell before I can register what happened or offer to help her with her crutches. With my fingers brushing the spot where her lips met my skin, I watch her crutch into her flat, that song from before coming back to me.

> *She's looking at me again*
> *And again, I can't breathe*
> *Because those eyes are full of wonder*
> *And that heart is full of hope*
> *And those legs can't stop running*
> *Searching to find a home*

CHAPTER FIFTEEN

Rachel

It's a Sunday, but I'm going to the lab. I don't want to ask Isla to drive me so I'm taking the bus. Because I kissed Isla. Just went and kissed her. On the cheek, but still. It was a quick cheek peck, which friends give each other all the time. Not me to my friends, but whatever. Maybe I do that now—kiss my platonic friends who I am undeniably attracted to on the cheek. How European of me.

So not a big deal, but now I need a distraction. Do I regret kissing her? No. Of course, I don't. Because it was a kiss on the cheek and I'm being overdramatic. I'm being overdramatic because now I can't stop thinking about the last time we kissed and how that ended in such a disaster.

I hate how my mind always goes back there. My heart is ready to move on and let go, so why does my unintelligible, annoying brain keep bringing it back up? I don't want to think about this. We've cleared it up! She has explained why she reacted the way she did and I have accepted the explanation, even if I still don't like how it made me feel in the moment. Really. I *know* Isla now. I know she didn't intend to be cruel. She didn't intend to make me feel bad about myself or put something on me that I didn't deserve. She feels terrible about it. She reacted based on past trauma. I get it.

However, that cold feeling that spread over me then is creeping up on me now, only this time it is my own doing. I am awash with self-pity because I didn't have the guts to kiss her on the mouth.

I resist the urge to bang my head on the window beside me. Not kissing her was the right thing to do. I like Isla. I am attracted to Isla. But I do not want to date Isla. I want to be her friend. I do not want to be her girlfriend.

It doesn't seem like she does girlfriends anyway. Like with that one woman, Micky, she said she broke it off when it became too serious.

I'm too busy to focus on a relationship. Even if Isla does do girlfriends, she needs one who has time to dote on her because she deserves that kind of love. I do not have the capacity to give her the love she deserves. It's simple, really.

I'm through thinking about this. I am going to instead think about water. I mean, I'm going to analyze the samples I gathered yesterday from Loch Ness. I get off the bus and crutch walk my entire way to the lab building, which seems even farther with only one non-injured ankle. I look ridiculous. Half of me considers hitchhiking the rest of the way to campus. I push through, despite my chafing forearms.

When I arrive at the lab, I wash my hands, put on my white coat, and then take a seat in front of the microscope, leaning my crutches against the counter. The sterile smell of the clean lab comforts me immensely.

I drop a few drops of the water onto a slide and place it under the lens. "Fascinating," I mutter to myself, taking a picture of the sample that I can blow up on my computer later.

The buzzing of my phone drags me away from the eyepiece. It's Piper.

I answer and her face fills my screen. She's outside; sitting behind Nick's booth at the farmer's market, I assume. My brother sells homemade jam on the weekends and Piper likes to hang out with him for at least part of the time that he's there.

"You look cute. Why are you wearing a lab coat? It's Sunday."

"I'm doing extracurricular work. Isla took me to Loch Ness yesterday, which is water that I haven't been able to sample before. I just started looking so I'm not yet seeing evidence of microplastics in this first sample, but the microalgae I'm looking at are showing signs of…" I trail off. "Sorry. You don't care."

"Hey now. I do too care, but I don't understand half of what your genius brain says. Did you get my package?"

"Yeah," I say, chest warming. "Thank you for the ranch. Tell Nick I don't need jam in every package."

She laughs. "Yes, you do! It's so good." She pauses for effect then asks, "So, Isla took you to Loch Ness yesterday? That's where I fell in love with your brother."

"Well aware, babe. And no, before you ask, I did not fall in love with her. I do really like her though. As a friend. She's been wonderful."

"I hope she stays that way. Wonderful, I mean."

I understand what she's not saying—her caution for me. "You've always been better at holding grudges than me. I'm over what happened that night. It's okay."

"Fine. All I want is for you to be careful and to spend time with people who care about you."

"I am trying my darnedest."

"Good. Well, tell me about your day. Beyond the samples."

I give her the gist. "We also stopped to get gas at this random station. I hobbled in to pee and the little store was packed to the brim with camping gear and every other random essential you could need. But it was also super cute because there was this big green rainboot painted on the side and I—"

She cuts me off with a screech. If I wasn't used to this, I would have flinched. "The Green Welly Stop! You stopped at the Green Welly Stop!" She angles her head away from the camera. "Nick! Nick, Rachel stopped at the Green Welly Stop!"

"No way!" he shouts back, likely busy bagging up someone's jam purchase. "That's where we were stuck at the charging station!"

She turns back to me. "It's where we had sex for the first time."

I laugh. "Oh my god. Ew, by the way. I didn't even realize. Wow. Well, not to make you bitter, but Isla has a car powered by petrol so the drive was uneventful."

"I am bitter, thank you."

"So, what have you got going today?"

"We just got to the farmer's market a bit ago and customers are already flocking to Nick. Probably because he's hot." I hear Nick snicker in the background and I roll my eyes. "I'll hang out here for a couple of hours, but then I've got a few errands to run. Other than that, not much."

"That's fun."

"Not as fun as microorganisms in Loch Ness freshwater samples!" she says enthusiastically.

•••

Isla picks me up like normal on Monday morning. I should bring up the kiss. I don't. Neither does she. Probably because it was a kiss on the goddamn cheek and is not that big of a deal. I'm acting like a third-grader about it.

She asks, "Did you pack your Loch Ness samples?"

I should tell her I went to the lab yesterday, but I don't want her to think I was avoiding her or anything. Even though I was. I just say, "Yes," because I do have them with me.

I pick at my nails as she drives. I wish I had a nail file. I broke one this morning and I forgot to take care of it, so now it's all jagged and uneven. It's going to irritate me all day. I find myself needing to speak to distract myself from the broken nail. "I haven't spoken to my mom in two weeks."

"Oh?" she says, furrowing her brow. "Is that abnormal?"

I sigh. "Yes and no. This was pretty standard when I was in college, but once I moved back to St. Louis, I would see her more in person. I talked to her almost every day, even if just by text, when I first moved over here, but now, not so much. I haven't spoken to her since I told her I sprained my ankle."

"I'm sorry, love. Are you reaching out and she's not responding?"

I sigh again. "I haven't been reaching out. The thing is, I get tired of having to initiate our conversations, so I just…don't. And then two weeks pass and we haven't even texted."

She clicks her tongue. "Shouldn't always be your job to reach out. What about your dad? Spoken to him?"

"He's texted to ask about my ankle and my research a few times and I know he's relaying my responses to my mom. My parents are both so busy all the time, it's hard for them to remember to communicate with anyone but each other."

"That's a poor excuse."

"I know. I love my parents, I do, they're just…not totally there all the time. Like when I told them I was bi, I think I mentioned it in passing. Sometime in college, long after I told Nick and Piper, and they just let it slide by. We've never had a conversation about it. But I know they're fine with it. It was never a thing."

She purses her lips but doesn't say anything.

"What?" I prod.

She clicks her tongue. "Sorry, that kind of blows. Like it's better than them not accepting you for who you are or being weird and awkward about it, but still, even a simple rainbow cupcake during June helps show that even if they don't understand, they support you."

My broken nail becomes very interesting. "You're right. But I don't think they'll give me that unless I ask. I don't feel the need to ask that from them. I know they support me, but to show that they do through gestures that I'm sure they would deem silly is not the way for them." What I don't say is, silly or not, something like that would make me smile.

She pulls in front of my building and puts the car in park. Isla seems to understand my unspoken words as she offers a gentle indication of her head. "Having parents is rough, right?"

"Very," I say, undoing my seatbelt. "As per usual, thanks for driving me." The instinct to kiss her again washes over me so I open the door and leap from the car the best I can with my limited use of limbs.

I crutch speedily into the building to find Dr. Andonov waiting for me. They gesture for me to take a seat, so I do. "Rachel—morning. I was taking a look at the data you drew up last week. Interesting stuff. I'm assuming you noticed the increased percentage of microplastics in the samples we took a few weeks ago to the ones in the archives?"

I nod.

"Good. Good. Are you drawing up a report based on that? I know you're focusing more heavily on the effects of microplastics on microalgae and zooplankton, but do remember to consider all data even if it doesn't logically connect with your focus now—it might help to have it documented for other research branches down the line."

I nod again. "Of course. And since we're talking about it, on the microalgae, I was looking specifically at oil-degrading microalgae and bacteria, interactions between them, and I know I need a lot more data to form any conclusions…"

...

The following evening, I meet David at a pub around the corner from my flat. It's overcast but the sun is still staying out late in the evenings, so I don't mind the short walk. I lean the crutches against the booth, fall to my ass on the seat, then slide in.

"Graceful," he comments.

"Left over from my pageant days," I respond, grabbing the half-pint he ordered for me before I arrived to take a sip.

"Please tell me that was a joke."

I flash my eyes. "My grandma thought it would be a good bonding activity. It was not. I competed for one season. I was twelve, pre-puberty, a complete stick. But when I got dressed up, I was a sparkly stick."

"I think we found your stripper name. Sparkly Stick."

"Sounds like a vibrator. I like it." I take another sip. "How are things going with Callum?"

He beams so brightly at the mention of the guy he's seeing. "Really good. We got coffee the other day and he held my hand across the table the entire time. Which sounds so juvenile but it was so *right*. I haven't felt like this…like, giddy about someone *ever*. To the point where I get irrationally angry every time I realize I miss him." His head drops back in a groan. "He's just so…" His fists clench in front of himself and I think I sort of understand what he's saying.

I put my hand over my heart and sing with a tease, "You like the guy you're dating."

He sighs. "I really do." His eyes flicker up. "Speaking of people we like."

I turn around and spot Isla. She waves and starts to weave her way through the growing crowd in the pub.

"Were you expecting her?" David asks.

"Nope," I say, eyes glued on her.

"Do you want me to give you two some space?"

"No, of course not." I keep my eyes on her as she approaches the table, guitar case slung over her back. "Isla."

"Hiya, love. I saw you through the window. Figured I'd stop in for a hello, even though I saw you only two hours ago."

I smile back at her. "Want to have a seat? We were talking about David's boyfriend."

"He's not my boyfriend," David cuts in as Isla's eyebrows raise. "Yet. We were also talking about Rachel's *Toddlers & Tiaras* phase."

I scoff. "I was *twelve*."

Isla slides into the booth next to me, guitar settled beside my crutches. "Pageant girl, huh? I will need to see pictures." She steals a sip of my beer. "I have a gig at the pub 'round the corner tonight, but I can stay for a bit."

I'm waiting for an invitation to see her sing, but she doesn't extend one. I suppose I could ask, but I don't. "Good," I say and she offers me a smile that feels like it's just for me.

Isla leans forward in her seat to strip off her light jacket, revealing a cropped white tank. She's not wearing a bra and I can't help when my eyes immediately go to her chest, her small breasts outlined expertly by the white fabric, her nipple piercings especially on display. I gulp, hopefully not too loudly, and drag my eyes away.

If she notices my gaze, she doesn't say anything. She looks at David. "You speak to Ben recently?"

David leans back with a shrug. "No more than the usual TikTok exchange train. He's been quiet since I last saw him."

"He wants me to throw a supper party. This weekend."

"A supper party?" he questions with a scoff.

Isla's nose crinkles. "Something is off. I can't sort out what."

David shakes his head. "I agree. He's not saying anything though."

"Sorry," I cut in, "why is your brother wanting to throw a dinner party a sign that something is wrong?"

Isla and David exchange a look. Isla says, "It's hard to explain. Ben is always so…Ben. And he's been extra Ben lately?"

David nods. "But also, less Ben."

"Exactly."

My eyes narrow. "That makes no sense, but as long as it makes sense to you." I take another sip of my drink. "So, you're having a dinner party next weekend?"

Isla steals a sip after me. "Seems like. You free?"

"Of course."

She smiles at me again and *god*, it's like a spotlight is shining on me. It's ridiculous. I…I don't know what to do. I've never wanted to be looked at this badly by someone before.

Isla eventually goes up to the bar to grab her own drink, then we spend the rest of the time chatting until she has to leave. I'm enjoying watching Isla and David interact. I know they knew one another before me, but I don't think they have spent much time together. I like watching them become friends. My friends. It hits me suddenly that I have friends. Two of them. I knew that already, but here they are, sitting with me in this booth. It's not that I haven't always had friends, but they normally don't develop this quickly. I normally don't feel so intently correct about them. They are meant to be with me for life, like Nick and Piper. David and Isla are not replacements for them, of course—they're additions. More people to love. More people who love me.

Isla and David have stopped talking. "Where'd you go, love?" Isla asks quietly.

I jerk back to reality. "Sorry. Tired." I smile slightly. "I'm happy you two are here."

David lightly kicks me under the table. "Me too, Rach."

CHAPTER SIXTEEN
Isla

Ben and I are shopping for the supper party he is insisting I host. When I again ask him *why*, all he says is, "I have more friends in Edinburgh than out of it. This'll be more fun than if I host at home."

That's valid. David and I both live here, along with a handful of his mates from uni. Really, the only friends he has back home are his girlfriend and a few of the blokes from work. There used to be more, but they've spread out over the years. Some in Edinburgh, Glasgow, Inverness, London. I think one of his friends moved to Aberdeen? Maybe that's all that's wrong. He's lonely. I don't know why he won't admit that, though.

We're walking through the market, me pushing the trolley and him grabbing things seemingly at random and tossing them in. He's paying for most of this, so I'm trusting the process.

I consider bringing up the café, but I chicken out. "How's Molly?" I ask instead, realizing I haven't heard about her in a while. "Is she coming?"

"Molly who?"

"Molly your girlfriend of over three years."

"Oh. Her. We called it off."

I stop the trolley, causing the bag of frozen peas Ben has tossed toward me to miss and hit the floor.

"Islington, not cool."

"Sorry," I say, bending down to pick up the peas and resisting the temptation to throw them at his head. "You called it off? When? Why?"

He grabs the end of the trolley to pull it forward as I have stopped doing my job. "Aye. Back in May."

"*May?* Ben, it's August. You haven't thought to mention it?"

"You haven't asked."

"Well, I've been entirely self-centered lately. But you haven't brought her up. Though, I swear I've said something about her within the last few months and you haven't said a thing." I hold tightly to the trolley to keep him from pulling it forward. He turns back to me, dark eyes hard. "Are you okay?"

He looks away. "Fine. I ended it with her. It's not a thing."

"It so is 'a thing.' *Why?* I liked Molly."

"It wasn't right. That's it. It's not a big deal. Sometimes people don't work out. We didn't work out." He yanks on the trolley and I reluctantly start pushing it again. "Now I'm single, thirty, flirty, and thriving."

"You're twenty-nine," I remind him.

"Close enough." He holds up a bag of Jelly Babies. "You still hate these?"

"Yes."

He tosses them in the trolley. "How are things with Rachel?"

I flex my jaw at the change of subject. "Fine. Great. We're friends. Honestly, kind of my best friend, right now."

He twists back, hand on his heart, feigning insult. "I thought *I* was your best friend."

"David is your best friend."

"I didn't say you were my best friend, I said I was yours."

"Harsh. But yeah. Since Corrine and I stopped being as friendly, and Aileen has been sucked under by her boyfriend, yeah. You have been."

We find the register and Ben starts unloading the contents of the trolley onto the conveyor belt. "And you and Rachel are *just* friends? I thought you fancied her?"

I sigh. "It's not like that. Christ, give me the chance and I would date the hell out of her but I know if I made a move, it would not be reciprocated." Or worse, I'd make a move and she *would* reciprocate because she would feel like she'd have to because of all I've done for her. I don't want her to think I expect *anything* at all in return for all I've done. I don't. Aloud, I add, "Friends is safer anyhow. Though, the sex would be great."

Ben rolls his eyes. "You know, you don't have to have sex with all of your friends."

I huff and throw an apologetic glance at the cashier who is poorly pretending to ignore us. "I don't! Aileen and I have never slept together. And I have plenty of other friends I've never had sex with." I scoot him out of the way so I can finish unloading the trolley. "If you met Rachel, you'd understand. She's gorgeous. And brilliant. And funny. And the best person I've met. And genuinely seems to enjoy my company so…" I trail off when I realize Ben is laughing. "What?"

"You're *so* in love with her."

I shove past him so I can help bag the groceries. "I am not."

"Oh, so if I hit on her at the party on Saturday, you'd be fine with it? I mean, she's bi, right? And I look like this, so there's no doubt she'd be interested."

I punch him on the arm. "Bog off. She's off-limits. But *not* because I'm in love with her."

"Sure."

...

It's Saturday and Ben has been in my kitchen all day, cooking appetizers, main courses, and dessert. All the cooking is making for both a toxic and intoxicating mixture of every scent imaginable. I've got every window open and the front door cracked because it's hot as hell in here with the oven on all day. While all the invitees were asked to bring something, Ben decided that he did not trust anything to be good or not crisps and dip, so it would be better to prepare the food himself.

I've inquired more about his breakup, but every time I bring up Molly, he follows it up with a question about Rachel that I am not going to answer, so we're now avoiding talking about either of them. This is nice though, preparing this meal together. I love spending time with him like this.

"You know, we could do this together all the time," I say as I arrange empty dishes on my table, awaiting food.

He fills a pot with water as he asks, "Throw supper parties?"

I take a deep inhale. "No, I mean, serve food. Like, at our café."

"Be a while before that, though."

I march into the kitchen. "It doesn't have to be."

"I need to live in Edinburgh before we open the café."

"Then move here."

"I can't. Not yet."

"Then when?"

"Soon."

"How soon?"

He drops the spoon he's holding on the counter and weaves around me to open my fridge. "I don't know. I have things I need to take care of before I can move."

I groan. "I'm not asking you to move tomorrow. I just need a yes, Ben. Are we opening the café or not?"

He comes back around me, butter now in hand. "I don't know if I can. Give me time. Please."

"I've given you years. *Years.* I want to start the process." I grab him by the arm so he will look at me. "I'll do it alone. If you won't say yes, I'll do it alone."

"You've been threatening that for a while. Islington, you're twenty-five. It doesn't have to be now or never." His attention shifts to the stove. "I'm not saying no. I'm saying I need time."

My age is irrelevant. This is something we have been planning since I was sixteen. I cross my arms. "I've given you enough time."

We're interrupted by a knock on the door. I answer it to find David with four bottles of wine and the bloke he's seeing, Callum, in tow. Ben rushes out of the kitchen to meet him, snatching the wine and inspecting each bottle closely. "These are good," he says, impressed.

David's face is stone. "They are the exact kind and brand you asked me to buy, so they better be." He touches the shoulder of the man beside him. "Isla, this is Callum."

I reach out my hand to shake his. "Nice to meet ya." Callum smiles back and says the same.

Ben looks between them, then clears his throat. David stares back. "What?"

"Why didn't you introduce me?"

"Jesus Christ. Callum this is Ben, whom you have met thirty-seven thousand times before considering we all went to school together and he has invited you to multiple things throughout the years. Sometimes before he has invited me."

Ben grins at Callum. "I know, I know. But my presence needs to be announced whenever I enter the room."

I pat him on the back. "And we all appreciate how humble you are." I sniff dramatically. "Is something burning?"

Ben's eyes widen as he shoots back into the kitchen. I snicker and open one of the bottles of wine. "I'm sure Ben has specific plans for these, but he's being an arsehole so here we are."

Callum shrugs. "Fair enough." He grabs a wine glass from my table and holds it out for me to pour the wine. David follows suit and they soon situate themselves on the couch, whispering sweet nothings in each other's ears, or whatever couples do.

Around 7 p.m., the rest of the guests start arriving. Corrine and her girlfriend Madison, who always eyes me like she knows the number of times I have made her girlfriend come. Which, fair. It is a big number. A few of Ben and David's mates show up next. Aileen and her boyfriend make an appearance, which does surprise me even though she lives here. A few more of my friends come through the door. But no Rachel. Where is she? I offered to pick her up from her flat, but she said she had an errand to run so she wouldn't let me.

I check my watch. It's a quarter past. She's not the most punctual, but I told her she could show up any time after 6 p.m., especially since David and Callum were already planning to show up early. I go to text her to ensure she's okay, when I hear a knock at the door. I practically sprint to it.

I open the door to a plastic pot of blue flowers. The flowers lower and Rachel is behind them, eyes bright. "Hi," she says, balancing on her one crutch. "Sorry, I'm late. I got stuck in this in-depth conversation with Dr. Andonov on the phone this afternoon that lasted way longer than I thought it did. Then I showered later than I meant to because I went to the store between the conversation and the shower but my bus got stuck in traffic on the way back."

I can smell the fresh scent of body wash on her skin and am overcome by the desire to shove my face into her throat.

I open the door wider so she can crutch her way in. "No worries. We're just snacking while Ben finishes up the main course." I point to the flowers questioningly.

"Oh!" she says, thrusting them out so aggressively that she almost loses her balance. "For you. Normally I'd bake something but you said Ben didn't trust anyone to bring good food, and I figure he *is* a professional, and David was already taking care of the wine. I didn't want to show up empty-handed. I know you like Forget-Me-Nots."

I do like Forget-Me-Nots. Love them, in fact.

I take the pot from her and press my nose into the flowers. "Thank you." I gesture to the living room. "Everyone is in there."

David gets up to help her into the living room, putting her where he was previously sat on the couch. I see her say hello to Callum and hear a, "Nice to officially meet you!" David points to her ankle and she lifts it in response, saying something I can't hear. That's when I realize I'm spying on her from the hallway like a creep.

I pivot to the kitchen where Ben is plating his dish. "Smells good," I comment as I press to my tiptoes to grab a little tin bucket from the top shelf of my cupboard. It's covered in a thin layer of dust as it's been a while since I've used it. I know Rachel only bought the flowers as a host gift, but still. She took the trouble to buy my favorite flower, not just whatever random cheap arrangement she could find. It's the thought—that she put any at all into it—that is making me nauseous with joy.

I force myself out of my head, curving around Ben so I can

rinse out the bucket in the sink and transfer the flowers to it. I leave the flowers in the plastic pot and place them inside the bucket, a perfect fit, then bring them out as my table's centerpiece. As I set them down, I glance up to find Rachel's eyes on me. She smiles and I smile back, only seeing her.

Ben comes out as I start to make my approach to her, shouting, "Drumroll, please!" He's carrying a large dish with the main course.

David leans forward and drums his hands on the coffee table, shouting back, "Friends and enemies, our humble host, Bennett Pyeon!"

Ben sets the dish down on the table with a huge grin. To David, he says, "I love you."

David chuckles as he stands, pulling Callum up with him. "You said you prefer to be announced when you enter a room. You're welcome."

His hand covers his heart. "Och, a friend who listens to my deepest desires. Everyone needs a David."

"I agree," I hear Rachel say. David helps her up and she limps over to me, leaving the crutch behind for now, as people start grabbing plates and getting their food.

There are too many people to sit at my four-person kitchen table, so the plan is to disperse and eat around the living room like the adults we are. Rachel hangs back with me to let other people retrieve their food first.

Ben walks up to us with his arms crossed and eyes her dramatically up and down. "Ah, my competition."

"What?" Rachel looks at me, confused.

Ben makes a face of disgust. "For David, not Isla. Blech."

David approaches us, plate full of food. Callum is laughing with Corrine's girlfriend as they settle themselves back in the living room. "I'm allowed to have more than one friend, Ben."

"No, you are not."

David glances at me with pursed lips. "How about one friend per city? You don't live here."

Ben scoffs, his expression falling for a brush of a moment before he rights it back to outrage. Perhaps he's recalling our conversation from earlier. Or perhaps it's something else. "And whose fault is that?"

David sets his jaw. "Yours, dude." He glances at Rachel. "Also, it's nice to have a fellow academic as a friend."

Ben scoffs again. "I'm an academic."

"You are a baker."

"I have an MSc in baking science."

"That is not true and not what culinary degrees are called."

Rachel leans over to me and whispers loudly, "Should we leave them alone for this?"

I snort. "They do this all the time. Ben is jealous when the people he loves get shown love from someone else." I look to Ben. "Come off it. Rachel is a perfect person and we are both very happy to have her in our lives."

He sighs dramatically, but can't hide the smile itching at his lips. "Fine. But only because I have heard nothing but good things about you. Now, go eat. Come on. I've been slaving all day."

"I'm going to touch you," I warn before I take Rachel by the waist and help her toward the food. When I release her to put a plate in her hands, she whispers, "Perfect person?"

My fingers grip my plate tightly. "Perfect. Sexy. Brilliant."

Her cheeks pinken but she doesn't dispute what I said. Because I'm right. We load up our plates and go find open spots in the living room, Rachel on the couch and me on the arm beside her. Ben soon takes a seat across from us on the ground and close to David and Callum.

Rachel takes a bite and says, "Holy crap. This is so good, Ben."

He simpers and utters an unexpectedly bashful, "Thanks."

She takes another bite and swallows, then asks, "David said you're a baker? Just a baker? You could be a chef."

He smiles wider. "Fine, okay. I like you. Erm, the thing is, I love to cook and bake, but cooking is something I do more for me than baking. I can be experimental in a way I couldn't if I worked in a restaurant kitchen. Baking is more scientific. I can follow a pattern, and making the same thing over and over doesn't get boring in the same way cooking an identical meal over and over would." He shrugs. "I don't know. Makes sense to me."

She nods like it makes sense to her as well. "That's why I like baking. I know you and Isla have talked about opening your own café. You'd be in charge of the food end, I guess?"

I flinch at the mention of the café but Ben doesn't bat an eye.

He nods, "Oh definitely. If we ever get around to it. I already work in a café, so it's what I know. Isla is the one with the MBA. She would handle all the business aspects and I'd be back in the kitchen like the perfect house-spouse."

My mouth thins. "Indeed." I hate how casually he's speaking about this, like he isn't the only reason we haven't opened it yet.

Rachel cocks her head at me. "I don't think I knew you had an MBA? I knew you had your Bachelor's."

I'm inclined to shrink under her focused gaze, but I don't. "Oh, I probably haven't mentioned it. Not like I'm using it."

"Yet. You're going to run the café so well. You would even if you didn't have a degree in it." She turns back to Ben. "So, what's the café you work in now? It's near where you and Isla grew up, right?"

He makes a small noise of confirmation. "It's a little café at the start of a mountain biking trail. Laggan Wolftrax Center."

Rachel nearly spits out the sip of wine she just took. "No way. No way! Wait, hold on." She sets her wine aside, out of reach so she won't knock it over. "Oh my god. This is unbelievable. We've met before! You're Wolftrax man."

Ben's eyes flash to me, confused, before going back to Rachel. "I…what? I work at Laggan Wolftrax?"

"Okay, sorry. I…wait. There's so much happening in my brain, words are hard. I'll get there." She looks solidly at him. "In June. We were walking back from a bar—Hoot, actually—and we ran into you. Me, my brother Nick, and my best friend Piper."

Ben still appears confused.

Rachel groans. "Did you meet a man and a woman who were having trouble with an electric vehicle back at the beginning of June? Nick and Piper. Piper's hair is brown layered over blonde."

His eyes light up. "Oh, fecking hell. Them. Yes, I did. They were having trouble with a charger and I was trying to help them. She lost her necklace and I brought it back to her. You were there!"

"Wait," I interject toward Ben, "that couple you told me about was Nick and Piper? Rachel's brother and best friend?"

Ben laughs as he repeats. "Your brother and best friend. That's incredible."

Rachel laughs in agreement. "Piper is going to freak. I can't believe you're Wolftrax. I forgot you said your name was Ben." She pulls out her phone. "Mind if I FaceTime her? Prepare for some screaming."

The bubbling ringtone starts and soon Piper fills the screen. She's outside with a table full of jam behind her. "Hello, I thought you had a thing tonight?"

"I do," Rachel says. She angles the camera toward me. "Isla is here next to me."

"Hiya," I say stiffly.

"Hi! I like your lipstick."

"Thank you." I'm still trying to be cautious around Piper because I know one false move will make her hate me for life. I want her to like me.

Rachel turns the phone back to herself. "You will never guess who I just met. Isla's brother."

Piper furrows her brow. "Oh, that's fun. Is he like secretly famous or something?"

"No, no, he's normal."

"Hey!" Ben protests, so I kick him in the shin. He pulls his leg away from me with an angry pout.

"But do you want to know where he works? The Laggan Wolftrax Café."

I see the comprehension hit Piper. "Oh my god! Isla's brother is Wolftrax Ben! Nick! Nick! Come here! Rachel is with Wolftrax Ben!"

Rachel hands the phone over to Ben. He says, "Hi there."

She shrieks again. "Oh my god! This is so incredible!"

They continue to chat and I think Nick has come into the conversation. "Small world," I whisper in her ear.

She bumps me with her shoulder. "You know what's funny? After we ran into Ben, I was trying to get Piper to admit that she and Nick had a thing, so I said that running into Ben was like fate. She was being stubborn so she said back that maybe it was because she was supposed to introduce Ben to me. It turns out it *was* fate."

I narrow my eyes. "I'm not sure what you mean."

She laughs. "*This* is fate. Not meeting Ben, but meeting you."

My breath hitches. I could kiss her. I want to kiss her. Her words draw me forward and lyrics spring into my head:

Love, come home
Just come home with me
I'll be your home

She continues, "Like you're one of my best friends. I was meant to meet you."

"For sure," I say, leaning back and rerouting my thoughts.

Ben finishes talking to Nick and Piper and then hands the phone back to Rachel. She pockets it and leans into me as she continues to eat. I realize I've spent so much time looking at her, that I have yet to take a bite of my food. I dig in as well.

•••

At the end of the night, the flat has cleared out, leaving behind me, Ben, Rachel, and David. Callum has to be up early tomorrow, so he took off already. David and Ben are clearing up the living room whilst Rachel and I are in the kitchen washing dishes. I told Ben since he cooked, I would clean.

"I wash, you dry?" Rachel suggests, turning on the sink and grabbing a plate before I can protest.

"Suit yourself."

She washes the plate and hands it to me to dry. We continue this pattern silently.

Ben and David are laughing about something in the other room, but I can't hear what they're saying over the running water.

"We're taking down the rubbish!" shouts Ben as he and David exit, hands full.

Rachel grabs a spoon and holds it under the tap wrong, causing water to splash up on her face and all over her dress. She shrieks in surprise. I chuckle and use the towel I'm holding to wipe the water off her face.

She puffs out her lower lip dramatically. "I hate when that happens."

"Me too," I coo. I drop the towel, using my thumb to wipe away one remaining drop. My hand remains on her face for a second too long, but a second is enough.

Her lips crash into mine so suddenly that it takes my brain a beat to catch up to what is happening. When it does, my thumb traces the line of her jaw as my other hand slides to her waist, pushing her back into the counter. Both of us ignore the running water in the sink behind her as my grip on the fabric of her dress tightens.

The door on us is not closed after all.

Our lips slot together perfectly, drawn together like magnets. Her tongue slides along the seam of my lips before I let it slip into my mouth, meeting mine. I moan as she pushes into me, her fingers digging into my scalp.

What took us so long? Oh, her lips need to live on mine. It's where they fit best.

The front door slams closed and I hear David say, "I think there's a general rule against making friends with animals that live in rubbish bins, Ben."

Rachel yanks back from me, breath heavy and mouth swollen and red with my lipstick. She looks up at me, eyes wide, and says, "Friends don't kiss like that."

The panic in her voice is my cue to step away, heart shattering. Though, I keep that to myself. My face relaxes despite the instinct for it to screw up and start sobbing.

"They can. It's okay." The door on us is still not closed. It's open a sliver. If I'm patient, it'll open all the way. I clear my throat and reach over her to grab a plate to start washing. "I've got the rest of this. There's lipstick on your face."

CHAPTER SEVENTEEN

Rachel

Well, I found the courage to kiss her on the lips. And, hey, what do you know? It was a bad idea. Friends don't make out in the kitchen while doing the dishes. *Friendsfriendsfriends.* I want to bang the term into my head like a railroad spike.

I leave pretty quickly after that, ensuring the lipstick is off my face before I bother to look David in the eye. Though, he already knows me well enough to suspect something is up because as we climb into his car, he asks, "Things get frisky in the kitchen?"

I exhale through my nose. "That's one way to say it. How'd you know?

"The lipstick smudged on the corner of your mouth."

"I thought I'd gotten it all off," I grumble, using my thumb to rub the rest of the lipstick away. "We kissed but we shouldn't have. We're blurring the lines of something that shouldn't be blurred."

David frowns. "I hate to say this, but the Pyeon siblings are a mess, so maybe for the best? I love them both to death, but they're the kind of people who need true friends more than romantic relationships. People who can embrace their faults, etcetera without things getting complicated."

I pick at my nails, unsure of whether or not I agree with that assessment, at least for Isla. Everyone needs close friends, but I also think the right kind of romantic relationship would be great for her. Someone to love her and take care of her and make her breakfast and show her how much she is worth. Though, aloud, all I say is, "Yeah, you're right. No more kitchen kissing."

...

The rest of the week goes by in a blur. Neither Isla nor I bring up the kitchen kiss. Every morning, I wake up exhausted so I'm quiet on our drives to the lab, and every evening I leave with no energy, so I'm quiet on the way back. I haven't seen David since Saturday, finding it too difficult to go see him at Hoot (those stairs are a bitch with the crutch) and telling him he doesn't need to worry about coming to see me, so most of my nights have been spent doing more research or bingeing *Criminal Minds*. Luckily, the library has been majorly digitized, so I have access to most of the studies I need without having to go to the actual library.

Dr. Andonov has brought me a bunch of samples, doubling my material but also the amount of data I have to examine, so it's taking more and more time. Which I really love. I love having this much to focus on, this much data to compile and then comb through. I'm learning so much.

On Friday, Isla picks me up in the morning as per usual. She notes the dark circles under my eyes. "Seems like a good time to get addicted to coffee."

I give a faux dramatic gasp. "*Never*. There's enough caffeine in my tea." I take a sip of the cup she brought me. "Thanks, by the way. And don't think I'm not keeping a tally of how many things you have bought me. I will pay you back even if you don't want me to."

She groans. "If you dare to give me money, I will chuck it out the window."

"I'll Venmo you."

"I'd decline it if I had Venmo." She scoffs. "Venmo. What are you, a drug dealer?"

I laugh. "Right, you do bank transfers here. That is so not a thing in the U.S. I don't even know how to do it."

"We also use PayPal, but I'm not going to give you my username because I don't want your money. How do you pay your rent?"

"Via check."

"Och, you are ninety years old. My gran is the only one I know who still uses checks." She pulls up to the curb in front of the labs. "Around five o'clock again?"

"Yeah, if that's fine."

"It always is."

I go into the lab and get to work. I don't retreat from my microscope until late afternoon when my growling stomach alerts me of the passing time, urging me to fetch my very delayed lunch and an icepack for my ankle from the fridge. Once my lunch is gone and the icepack is warm, I go back to work.

A knock stuns me away from my notebook where I am handwriting research with a satisfying lead pencil. Isla pushes the cracked door open.

"Isla? Hey. What are you doing here?"

"It's half past five. I called but you didn't answer."

I look around the lab. I don't even see my phone. I must have left it in the kitchen earlier. "I completely lost track of time." I refocus on my work. "I should have texted. I am so sorry. I still have so much to do."

She wanders closer. "It's fine. I can wait."

"No, you don't need to do that." She gives me a hard stare. "Oh, shush. Seriously though. I might be here for a while. I can take the bus back."

"I don't mind. Really. I brought a book—trying out that whole reading thing you like so much." She pulls the book out of her bag to show me before stepping further into the room and closing the door. "You look stressed, though. You've looked stressed all week." She walks up behind me, standing close. "Anything I can do for you?"

I look back to my notebook, grabbing my pencil to finish the half-thought I had started writing down. "Like you don't do enough. Not unless you know a magic cure-all for stress."

Isla laughs lightly as she finds her seat, propping her legs up on the table beside mine, book closed in her lap. "Well, I don't know about a cure-all, but I do know something that can offer stress relief."

I don't look up as I continue to write. "What?"

"Rachel."

"That's my name," I say half-heartedly as I keep writing.

"Orgasms."

I drop my pencil and look up sharply, turning in my seat to stare at her. "Excuse me?"

She opens her book, but I can tell she's not actually reading. "Stress relief. A great stress reliever is orgasms."

"Oh." I grab my pencil, tip hovering above the page. "I'm not very good at orgasms."

I hear her book close and drop on the table before she stands up and strides over to me, standing above me with her mouth gaping. "You're not '*good*' at orgasms?"

My face burns. Goddammit. The topic of sex does not embarrass me, so why am I sweating? Oh, maybe because I am talking about orgasms with someone I have definitely thought about both giving and receiving them with. I mean, on the first day we met.

And a few times since.

"I've only had one orgasm before," I admit. Then expand, "With another person. Though, I will note that I figured out how to do it for myself rather recently. It still takes time. I'm still…working through the kinks. Like, I've tried a lot of different ways to get myself there on my own but wasn't able to until a year ago. Up until then, I was getting close but not passing the brink, and before orgasm number one, I wasn't sure whether I was having them or not. I mean, I knew I wasn't, but a part of me was like, what if I am? Is this really worth everything people do to have sex? And the answer was no, so…I'm still talking. Sorry."

"I like it when you talk." She drags a seat up and sits as close as possible without touching me. "Who did it?"

My brow furrows.

"Who gave you the orgasm?" she clarifies.

"Oh. His name was Parker. The one-night stand guy."

She leans back in her seat with raised eyebrows. "Wow. He would not have been my guess."

"I know. But he knew what he was doing. And he was so very…yum." I shake my head back to reality.

She leans forward again and says in a low voice, "How'd he do it?" This conversation has my heart pounding in my chest. Friends talk about sex. This is normal. But Isla sees the panic in my eyes so she continues, "Well, if we're using the scientific method, *something* worked before. You would think, as a scientist, you'd want to keep that in mind. Maybe test it again. How'd he do it?"

My tongue traces over my barely parted lips. "His mouth." The memory flashes over me, making my toes curl. But now Isla is in his place, gazing up at me from between my thighs.

No, I command myself, shoving that image away.

"Did the other guys ever use their mouths?" she asks.

I twirl my pencil in my fingers. "Yeah, but not a lot. Neither of them liked it that much. And both were not great. Whenever they were down there, it was like they couldn't wait to be done."

She scoffs. "That's literally the most demented thing I've ever heard. This Parker bloke, he was good?"

"Very. Uh, and he seemed to enjoy it, which made it better. For me."

She cracks that half smile. "Funny how that works." She scans me up and down slowly and, almost as if she can't control herself, says, "Rachel, let me assure you, if I ever get my mouth on you, I will never want to remove it."

I gulp. Is she…offering? I suppose I wouldn't be against it. I may have said no more kitchen kissing, but this would be lab sex. Totally different. It would satisfy a carnal need that has been gnawing at me since I met her. It's Isla so I would feel safe doing this with her, and it doesn't have to mean anything. Isla too has expressed the desire for casual in her romantic life so, maybe this wouldn't be a bad idea.

Finally, I say, "I can express the same sentiment." Then I return to my work, feeling her eyes burning a hole in me. Daring me to look up at her. I don't. Eventually, she drops back into the chair beside mine and opens her book.

My face is fire engine red. I know it is. Well, it always is. I keep working, but I also keep glancing up at her, immensely distracted by the way she's chewing on her thumbnail as she flips through the pages of her book. I'm practically drooling. Foolish, ridiculous biology. I shake my head and stick my eye back in the eyepiece of my microscope, snapping a picture of the slide. I note what I'm seeing, then glance back at Isla. I look back to my work, but soon find myself staring at her again.

This time she catches me.

Isla raises an eyebrow, then scoots her chair closer, tossing her book to the side. "Want to show me what you're working on?"

"Sure," I ground out.

She leans toward me, settling her head next to mine as she peers over my shoulder.

"It's a zooplankton. Did you know nearly every zooplankton species can ingest microplastic?"

"Huh, that's interesting."

My mouth perks. "It is. It's also bad. Their consumption of microplastics has negative impacts on the marine ecosystem." I look at her, face still so close to mine. I'm staring at her lips and she undoubtedly notices. Because I feel the need to say something, I say, "I like that lip color. Have I verbalized that to you? I think it a lot."

"It's my favorite, as I'm sure you can tell." She smiles wolfishly. "Spend a lot of time thinking about my lips, do you?"

I could lie. I could *lie*. "I think about that color." My tongue barely traces my bottom lip as my focus flashes to her eyes.

"Want to try it on again?" she asks, glancing at my mouth.

Everything about our first kiss soars through my mind—only the good parts. The way her lips felt on mine. Her grip on my hips, her heat on my skin. Then the kiss in the kitchen comes to me, the memory of her tongue sliding against mine causing me to squirm.

"You're distracting me," I murmur. Then I clear my throat and say with what I hope is a lighthearted laugh, "Seriously, I need to get this done."

She leans back with a nonchalant shrug and says, "Sorry. I'll stop being so 'distracting.'"

"Thank you." I finish the note I'm in the middle of writing.

Then I drop my pencil on the counter, swivel my chair, grab Isla's face with both my hands, and pull her lips to mine.

If she's surprised, she doesn't show it. Her mouth opens and her tongue casually slips into my mouth like it belongs there. *Shit.* I think it does. Her kiss deepens. I drop my hands from her face and reach out blindly for her hips, grabbing them and pulling her so she's climbing from her chair into mine, straddling me. Her teeth sink into my lower lip, tugging it toward her and pulling a true whimper from the base of my throat. Fingers finding their way to the scrunchie in my hair, she yanks it out as her kisses move to my neck, sucking hard enough to mark me as hers.

Into my neck, she asks, "How many people are usually in the building this late?"

I'm confused by the question, my head clouded by the pure bliss of her mouth on me. "On a Friday night in the middle of the summer? None." I have to suck in a breath as her lips sweep searing kisses across my throat. "It's probably only us. Maybe a janitor or security guard, but they're normally stationed up on the ground floor. Why?"

She stands abruptly, climbing off me with that crooked grin on her face as she places her hands on the arms of my rolling chair and pushes me to the far wall, nestling the chair back against it. I don't even bother to question what she's doing because, clearly, she has a plan.

Her hands caress my bare legs beneath the hem of my skirt as she kneels in front of me. She kisses my thigh, saying into my skin, "I promise to thoroughly enjoy it."

I catch her meaning quickly. "Wait, before, that wasn't me

asking you to…or like saying I *need* you to try to give me an orgasm or whatever."

"Do you not want me to?"

My pulse sings with want. "That's not what I'm saying."

"Then, love, I will certainly be giving you an orgasm and I will be using my mouth." She kisses my thigh again, this time a little higher. "And I will revel in every fucking second of it." She runs a tongue up my leg and I involuntarily spread them wider. "Don't be afraid to ask for what you want. I will always give it to you."

"Okay," I whisper. "Then, I want your mouth on me."

"Done." Her mouth continues to move up toward her goal as she murmurs, "I like that you wear dresses to the lab."

"They're easier to put on than pants with the ankle," I say honestly. I'm bad at dirty talk.

"Sexy," she says.

I know I should shut up but I have to add, "You know, I still haven't ever done this with a woman." A coolness spreads through my chest as I recall the previous rejection after I admitted this fact.

Her eyes meet mine with a serious look. "That's alright, love. I'll help you find your way." She places another searing kiss. "I'll take care of you." Her hands glide up, pausing when she gets beneath the hem of my dress. "May I?"

"Yes," I say. "Whatever you want."

Her grin turns devilish. "Good girl." I revel in the praise. Her hands slide up to my hips and find the waistband of my panties. She hooks her thumbs underneath the sides and pulls. I lift my ass to help her get them off and watch as she guides them down, removing them from my legs one at a time. With nowhere else to put them, she shoves the panties in her pocket. A rush of carnal desire spreads through me.

Her fingers skim around the bare edges of my sex but don't quite touch. "You're soaked."

"*You* are kneeling before me," I say breathlessly. She always looks beautiful, but in this position with her hair loose and wild, her oversized T-shirt dropping off one shoulder, and her hands on my skin, she is mesmerizing.

She smiles, biting her lip. Her thumb brushes over my clit and a teasing jolt travels through my body.

"Isla," I squeak.

"Save that voice for when you're screaming my name," she orders before placing a kiss on the crease of my leg, so close. My legs spread wider, welcoming her. Begging her without words.

But soon, I need the words because I say, "Touch me. I need you to touch me."

"Little wider, love."

I do as commanded.

Her mouth connects with me. My fists clench as her tongue traces a strip up my center before settling on my clit. She sucks gently and all the air rushes out of my chest. Only for me to draw it back in with a sharp gasp as her tongue focuses in.

I've never had sex in public before. Public make-outs, sure. Of course, it's not like we're splayed out in the middle of the Royal Mile—we're behind a closed door in a practically empty building, but still. All of my previous sexual encounters have been confined to a bedroom, or a dorm room, or a shower, or—

Oh god. "Isla," I whine. My fingers find her hair, locking tightly in the curls as I hold her mouth to me. Her and her tongue are suddenly the only things I can focus on. My hips urge toward her, seeking more. As her grip on my thigh tightens, her tongue flicks across my clit and *shit*.

The pleasure courses through me as my eyes flutter closed,

letting her lick me into oblivion and back as I come hard, arching forward.

When my soul finds its way back to my body, she pulls away, lips shining with traces of my arousal. She looks extremely satisfied with herself.

"See. That's what you like." She licks her lips and says, "I'd like to run another experiment. Think you can stand if you lean most of your weight on me?"

My chest is heaving as I try to recover. I'm sure as hell going to try. "Yes."

She stands and pulls me up with her. With her arm around my middle and my arm around her shoulders, she takes my injured leg so that it is resting over the back of the chair, hovering so there is no pressure on my ankle. Also, effectively spreading my legs apart.

With her face inches away, her eyes lock on mine as her hand moves between my legs. A spark fires through me as her fingers pass softly over my clit and explore lower. I moan loudly, already feeling like Jell-O from that much-needed release. Two fingers dip into me, pulling a gasp from my lips. I nod to let her know I'm okay. She gently moves her fingers deeper, tracing my inner walls, working me open. As her fingers curl inside of me, the heel of her palm massages against my clit. I'm breathing heavily through my nose, my eyes squeezed closed, but then her fingers scrape against the perfect spot and my eyes shoot open as I moan, focus locking on hers. I can't bring myself to close them again. The way she's looking at me as she pleasures me is nearly orgasmic in itself.

"Look at you," she says in the husky voice I love. "So pretty, riding my hand. You're going to come for me again, okay?"

I nod and grind my body on her hand, our faces still so close, exchanging breath.

"*Fuck*, Isla."

The second orgasm is building; I am one false move from exploding. *How* is she doing this? I swear I have tried some of these moves on myself before, but *god*, her touch is on another level. With a quivering hand, I pick up my skirt so I can watch how she touches me. There are traces of her lipstick on and in between my legs, the sight making me whimper. As she curves her fingers, my body cries out, soon followed by a cry from my lips. The shock of my release is so intense that tears prickle in my eyes. I pulse around her fingers, hesitant to free them as she pulls out of me gently.

"Fuck," I heave again, worried about my ability to remain standing. I lean heavily on her, body trembling. She pops a quick kiss on my lips that I chase after before pulling her hand away fully and dipping those two fingers into her mouth, eyes staying locked on mine as she drags them through her lips, hand drenched from me. I feel like I'm going to come a third time just watching the way she licks me off of her. *Scottish Goddess.*

I don't know how words work anymore. I'm sure I'm staring at her with a bizarre look on my face, my mouth half open as I try to learn how to breathe again. Once I can manage a single syllable, I say ridiculously, "Thanks." I finally let my skirt drop back into place.

She snorts, her eyes lifting quickly to the ceiling. "You're welcome. Feel better?"

I make an incomprehensible noise of confirmation, unable to grasp that I am still standing with my legs spread, dumbstruck as I stare at her. Dumbstruck mostly by the intensity with which I want her. I want to taste her on my lips, I want my fingers inside of her, I want to be pressed against her, skin to skin, I want to hear her moan my name, I want *her*. And while I want to say all of this, aptly express my desire, all I find myself saying is, "I owe…I mean, I need…" God, where are all the goddamn words? My IQ measures at moderately gifted. I scored a 35 on my ACT. I have a BS in Biology and an MS in Marine Biology. And yet, a simple sentence is beyond me. "Do you want me to, uh…I mean, should I…?" This woman has finger-fucked every brain cell out of me. I can't complete a full sentence.

"Naw," she says, finally loosening her hold on me, letting me fall back against the wall.

I remove my leg from where it was slung over the chair, leaning heavily on my good ankle. I stay pressed against the wall as she grabs a paper towel to clean off her hand, then gathers her things and struts out of the lab.

"What the hell?" I say aloud as the door clicks closed behind her.

Nope. No. She is not doing this to me again.

CHAPTER EIGHTEEN
Isla

I'm running away. Like, I am actually running right now. All the way to my car. Shit. *Shit.* I keep trying to suck in a full breath and I keep failing, the misty weather not helping my lungs. My pounding pulse echoes in my ears so loudly that I can't even hear the door of my car opening. I throw myself into the driver's side and gun it away from campus, pulling off to the side of the road as soon as I can. My forehead meets the steering wheel as I ride this out. I heave in and out, trying to focus my breath, but it's just increasing speed.

When my brain clears and my breathing returns to normal, I finally note the tears escaping my eyes. As I drive home in the steady rain, they don't cease.

Rachel isn't using me. Rachel isn't going to turn on me. I hate that that happened. I hate that my brain reacted like that. I hate that godforsaken word. "Owe." I don't want her to owe me anything. *Dammit.* I've run out on her again. Why do I keep doing this? I groan, slapping my hand against the steering wheel. The last time I tried to retrace my steps to her, she was gone. I suppose this time a phone call should suffice.

Pulling in front of my flat, I angrily put my car in park, get out, and slam the door behind me.

The taste of her is still in my mouth. I have spent months *wanting* her like that and once we finally got there, I bolted. Again.

I stomp through a puddle and then up to my flat, happy to find it empty. Aileen is at her boyfriend's, I presume. I drag the bottom of my shirt down my face to dry it from the rain and my tears as I pace the living room, trying to muster up the courage to pull out my phone.

A knock pounds on my front door before I can even make the move for my mobile. *Who is that?* I stalk over to the door, wondering if my downstairs neighbor is complaining about me walking too loudly. It's happened many times before—I'm a stomper. However, when I peek through the peephole, I see an angry blonde woman.

I take a deep breath, then I open the door.

Rachel barges inside without waiting for an invite, her singular crutch furiously slapping against the hardwood.

"I cannot *believe* you dipped after that! Honestly, what the hell?" She whirls around to face me, letting the crutch crash to the ground. Her wet hair is sticking to her forehead, tangled strands dripping water onto the floor. "First of all, you stole my underwear, which made my bus ride here *very* unpleasant. Second of all..." She trails off and cocks her head. Her voice instantly drops to gentle. "What's wrong?"

I shrug, looking away. "Nothing. Sorry. I shouldn't have left."

She limps closer to me. "Don't lie to me, Isla. Something's wrong. Your eyes are red. You've been crying." She grabs my shoulder. "Talk to me."

I nod quickly, feeling tears brim my eyes again. I lead the way to the couch so we can sit down. She falls ungracefully down beside me and I kick myself for not assisting her.

"Talk to me," she says again, hand resting over mine.

My lips purse. "I freaked," I mutter. "Sorry. I couldn't breathe and my heart was beating out of my chest. I had to run. I had to get out of there. I don't know why. I do that sometimes. Just freak."

She scoots closer to me. "It sounds like you had a panic attack."

"I don't have panic attacks."

She searches my face, fingers tightening their grasp. "I think you do, Isles."

My voice catches. "Those are panic attacks?"

"It sounds like it, yeah. It's okay. It's normal. It sucks, but it's normal."

"Oh." So…so that first night with her. That was also a panic attack? Huh.

"Do you want to talk about it?"

I sink back into the couch. "Yeah, yeah. Let's talk about it." I cover my face with my free hand. "I don't know how to explain. I just…I get weird about people owing me things. Like, them doing things for me because they feel like they have to. Not…not because they want to."

Her thumb traces over my hand, staying silent to let me explain at my own pace.

"That's why I hate it when people say they have to return a favor, pay me back, do something in return for me. Like my time, energy, gifts, or whatever is just me exchanging goods or services in return for something for me. Something selfish. Which I know is my mum's fault. She would always tell me to do things for people so they would owe you things in the future. Nothing about doing things for general kindness or love. But that wasn't all."

I inhale. I don't like talking about Kenna, but I need to.

"And I think one of the things that started triggering the…the panic attacks was when I was dating my ex. Or I guess more so when we started to break up." I quietly groan. This is going to be harder than I thought. I glance at Rachel, who is still regarding me expectantly. "Kenna was not out when we started dating, so it was all very secretive. Like, I was fine with it. We were young. Everyone comes out at their own pace and I wasn't going to force her out of the closet. But she also had some negative internalized notions about queerness that she would often put on me, which is a whole separate thing. She would go back and forth all the time, telling me things like I'm the only woman she's ever been attracted to. Sometimes she'd act like it was a good thing. Sometimes a bad thing. But when we were breaking up…" I swallow. "When we were breaking up, she told me she didn't even like having sex with me. She said she liked what I would do for her, but whenever she would have to 'return the favor,' she didn't do it because she wanted to, but because she felt like she had to. Because she *owed* me. And that…that made me feel like shit. Like I was forcing her to have sex with me. Like none of it was consensual when I know it was. She said yes. I didn't force her or beg her—she offered. It was mutual. And it was often she who initiated it. Then I start to question if I'm misremembering it." I shake my head. "It's complicated."

Rachel squeezes my hand. "Isla. I am so sorry. So, so sorry. So, when I offered, that's what triggered it?"

My shoulders hunch. "Sorry. You said the word 'owe' and it sunk its claws into me."

"Don't apologize," she says instantly. "Please. I want to be more careful with my words."

She wraps an arm around my shoulders and I lean into her,

letting her hold me there. Knowing how difficult initiating touch like this is for her, knowing that her arm is around me because she *really* wants it there, almost makes me start crying again.

She asks, "That night after Hoot, you had a panic attack then too, right?"

"I…I think so."

"Okay. I know I said something about you taking care of me. Was that all?"

"You also said I was 'perfect.' I know you didn't mean it in a bad way, but it made me spiral."

"You *are* perfect." Her fingers tangle in my hair as she says, "Please, in the future, if anything happens that triggers a panic attack, don't feel like you have to run from me. Run toward me, if anything."

I snuggle into her. "I'll try."

"If you do run away, I'll run after you."

We stay like that for a while with my head nuzzled in her neck and her arm around me. Eventually, she breaks the silence with a quiet admission. "I meant it when I offered."

I close my eyes. "It's fine, love."

She sits up to make me face her. "No, Isles, I need you to listen to me." And I do. Because she called me *Isles* and I fucking love that. "You cleared my head of every intelligent thought. What I wanted to say was how much I *want* you. How much I want to touch you. Taste you. Kiss and lick you until I'm sending you into spasms." I gulp, feeling a thump between my legs at even the suggestion. "And trust me, everything I want to do to you is because I want to. It's completely selfish. It's all for me." She gets as close to my face as she can without touching and whispers, "Understood?"

"Understood," I say back. Then in an attempt to lighten the

mood, I say. "Some other time, then? Next time the ongoing sexual energy between us becomes too much for you?"

Her mouth twitches. "Yeah, good plan."

I pull back and settle into her side, her arm still around me. I want to kiss her again, resume where we left off. Ensure she doesn't go home for the evening. But even with that little speech she gave, I don't believe that's what she wants tonight, so I say, "Just know that I am always happy to be the mate you go to for some casual stress relief."

Casual is what will work for us. I have to be sensible about this. I know how much of her heart she is willing to give me, and it's not nearly as much as I would give to her.

...

The next day, I'm walking to meet Ben at a café for breakfast. He took the day off from his job and I'm just giving a few tours today so I was free to meet up. For once, the subject I am anxious to bring up with him is not our café, it's Rachel. When I'm about a block away, my phone aggressively buzzes in my pocket. I pull it out and squint at the name. It's Ben.

I answer, "I swear to god if you're canceling on me—"

He cuts me off, "No. No, I'm already at the café."

"Oh. Well, I'm close—"

"I'm not alone."

I pause in the middle of the pavement, causing whoever is walking behind me to swear as they swerve around my abruptly still body. I pull off to the side. "Please tell me you're talking about David."

"Unfortunately, no." He clears his throat. "I may have mentioned to Mum that I was coming 'round yours today and she asked if she could tag along."

"I doubt she asked, rather insisted. Why didn't you warn me?"

"I knew you would refuse to come and then I would have to deal with the wrath of our mother. Which is entirely unfair."

"Where is she now that you're calling me?"

"In the toilet, getting ready to complain about the state of it as soon as she exits, I'm sure."

"Bollocks." I hang up the phone.

Leaning against the building behind me, I force myself to take a few deep lung-fulls. It's fine. I can do this. It's just lunch with my mother. Last night, Rachel mentioned that I may want to consider anxiety meds for the panic attacks. If seeing my own mum fills me with this much anxiety, maybe she's right.

Eventually, I force myself to keep walking. Before I open the door, I see Ben and my mother sat across from one another at a square table. Her blonde hair is in the normal tight bun she's kept it in for as long as I've known her, but now there are a few strands of gray running through it. She's talking and he's nodding, so I assume she's complaining about the state of the toilets. Since I picked the location, it's probably my fault.

When I enter the café, Ben hops up to hug me. My mother does not and I don't bother to try to initiate one. I slide into the seat next to Ben so we're both sat across from her.

"Hi, Mum," I say finally. "I wasn't expecting you."

She huffs, ice-blue eyes shooting to the sky. "Well, you never come see me so I was forced to come here to you."

"Yes, because coming to the city of Edinburgh is such a hassle."

She huffs again, this time at my tone.

"No Da?" I ask as a way to ease the tension.

"No, no. It's the second Saturday of the month. You know he's always at the market on these Saturdays."

Right. For as long as I can remember, my dad would drive over two hours to visit an East Asian grocery store in Glasgow to pick up "the goods." My father was born in Scotland, but his parents had emigrated from Korea. Though Scotland is not best known for their abundance of access to Korean delicacies, my father did manage to find the best grocery store for anything he could need to make kimchi, japchae, tteokbokki, amongst other dishes. I used to go with him on these treks, but they stopped when I moved away. Though, that didn't stop him from inviting me for the first year or so. I miss going with him. I suppose *I* could always re-initiate the continuation of a joint journey.

The waiter comes by and places a cup of tea before Mum. I order a coffee and as soon as the waiter is gone, she says, "I'm surprised you could meet today since both of your jobs have you working on weekends."

Ben sighs, reading her undertone. "We work in a café and a shop. Nothing wrong with either of those. Or with Isla's tour guiding. Can you see us as lawyers or doctors or accountants?" He turns to me and says with a wink, "Though, I would thrive as an accountant."

I roll my eyes.

Mum holds her hands up in surrender. "I didn't mean anything like that. I was just saying it was nice we could have breakfast today."

"Sure," Ben and I say together.

The waiter soon returns with my coffee and I am thrilled to finally have something to occupy my hands with. Before I take my first sip, I take off my outer layer, suddenly overheated. When I do, Mum's eyes catch on my arm.

"That's new," she comments, eyes like daggers piercing the tattoos on my arm.

"I've been growing the sleeve for a while," I say.

"I meant the guitar."

I'm genuinely astounded that she can zero in on the one she hasn't seen before. "Oh," I say. "It's about two months old now.

She tuts. "I've never understood tattoos."

"It's simple ink on skin," I say.

Her lips wrinkle. "I meant the desire for them, my dear. Your brother doesn't have any."

"He has one on his back," I say at the same time Ben says, "I have one on my back."

"Visible ones, I mean. That," she gestures vaguely at me, "is out in the open, unless you wear long sleeves."

"I like for people to see my tattoos. Corrine is a beautiful artist—I should show off her work."

Mum's nose scrunches at the mention of Corrine but she doesn't make a comment. Though, because of the mention she must now be forced to ask, "Are you seeing anyone right now?"

"Not really," I say because I don't feel the need to get into the complicated airs of my situation with Rachel.

Mum smiles tightly. "Good. Well, one of my friends has a son—"

I cut her off. "I'm a lesbian, mother."

"Still? I figured you'd go back to liking both."

"Nope."

"Well, maybe if you meet my friend's son—"

I cut her off again. "Does he identify as a man?"

"Yes?"

"Then, no."

She clicks her tongue. "I only want you to be happy."

The waiter brings our food. Ah, now I have something more than coffee to occupy my mouth with. I'm anxiously anticipating the real reason she's here today. I know my mother and I know she is not here to grill me about my love life.

We're all quiet as we eat. I tense with each bite like I'm waiting for a bomb to go off. Finally, my mother puts down her napkin and says, "I hear you and your brother are still wanting to open a café."

Ben and I exchange a look. His hand moves so he's gripping my wrist, thumb placed on my pulse. He's been doing this since we were wee—for whatever reason, it does great to calm me. If he's doing this, my mum is surely about to say something that could set me off.

"Yeah," Ben finally responds for both of us. "We've talked about it."

Mum frowns. "Well, I know you don't have enough money to do this. Neither of you work in careers where you earn much." We both just look at her so she continues. "I'd like to offer a contribution."

My breath hitches and Ben's grip on my wrist tightens.

"Why?" I manage to ask.

"To help."

"No," I say. "You don't offer anything just to help. You taught me that yourself. If we take this money, what do you want?"

"You come home weekly to see me."

My brow scrunches. "This isn't *Gilmore Girls* and that is too far a drive to be made once a week. What else do you want?"

Her chin lifts. "I want my children to be happy. To have a job they're not embarrassed about."

Ah. There it is. Ben's grip tightens almost to the point of pain. As calmly as I can manage, I say, "You mean, you want us to have a job that *you* aren't embarrassed by. You don't like us working in a shop and a café for other people, but if we own it, that's something else entirely."

Ben adds quietly, "And you contributing money to it would help you claim some control."

Mum scoffs. "Well, you can't blame me. You are both so bright and yet *this* is what you've done with your lives."

That's it. I push myself to my feet, pulling out of Ben's grasp. I look at him apologetically as I say, "I need to go."

He nods with understanding.

I glance at my mum. "Bye, Mum. Thanks for the offer, but I would rather owe money to a bank for the rest of my life than owe a single penny to you."

I storm out of the café, walking blindly without any clear intention of where I'm headed. Soon enough, I find myself pushing through the doors of Josie's shop. She looks up at me, mouth open and poised to ask what I'm doing here, but with one glance at my face, she closes her mouth. The store is empty so she gets up from behind the counter without a word and walks over to the door to flip the open sign to closed and put on the latch.

"Early lunch hour," she says. She puts an arm around my shoulders and steers me to the backroom.

She plops me down on the couch and switches on the kettle. As the water heats, she takes the seat across from me.

"What happened?"

"Mum happened." I shake my head. "I don't understand how you were ever friends with her, Josie."

Josie leans back in her chair with a lift of her shoulders. "People change. That's all I can say. The woman I was chums with was kind. She danced on top of tables. Had the loudest laugh in the room. The woman she grew into is not that. I held on to her for so long because while she changed from who I became friends with all those years ago, she produced two of my favorite people in the world and I couldn't let them go." The kettle whistles and she stands. "I still can't. You and your brother are my greatest gifts in the world. I hope you know that."

My eyes well with tears. "Thanks," I mutter. Why is it that some people are gifted with the perfect mothers and others have to find them in other people? I'm lucky to have found Josie.

She hands me a cup of tea that I sip from gently, knowing it's too hot. I go through what happened at lunch and Josie tisks.

"I don't know what happened to make her this way." She sips her tea. "Is Ben alright that you left him behind?"

"He's better at dealing with her than I am."

Josie nods. "Well, pet, you know if you do need money for the café, I can offer some." I open my mouth to reject her offer, but she cuts me off. "Don't consider it a loan. Consider it an early dip into your inheritance."

"My inheritance?"

"I don't have any weans of my own. All I have is going to you, Ben, and my sister's son."

More tears well in my eyes. Josie moves to sit beside me and wraps her arm around my shoulders. She presses a kiss to the side of my head. "I love you like my own. You're more than I or anyone could ask for."

I settle into her warm embrace. "Thanks, Josie. I may still go with the bank loan, though. I am determined to do this on my own. Or on my own with Ben. Either way."

"I understand. Let me know if you change your mind. No harm in having me *and* the bank behind you." She clears her throat. "Since you're here, I may as well put you to work."

CHAPTER NINETEEN
Rachel

I spend my Saturday anxiously waiting for Piper to wake up so I can call her. I go to the store. I make brownies from scratch. I text David about things other than Isla hoping that he'll bring her up so I can talk about this with someone. Half the pan of brownies disappears before they fully cool. I check my phone to see if Isla has texted. Nothing.

Casual. She said that word last night. I can be casual about this. I've done casual before—that situationship in grad school.

Though with Isla it's different because we're friends. I was not friends with situationship guy. When we weren't, you know, there wasn't much to talk about. Isla and I didn't lay down terms for what exactly we're doing. If it was a one-time thing. If it'll be a hey-if-you-wanna kind of thing. Or if we'll officially enter into a FWB relationship. But one thing I know for certain is neither of us wants a relationship.

I wanted to call Piper the second after Isla dropped me off last night, but Nick had a softball game and Piper was there, cheering him on.

12:30 p.m. hits and my phone starts to ring. For a moment I

think it's Piper, sensing how much I need to talk to her, but it's not. It's my mom. I haven't talked to my mom in almost four weeks. I answer with a cautious, "Hello?"

"Hey, sweetie. How are you? How's the ankle?" I can hear her set a mug presumably for coffee down on the kitchen counter.

"I'm alright," I say, because I do not need to tell her about what happened with Isla last night. "Ankle is healing."

"That's good." I hear her pour the coffee in the mug. "I woke up this morning and realized it has been nearly a month since we've spoken. A month! How did that happen?"

I readjust the icepack on my ankle as I shift on the couch. "Neither of us reached out to the other."

"Well, that'll do it. Sorry, hon. You know how I can get. All the days blend together and then suddenly I haven't talked to my daughter in a month."

"It's okay," I find myself saying.

"It's not," she counters. "You can tell me I'm a shitty mom."

"You're not a shitty mom."

She sighs. "Well, thank you, but this wasn't one of those 'Oh, so you think I'm a terrible mother,' things. I'm a bad communicator. We can both admit it."

I laugh lightly. "Fine. You're a bad communicator."

"Thank you. I think I'm used to you living with me or within driving distance. For years since you graduated undergrad, I saw you at least once a week without question, so when did I have to worry about calling? And now we're both so busy, you don't have the space to remember to call either."

I finger the scrunchie around my wrist. "I have to admit something."

"What?"

"I didn't reach out on purpose. I wanted to see how long it

would take for you to reach out to me."

She clicks her tongue, annoyed at herself, not me. "Well, good experiment. I'm sorry about the results. Is there a day that works for you? We can schedule weekly calls."

"I'd like that. Sundays would be best."

"Sundays work for me as well—starting tomorrow! Let's save the chatting for then, okay?"

"Okay. That works for me."

"Bye, sweetie. Love you."

"Love you too." I hang up, pleased with that interaction. I'm not sure I will ever get to know my mom very well, but I suppose I can start trying.

I check my watch with a groan. I still have time to waste until I can call Piper. I make it to 1:30 p.m., 7:30 a.m. her time, and press call.

When she answers the FaceTime, she is still in bed, which makes sense since it's a Saturday. Though she's an early riser no matter the day of the week, so I thought she'd be up by now. But judging by the fact that I vaguely recognize the sheets from when Nick texted me to ask if they were a nice color (they're tan) before he bought them, she's in Nick's bed.

"Morning," she says with a yawn, palm over her widening mouth.

Nick pops his head into the frame, hair tousled with bedhead. "Morning," he follows.

"Morning," I say back. And god, with that one word, my best friend catches that I need to talk to her alone. I love her so much.

"Nick," she says, "can you go get the coffee started? Please?"

I can't see him, but I know the face he's making: narrowed eyes before the moment he catches on. "Sure," I hear him say. There's a rustle of sheets and covers as he gets up from the bed.

"Which do you want?"

"Khaldi's?"

"Ooo, yes. The dark roast is my favorite."

"Damn right, sunshine. Thank you."

His head quickly comes back into the frame as he bends over the bed to brush a kiss against her cheek. "Love you," he whispers so softly I almost don't hear him. "Talk to you later, Rach," he calls as he exits my sight.

"Thanks!" Piper shouts after him. "Love you!" She looks back to me. "What's wrong?"

"I..." I start before trailing off with a shake of my head. "Wrong is too strong of a word because nothing is *wrong*, I'm just...having complicated feelings."

"Let's talk them out. See if we can uncomplicate them."

My fist covers my mouth, muffling my words. "Isla and I had sex yesterday."

Her eyes light up. "Yay, okay. Are we happy about that?"

I drop my hand. "Yes, we are. Because it was...*wow*." I go into brief detail about our exploits, leaving out Isla taking off and me following her back to her place because she had a panic attack. She was embarrassed about it, so even though she shouldn't be and Piper of all people would understand what she was going through in terms of brutal anxiety, it's not my place to share.

Piper nods approvingly. "I'd high-five you if I could. So, I'm missing why things are complicated. You guys like each other, right?"

"We do. As friends."

"Friends don't have sex."

"They can."

Her head swirls. "Okay. Sure. I guess I just don't have sex with my friends and have never known you to have sex with yours."

"Because I haven't before."

"Because you like Isla as more than a friend."

"I'm sexually attracted to her but I don't have time for a relationship. She doesn't want one either. Last night she said she was 'always happy to be the friend I go to for casual stress relief,' which said to me that she is also only interested in being sex friends."

"Fuck buddies or friends with benefits."

"I was happy with the term 'sex friends.' But…" I cover my face with my hands and blow out a puff of air. "Sorry, I have multilayered data for what I'm trying to say and work out. I'm having trouble organizing it into words."

"Take your time, Rach. Nick won't come back in here until I give him the all-clear."

"Okay, first point I want to bring up. Isla has this friend, Corrine—"

"The tattoo artist?" Piper interrupts.

"Yes. Shush. She hasn't gone into extreme detail about her with me, but I know Isla and Corrine were close friends before they started sleeping together. And I know they never had big feelings for one another. When Isla started dating her ex, Micky, she and Corrine stopped sleeping together. But they also stopped talking. Like, they weren't even friends anymore, so they basically broke up. Then she and Micky broke up, and she and Corrine started things up again. Then Corrine got a girlfriend, and while this time they're still friends, they're not close. I don't think they ever hang out unless it's one, tattoo related, or two, with a larger group."

"You don't want to be Corrine."

"No. I love being Isla's friend. I don't…I don't want to ruin the friendship we have by forcing our relationship into the specific category of friends with benefits. I don't want sex to be the only reason we hang out. Especially if she starts dating someone and we break it off and then never talk again. I don't want that to be what happens."

"That's understandable. One question though, are the options definitely only friends or sex friends? Nothing more? You're sure you don't want something more? But do you not want to risk your friendship for a full relationship?"

I click my tongue. "That was four questions."

"I'm not a mathematician."

"A relationship is not what I need right now. I don't have time and she's said a million things to imply that she is looking for anything but serious. If we were to date, I can see myself being unable to be there for her. I have so much going on with my Ph.D. And…I have two friends here, her being one of them. What if we start dating and it doesn't work out? I mean, our friendship so far has not been without its rocks. What if a relationship is not in the cards? Staying friends is easier."

Piper rests her chin in her hand. "It sounds like you've made up your mind, Rach. You want to be friends with her. Nothing more."

I sigh. "That's the conclusion I was seeing too."

"But…" she starts.

"Oh no."

"*But* you haven't known her for very long. I mean, two months, but you've only been friends for one month. I say, don't rush into things. Talk to her, for one—"

"I was planning to." Eventually.

"Good. And maybe let things play out. Don't be afraid to let it grow into something more with time."

…

After taking the full weekend to think things over, I get in the car with Isla on Monday with the full intention of talking to her about what happened, but she doesn't give any indication to the fact that her fingers were inside of me on Friday.

I ask, "Are you okay?"

She looks up, oddly startled by the question. "Fine. Just a bit knackered."

"Is that all?"

"Naw," she admits. "I saw my mum on Saturday. She was rude and mildly homophobic, as per usual. I'm fine though. Knackered, like I said."

I purse my lips. "Anything you want to talk about?"

"Not really."

My chest pinches. I wish her answer was yes. "Okay. Let me know if you change your mind. I'm here."

Her eyes crinkle at that. "I know. Thank you."

Quiet takes over the car. The one subject I can think to bring up instead of my planned topic of discussion is how I finally spoke to my mom, but that would be the absolute worst thing to mention right now. We need to talk about Friday because I am incapable of being casual about this until we establish our baseline of casual.

"I want to talk to you about something," I say.

"Oh," she says, glancing at me out of the corner of her eye. "Friday, yeah?"

"Exactly."

Her mouth thins. "You regret it? Love, it was just a friendly way to blow off steam."

"I don't regret it at all. Isles, I don't want our friendship to be about sex. *Only* about sex."

"Oh? I don't think I understand what you're getting at."

"I want to be your friend, Isla, but I don't want to be a friend with benefits where the benefits come first. I want the friend part to come first. I think…I'm not opposed to what happened on Friday happening again, because it was so, so great, but I don't want what's between us to become a friends with benefits thing or a situationship. I don't want each time we see one another to have an ulterior motive. Unless…" I trail off, afraid to finish my sentence.

"Unless?"

"Unless that's all you want," I finish quietly.

"I'm going to touch you."

"Okay."

Keeping her eyes on the road, she grasps my hand firmly. "That is not all I want. The reason we became friends is not because I wanted to get in your pants. Don't get me wrong, I was dying to, but you're a whole person. I like all of you, not just the fun parts." As we're stopped by a red light, she says, "We can take sex out of it completely." She pauses, chewing her lip. "Or we can keep sex on the table for special occasions."

"Special occasions?" I repeat.

"Sure. After a stressful day or if we're feeling particularly frisky. We can define it as it comes up. We can still see other people, *should* see other people. But maybe we exchange a few orgasms here and there, if you'd like. Our friendship will always come first. I will never booty call you or want to see you with a sex-only mindset."

I huff out a laugh. "I'd like that. But, I will note, I don't date much. Or, ever. I don't date."

"I haven't been dating much recently either." She drums her fingers on the steering wheel, staring ahead. "Maybe I should. Both of us should. Get our wiles out with other people."

I nod, trying to cover up the twist in my gut that comes with the idea of her seeing someone else. That's misplaced jealousy that I have no right to. "So, friends?"

"Friends." She purses her lips like she wants to say something more. I'm waiting for her to, but nothing else comes.

That's fine. I'm okay being her friend. However, just having her beside me in the car sends a sizzle through my chest and a shiver down my spine. I still *want* her. I'm not sure how long it'll be before that becomes a problem.

...

At the end of my day, I have Isla drop me off at Hoot instead of home because it's been forever since I've seen David. Also, I have finally bucked up the courage to go see him at the bar. It's a pain in the ass getting down the stairs with crutches, but now that I only have to use one, it should be easier.

He eventually comes out into the stairwell saying, "I can hear you struggling. It's been ten minutes, Rach, and you're only halfway down."

"I'll get there when I get there," I say as I attempt to carefully lower myself onto the next step with my crutch balanced precariously. "I'd get there faster if this wasn't such a hoppin' place. I mean, it's 6 p.m. Why is it so busy? Did it blow up online or something? I keep having to let people pass me by. And no one, not a single one, has offered to help. If I was back in St. Louis, I'd've been there already. Someone would have walked by and offered to carry me down the stairs."

David sighs and shakes his head. He stomps up the stairs to where I am standing, takes my crutch away from me, and then walks back down the stairs and into the bar. I am too speechless by what just happened to even complain.

When he comes back out, I ask, "What the hell are you doing?"

"Incoming physical contact," he says as he scoops me up into his arms like a baby, earning a surprised gasp from me, and lugs me down the stairs. My face burns as he carries me.

As we enter the bar, I deadpan, "Well, this is romantic."

"You're not my type," he deadpans back as he sets me on my usual bar stool. When he loops around the bar to face me, he's grinning. "But unfortunately for me, I'm everyone's type."

My eyes roll. "Yeah, yeah. You're cute and you know it."

"So," he leans forward with his elbows on the bar, "you're normal grumpy, but glowing. Do you feel better ankle-wise or has someone else entered the chat?"

I look around to see if anyone is listening, even though I know no one cares. I lean in and say quietly, "Isla and I sort of hooked up Friday night."

He raises an eyebrow and leans in as well, matching my volume. "Define 'sort of.'"

I purse my lips. Listen, I have no issue talking about my sexual exploits with Piper and I don't mind talking about sex in general, but with David in a crowded bar about myself? I can do this. "Let's call it mouth stuff and a fingering in my lab. And two orgasms. Both mine because she didn't give me the chance to reciprocate."

He backs up and crosses his arms, pulling an impressed face. "I'm not sure I would call that 'sort of.' So, are you and her going to finally be a thing?"

I blush furiously. I wish I didn't. I hate it when my face goes red without my consent, showing off emotions I'm not ready to share. "No. It was a one-time occurrence." I drum my fingers on the bar. "A one-time occurrence that has the potential for additional one-time occurrences, but nothing serious."

He nods, knowing how I feel about being in a relationship

right now. "Makes sense. When is your doctor's appointment?"

My face cools with the change of subject. "Wednesday afternoon, if you're still good to take me."

"Of course. This is the big one, right?"

"Right. They're gonna check out the ankle and see if it's finally fine to walk on without assistance. Either way, they're probably going to give me a bunch of physical therapy exercises to do and tell me I still need to be careful, and blah blah blah."

"Ugh," he says dramatically. "Annoying doctors and their annoying medical expertise telling you to be careful on your uncool injuries."

"Hey! It's not an 'uncool' injury."

"You twisted your ankle on a curb, darling. I would never call that cool."

I laugh. "Fine, fine. It's not cool. But it *was* painful."

I'm happy to be back here with him. While I've been spending more time with Isla on our drives, I've been lonely without seeing David at the bar a few nights a week. The ankle sprain threw a wrench in me settling in, but I'm getting back to it. The clock has resumed. I have a chance, a real fighting chance, of being happy here.

• • •

As of Wednesday afternoon, I no longer need to use crutches. The doctor gave me the all clear and everything feels great. Honestly, I was probably on the crutches longer than I needed to be, but there is nothing wrong with extending a little caution. I take the bus to and from campus on Thursday and Friday, despite Isla's many protests. I'll miss our drives, but there is no reason she needs to keep wasting gas money on me.

I don't see or talk to her until Saturday.

How are those new legs working out for you?

Good. Everything feels fine

What are you going to do with all that freedom?

I was thinking...walk?

That's a nice activity. Might I suggest another?

Like what?

Have you taken time to explore more local spaces in Edinburgh? Besides pubs, I mean. Queer spaces, maybe?

I gnaw my lip as I contemplate my phone. The answer is no. Should that have been one of the first things I did?

Not yet. I'm not very good at being a part of the community

There's no right or wrong way, love. Do you have any friends back in the States who are queer?

I don't have many friends in general, I would like to start by saying. But, not many. Piper's demisexual, but beyond her, no one close

Well, there's a step up for Scotland. Your two best friends here are a lesbian and a gay man

True

So, what's your idea for tonight?

Dancing, if your ankle can take it

I like dancing. I'm not a huge club person, but dancing is fun. Though, I frown at what I'm wearing. Jeans and a T-shirt. Something I'd wear to the beach for samples (now that I can do that again!) or to the lab. I pinch the soft blue fabric of my T-shirt between my fingers.

Okay. Sounds fun! I'll need to change into something less science-y

But I like your science-y clothes

• • •

When Isla picks me up at my place, I've changed into a short black skirt, white sneakers, and a rust-colored, cropped T-shirt.

Her eyes roam over me as I exit my front door, but she doesn't say anything.

"What?" I ask, stance defensive. "Am I not dressed right?

I catch a flash of her pink tongue against maroon lips. "I like you in anything and nothing," she says seriously. "But you look really good. You should show those legs off when you can." She pivots away from me and starts walking with purpose. "Maybe you'll catch the eye of someone special tonight."

Right. Other people exist in this city. It's odd how often I find myself forgetting that.

We catch a bus to a dimly lit club with a smattering of people inside. An appropriate amount of people, in my opinion.

"It'll fill up more the later it gets," Isla confides. "We're here sort of early."

"Cool," I say. We head to the bar and order drinks. While I like dancing, I usually need at least one in me before I can truly let loose. I know no one is judging me when I dance, but I don't like being perceived by strangers.

We drink and chat, and as the club fills up, Isla introduces me to a few friends (because of course she does). Soon enough, Corrine and her girlfriend Madison show up with even more friends. Eventually, Isla pulls me to the dance floor, multicolored lights swirling around us. She gives me my own space as we dance, which I appreciate, and soon enough I lose myself in the music. The hour grows later, the music gets louder and the lights lower.

Isla yells in my ear, "I'm going to go grab us another round! Be right back." She glances behind herself, then leans back in. "There's a woman who's had her eye on you for a bit. Make eye contact." Then she's gone, back toward the bar.

I give a thumbs up, but keep dancing. Cautiously, I lift my focus to the woman Isla was referring to. She's gorgeous, with light eyes and a hot pink pixie cut. With the invitation of eye contact, she comes up to me, saying something I can't hear, but I find myself nodding and soon enough we're dancing together. I glance over at Isla and see her head thrown back in a laugh as she is talking to Corrine at the bar, the drink meant for me forgotten beside her. Corrine has a girlfriend and Isla is not mine, yet I cannot help the jealousy snaking through me. I shove that feeling down deep in my chest.

The woman I am dancing with grabs me by the hips and I try not to cringe under her touch. This is normal, I tell myself. Normal people are okay with being touched by the pretty people they dance with. I can do this. I can be flirty and free and normal. But soon her touch is too much so I pull away, keeping a smile on my face. We dance without touching for a little bit longer before she puts her hands back on my hips. Again, I succumb to it, telling myself that this is fine. She's pretty. She seems nice. Just because I don't want to touch her right now does not mean I am displeased by the attention.

But then it overwhelms me again and I pull away.

I can't hear her, but I read her lips as she asks if I'm alright. I nod, confirming I'm fine. She grabs my hips again, and this time I must visibly cringe because she drops her hands, affronted. She says something I can't hear again, so I ask, "What?!"

She yells in my ear, "I said, am I bothering you?!"

I shake my head. "No, no! It's not that!" I swallow a breath before I lean back into her ear and explain, "I'm not huge on physical touch. I'm enjoying dancing with you but I would appreciate it if you would touch me less for now."

I draw back, proud of myself for setting boundaries. The woman nods and smiles. We dance until the end of the song, but she soon drifts away.

Got it. It's fine. I'm the one who made it weird. I'm the one with something wrong with me. I'm the one who can't just be normal.

I search for Isla in the crowd and see her dancing with Corrine, Madison, and one of the other friends she introduced me to earlier—Hannah. I try to make my way over to them, but there are suddenly so many people in here. When did it get this crowded? I get stuck in a glob of people; sweaty, moving bodies touching me on all sides, brushing against my bare skin, and it is too much. *Too much.*

I don't even make it to Isla before I burst out of the hoard of people and race toward the exit.

Once I emerge onto the cool street, I can breathe. I lean against the brick wall of the club, taking in a few mouthfuls of air and enjoying the distinct lack of strangers touching me.

A hand on my arm causes me to jump but I relax when I recognize the hand as Isla's.

She doesn't let her hand linger as she asks, "Everything okay?"

"Yeah," I say with a sharp nod. "I'm good. Got overwhelmed. So many people, you know?"

"Aye, it got crowded in there." Isla nestles up next to me against the wall, still leaving a sliver of space between us. "What happened between you and that woman? She was gorgeous."

My thumb scratches at the clear polish of the opposite pointer finger. "She was. I set a boundary and she wasn't a fan. It's fine. She knew what she wanted tonight and I wasn't going to give it to her. I get it."

Isla cocks her head to the side. "What boundary? Did she want to sleep with you?"

"No," I say. "Well, actually maybe. Probably, but no. We didn't get that far. I asked her to touch me less. I tried to explain that it didn't mean I wasn't interested, but I don't think she understood. I get it. Normal people don't mind touching the people they're flirting or dancing with."

She scoffs. "What's this talk about normal people? It's perfectly normal to ask someone to stop touching you if you don't want to be touched. If they take that poorly, that's on them."

My head lifts with a sudden lightness. "You think?"

"You only had to tell me once, love. Now, I let you initiate the touch. Or I ask or warn you before I touch you. And I still want to be around you. It's not hard."

That's true. I don't think I realized she was doing that. "Thank you," I say softly.

"Don't thank me for human decency." She pushes herself up from the wall. "You ready to get out of here?"

I push myself up as well. "We don't have to if you're still having fun. I might just head home on my own."

Isla shakes her head. "Naw, I'm done. Corrine and Madison were making gooey eyes at each other and Hannah was flirting hard with someone, so they're all probably going to take off as well."

I cock my head. "No one you would rather go home with? Someone who might give you a little more fun than me?"

She looks at me like I'm being ridiculous. "There is no one I would rather spend time with than you, Rachel."

Goosebumps prickle my bare arms because of the way she says my name. I believe her.

My face heats as I say, "Me too. Well, I'm not quite ready to go home. I've been wanting to go back to Calton Hill in the evening." I give her a hopeful look.

She beams. "My favorite view in the city and my favorite person in the city, all together? A perfect night, you've just proposed." She sets off, knowing the direction without pause. "Let's go."

CHAPTER TWENTY
Isla

As we climb the steps of Calton Hill, I ask, "How's the ankle?"

She seems surprised by the question. "Totally fine. A little stiff. I sort of forgot about it."

"Well, if it starts to smart and you need me to carry you home, I will."

She snorts like I'm not entirely serious. "I'll keep that in mind."

We reach the top and I let myself watch her as she takes in the sight with the same wonderment she held the last time we were here.

"What do you think?" I ask softly.

"It's beautiful at night," she breathes. "You can see farther during the day than at night, obviously, but there's something magical about all that inky darkness surrounding the city. Endless possibilities, endless everything."

"I like that. When we're up here at night, it's like all those possibilities are just for us."

She inches closer to me. "You know, you don't need to warn me anymore."

I turn my head toward her, squinting in the dim light.

She expands. "Before you touch me. You don't need to warn me. It's welcome. I mean, I still don't like it excessively, but I'm not afraid to tell you when to stop if I need you to stop. If I don't tell you to stop, you don't need to."

The corner of my mouth perks, but I don't say anything. I hook a pinky through hers, inching closer to inhale the scent of her shampoo, crisp and clean. She sidles up by my side like that's where she belongs.

That little green monster wormed its way into my chest when I saw her with that woman tonight. I couldn't keep my eyes off of them, as much as I tried. When I could no longer see Rachel, my entire being went into red alert, thinking they'd left together. But then I caught a flash of blonde hair exiting in a hurry, so I followed. I'm glad I did. Immense satisfaction passes over me because here we are again. Rachel may have been dancing with a beautiful woman who I pushed her toward, but right now she is with me.

The idea of dating other people was a preposterous one, anyhow. I can't even fathom the thought. We'll be fine to not date at all and keep orbiting around one another, experiencing whatever this is between us without putting words to it—as all healthy adults should strive to do.

I'd be content to stand here all night in our own little universe, but then we feel the first drop. Then another. And another.

"Shite," I say as the rain starts to come down harder.

Rachel shrieks and follows me as I race back down to street level, ignoring all of the places to seek cover up on Calton Hill. We run like we're trying to pass between the raindrops, until the storm calms to a drizzle. Rachel grabs me by the arm to pull me under an awning. She heaves for breath, lost from both the physical activity and her laughter.

She looks at me and lets out a harsh screech, slapping her hand over her mouth to stifle the laughter.

"What?" I ask, a laugh bubbling in my throat as well. "Is my makeup running?"

She nods. "Sorry," she manages to get out in a wheeze. "It surprised me."

I pull out my phone so I can inspect myself in the camera. I let out a sharp hoot. Black and maroon streaks run down my face from mascara and eyeliner. My lipstick, however, is firmly in place. "I look ridiculous," I moan.

"You look as gorgeous as always." She uses a thumb to wipe at my face, unsuccessfully clearing off the makeup. "If anyone can pull this look off, it's you."

I smile. "You think?"

"I do."

Gooseflesh I convince myself is from the cool rain prickles on my skin. We both creep forward, sharing our breath before she looks away, focusing on the sky.

"The rain seems to be lightening up," she says.

I pull back, internally scolding myself. This can't be more than what it is. We can't be kissing in the rain, engaging in something as romantic as that. I keep fooling myself into believing that the path we're heading down is one consisting of anything more than friendship.

"We should go home, I guess."

Her shoulders slump. "I guess."

I wipe at my face with the back of my hand, working on clearing the streaks of makeup, as neither of us attempts to leave where we stand. In that case...I look around conspiratorially, unwilling to let my time with her end. "Unless you would rather stay out?"

Her eyes brighten. "I'm wide awake. What else can we do?"

I shove my hands in my pockets and walk off. "We can keep existing in my favorite city in the world."

Rachel seems content to wander with me, so we do just that. Without even thinking about it, we are retracing our steps from the first day we met. Suddenly, we've been walking for thirty minutes and we find ourselves in front of the space I hope to house my café. I pause with a sigh.

"I have to do it by myself," I say. Even after Mum brought it up, Ben still won't commit. I asked him about it again and he said I needed to give him some time. It wasn't time yet. And that when it is time, he'll be ready. He said the word "time" a lot. Then he made a joke about thyme. But the thing is, for me, it is time. I'm doing it myself. I'm getting the loan and if that isn't enough, I'll accept Josie's help. If Ben wants in later, I'll be more than happy to have him.

I haven't told Ben yet. It's his feet dragging that got me here, but regardless, I feel like he'll be upset.

"Good. You should do it yourself. You shouldn't have to wait on other people to take charge of your dreams."

I nod once. "I shouldn't."

An opening door startles me and I swivel quickly to the sound. The woman exiting the antique shop also seems startled by our presence because she drops the box she was holding, whatever is inside clanking and hopefully not shattering as it clatters to the ground.

"Shit," she says, bending down to open up the box, inspecting everything inside. "I wasn't expecting anyone else to be out here this late."

"Sorry," Rachel says. "We were just…loitering."

After determining everything in the box is fine, the woman

stands, jerking to flick one of her two ginger braids over her shoulder. "Public street," she says with a shrug. "I need to stop being surprised by the presence of other people. I jump if I turn into an aisle with another person in it at the supermarket." She faintly shakes her head. "Were you actually loitering or were you trying to get a moment alone that I've now interrupted? This is a quiet street at night. Good place to be alone." She shifts the box, digging a set of keys out of her pocket.

I explain, "We were looking at this space. I'm opening a café and I've had my heart set on this location."

She looks suspicious as she locks the door she just exited. "You sure? It's been vacant for so long because it's a terrible location. Quiet street during the day as well. We survive because we sell a lot of specialty items you can't get anywhere else."

I don't let her discourage me. "I have a good feeling about this place."

The woman lets the keys hang on her fingers, tapping against the box. "Up to you. If you're set on it, the owner is planning on lowering the tenancy price in a couple of weeks since they're having so much trouble letting the space."

My eyebrows perk up. "Wait, really?"

"Yeah."

"It's like fate," I muse.

"Yeah. Or the terrible real estate market," she says. "Anyway, this box is heavy and I have to carry it up these stairs." Her elbow points to the door of a flat I assume is above the antique shop. "Have a good night."

As she opens the door to her flat, Rachel and I look at each other, eyes both glowing with excitement. My café has suddenly become a lot more real. If they're lowering the price, I need to jump on it as soon as possible.

"I think that was your café angel," she says.

"I think she was a grumpy antique shop owner who wouldn't hate me as a neighbor, but I'll take it."

...

I spend the next few days honing in my business plan, staring at the loan application, and doodling signs for my café. Oh, and picking up as many tours as I can manage. I've been doing this for a while and saving as much money as I can, but now that I have officially decided to do this by myself, I need to get a move on. I have a good chunk of money in my savings account, but not enough. Not nearly. If I keep working hard, I can at least be a little more comfortable when the time comes to spend it all.

Coming off of a 9 a.m. tour, I push my way into the music shop.

"You're early," Josie says without looking up from her phone.

"Only a bit."

"Two hours," she corrects. She sets the phone down. "It's fine. I can put you to work. The back room is a mess if you want to get a start on organizing."

"I'll get on it," I say, moving to walk past the counter. Then I swivel back around. "Josie?"

"Hmm?"

"I've decided to open the café by myself. Without Ben."

She props a hand on her hip and looks at me seriously. "And he knows this?"

"I've threatened it before." She raises one eyebrow at me so I add, "But, no. I haven't told him. He won't commit. I can't keep waiting for him."

She nods. "I understand. And so will he."

"I hope so." I pick at my fingernails. "But…since I am doing this alone, I was wondering…" I look back up at her with pleading eyes. "I was wondering if your offer is still on the table? I'm still going to apply for a small business loan, but having you as an investor would offer a great cushion. I would pay you back every penny, even if it takes me to the grave."

She laughs, a loud cackle that I have always loved springing from the base of her throat. "I'll be in the grave long before you, pet. No matter. I'm happy to give you the money. I was already planning on it." She settles back down on the stool behind the counter, rotating it toward me. "You found a location yet?"

"Yeah." I lean my elbows on the counter across from her, telling her about the spot I've had picked out for years.

"Next door to that haunted antique shop?" Josie asks. I nod. "I know the owner. Carolyn. She's a bit off in the head, but in a good way."

"The ginger-haired woman?"

"No, no. That's her niece. Great niece, I suppose. Melanie or Melinda or something. Carolyn's an old bat, like me."

"You are far from an old bat," I argue with a laugh.

She waves me off. "I suppose the woman has twenty years or so on me. She's good people. Will be a good neighbor to you." She gestures to the back room. "Now, get to work. I am not paying you to stand here and chatter with me all day."

Once the back room is sufficiently organized, Josie and I swap places, her heading to the back and me taking residence behind the counter. It's a relatively busy day, so the next time I hear the bell over the door chime, I hardly glance up from the customer I'm assisting at the register to call, "Hiya!"

When I hear a familiar voice say, "Hi," my head rockets up. Rachel, hair in a low bun beneath her favorite ball cap. I can't help the grin that grows on my face.

I wrap up with the customer as she approaches the counter.

"To what do I owe the pleasure?"

She adjusts her backpack. "I was in the neighborhood—had to stop off at my flat before heading to the lab. Dr. Andonov and I were gathering samples this morning. Also, I've never seen Josie's shop—it's super cute." She places an iced coffee on the counter. "I brought you this."

I accept the drink with my heart pounding out of my chest. Perhaps caffeine is not the best idea right now. Oh, well. I take a sip and say, "Cheers, love."

The door to the back room swings open and Josie exits, saying, "Isla, would you mind…" She trails off when she spots Rachel. "Oh, I'm sorry. I didn't realize you were with a customer. Busy day, today is."

"Naw, Josie. You're fine. This is Rachel."

Her eyebrows raise. "Rachel, is it? Well, you're gorgeous."

Rachel's cheeks go pink, making her freckles stand out. "Thanks," she says with an awkward laugh. "Josie, right?"

"Right," Josie says, sweeping around the counter to pull Rachel into a swift hug. I don't see it coming in time to warn her off but Rachel accepts the embrace. "I was starting to think you didn't exist."

"Hey!" I protest. "I haven't had to make up friends since primary school."

Rachel looks at me with big, soft eyes. "You made up friends?"

I shrug. "Believe it or not, I didn't use to be that great at making them. Long past that, though."

She reaches across the counter to squeeze my hand, keeping her attention on Josie. "It was so great to meet you. Finally."

"You too. Maybe I can take you girls out to dinner soon?"

"That would be great."

"Aye," I agree. "That would be lovely, Josie." My heart

continues to try and burst from my chest. Two of my favorite people finally meeting is a lot to take, but it fills me with an unfiltered sort of joy.

Rachel squeezes my hand again, perking up at the echo of the one o'clock gun in the distance. "That's my signal. I've got to go, but I'll see you soon?"

"Count on it."

...

I hang about Josie's shop working on my business plan far after close, Josie herself having left hours ago. I intend to head back to my flat, but as I gather my things, I spy the coffee maker Josie keeps in back. I'm out of coffee at home. It won't hurt to stay here a little longer. I get the coffee maker going, then re-open my laptop and settle back on the couch.

I am quickly distracted from my business plan once I start messing with this 3D layout program to set up a virtual diagram of my café. I place all the tables where I want them to go, set up the counter, set up the kitchen. Ah, the kitchen. I'll need to hire a baker if I'm to be doing this without Ben. That's fine. I can manage that. I need to add that to my business plan document, though. Before I do so, I pour myself another cup of coffee. I settle back down with it and open up my business plan to add that note in the section about staff.

I go back to the 3D model and keep playing with it for a while. I move a table slightly to the right and...oh, wow. It's perfect. It's *perfect.*

Without thinking, I snatch my laptop and am out the door, locking it behind me, running in the direction of Rachel's flat. It's spitting rain outside, but I hardly notice.

I ring her buzzer a few times before a cautious voice answers, "Yes?"

"It's me," I say.

A pause. "Isla? It's 2 a.m. What are you doing here? I'm not wearing pants."

It's 2 a.m.? Bollocks. I did not realize how late the hour had grown. "Damn. Sorry. I was just excited. Not thinking. I'll let you sleep." I turn to head home, my excitement fading into embarrassment at my impulsivity.

Her voice makes me swivel back. "No, no. Come up."

The door buzzes open and I push through, making my way up to the first floor to find Rachel standing in her open doorway, arms crossed. Unfortunately, she's donned on bottoms. Black sweats rolled at the waist under a ratty T-shirt that says: KISS ME, I'M A BIOLOGY MAJOR.

"What's wrong?" she asks.

"Nothing," I insist, holding up my laptop in proof. "I wanted to show you something. Last I checked the clock it was half past ten, which I know is still late, but I figured you would be up."

She looks me over, up and down, her eyes wary. "Are you drunk? High?"

I groan, shoulders drooping. "No. I am completely sober. Is that new?" I point to a wooden coffee table in the middle of the living room as I head toward it.

"Yeah. David and I found it at a resale shop yesterday."

Kneeling, I set my laptop on the table—noting that this would be easier if she had a kitchen table, but such a table has not yet found its way into her home. I open the laptop and show her the 3D model of the café, pointing out every little bit I've spent, apparently, the last three hours working on.

She kneels beside me and nods in approval. "I love it. I cannot wait to see it in person."

"Me too. Hopefully sooner rather than later. Josie gave me her word today that she would act as an investor, and I have been taking on so many tours this week that my pockets are literally weighed down by tips. I've been working on this instead of my loan application, which I know, I do need to fill out and submit, but I'm not convinced my business plan is in peak condition yet—"

"Oh my god," she cuts me off with a laugh. "That's what it is."

I close my mouth, swallowing the end of my sentence so I can ask, "What?"

"You're not drunk or high. You're overly-caffeinated. Isles, how much coffee have you had tonight?"

I shrink, feeling a microscope on me. "I don't know. A cup? Two?"

She raises an eyebrow at me.

"Perhaps three. Plus the coffee you brought me at the shop. And of course, one or two cups this morning."

Her thumb catches my face to trace under my eye—surely the dark circles there. "And when was the last time you slept?"

"Last night."

"For how long?"

"Enough."

"How many hours did you get, Isla?"

I do quick math and then consider whether or not I want to lie. I don't. "Maybe two. Or three. Hard to tell."

She blows out a puff of air. "Right. And how many hours the night before?"

I carefully regard the floor. "The same, I'd say."

"Isla, you need to sleep."

"I sleep!" I argue.

"Not enough!" she argues back. She groans, stalking off to her bedroom and coming back moments later wearing shoes. She picks up my laptop from the coffee table and gestures me toward her front door. "Come on. We're going to bed."

"Are we now?" I say, lifting my eyebrows in what I hope is a seductive fashion.

She doesn't acknowledge it. She grabs her keys off the hook by the door and starts down the stairs, leaving me behind in her living room. I chase after her, arguing, "I'm fine. I was planning to go to bed after I saw you. I swear I didn't realize the time."

"That's the problem. You're not paying attention to the time and you're not taking care of yourself. You need to take care of yourself."

"I do."

She whirls on me. "Well, take care of yourself better!"

I step back at the tone. "Okay," I murmur, not sure what else I can say.

She pinches between her eyes. "Sorry. I'm sorry. *I'm* exhausted. It's been a busy week. I know it's not that simple, but can you promise me you'll try? I'll do anything you need me to do to help, but Isla, I want you to be well."

I catch up to her, throwing an arm around her shoulders as we start again in the direction of my flat. "I know, love. And I appreciate it. I'll try. I just have so much to do for the café."

"I know. I know. I do." She leans into me as we walk. "Anxiety meds may help you sleep better. If you've thought any more into trying those out."

I wrinkle my nose. "I've thought about it." In all honesty, I have. I've looked into psychiatrists—I just haven't gotten around to making an appointment.

We make it back to mine and head upstairs. I'm amazed to see Aileen when I open the door, dark hair in a bun atop her head and slippers on her feet. She seems surprised as well. "Figured you'd be out for the rest of the night." She looks around me at Rachel. "Hiya. Good to see you again." Her gaze flicks back to me. "I'll be in my room."

"Hey," Rachel says back. "I'm just here to force her to sleep, then I'll be out of your hair. Isla, go wash your face and get ready for bed."

Aileen slips into her room and closes the door.

Rachel asks me, "Do you guys have non-caffeinated tea?"

"We have chamomile in the cupboard."

She squints at me for a second, then understanding crosses her face. "Oh. You said chamomile. I swear I can usually understand every word you say, but that one in the middle of the night got me." She shakes her head. "Go wash your face."

"Bossy, bossy," I tut as I do as she says, getting ready for bed. Once I'm done in the bathroom, I strip myself of my trousers and climb into bed.

When my tea is prepared, she meets me in my room and sits gingerly on my bed, handing me the mug. "Drink, relax, sleep."

"You could sleep over," I offer, fingers mentally crossed. "It's late and I know you want to monitor me."

She stiffens. "I hate sharing beds with people, if I'm being honest. I can share with Piper because we've been sharing a bed for years and I know to expect her to spider-monkey grab me in her sleep. But with anyone else, I don't know what to expect. I don't like unpredictability in vulnerable moments. Like, sleep."

I gently swirl the tea in my mug, unsure of what to say because I wasn't expecting such a serious answer to my flirty question. Instead, I ask my own. "Could you share with someone else, though? Ever?"

She nods. "Yeah. I would figure it out and get used to it if I was dating someone."

"But would you enjoy it?"

"Probably." She smiles. "No, yeah, I would. Because it would be about more than predictability. If I was dating the right someone, their presence would be comforting enough that I wouldn't care."

I sip my tea. Good to know.

"I should go," she says quietly.

"It's late," I agree. "At least call me on your way home? So I know when you make it?"

She leans forward and presses a kiss to my forehead, a surprisingly simple gesture that I know means a lot coming from her. I lean into her lips, wishing they would stay, before she pulls away and whispers, "Okay."

Moments later, I hear my front door close, and moments after that, my phone buzzes on the bed beside me. I answer, "Hello, love."

"Hi," she yawns. "I'm too tired to chat, mind walking in silence with me?"

"Of course." I finish my tea as she walks.

"I'm home," she announces about ten minutes later. "You can go to sleep."

A wave of disappointment thrashes in my chest. "Okay. 'Night."

"Goodnight."

I expect her to hang up, but she does not. I still hear her breathing on her end of the line. I won't be the first to hang up. Never. I turn out my lamp and slide deeper under the covers, laying my phone on the pillow beside mine. I fall asleep listening to the sound of her crawling into bed, the music of her deepening breaths lulling me under.

CHAPTER TWENTY-ONE

Rachel

My next week is spent gathering even more samples and logging a lot of time in the lab. I'm getting far with my research into microplastics' effect on marine life. I mean, far in the sense that I have gathered a ton of data. But there's still so much I don't know. Years' worth of research to be done. Because I know that, I stay at the lab past 8 p.m. multiple nights this week.

Finally, on Friday, I manage to get myself out of the lab by 5 p.m. so I can go home and shower before meeting up with David. Once I get out of the shower, there is a text from him waiting for me.

Change of plans. We're going to McFleet's instead

Works for me. Any particular reason?

Isla is playing tonight

Oh, cool. She never invites me to see her sing. Will she be fine that we're there?

Oh, that makes sense. That makes a lot of sense. She doesn't ever want anyone to feel obligated to do anything for her. *Shit.* I should have been trying to go see her much sooner.

When I arrive at the pub, I glance around the room to check if Isla has shown up yet. I don't see her, so I settle at a table with David, both with cold pints in front of us. I can't help but glance at the door every five seconds to see if Isla has arrived.

"Her set starts at half past," David says.

"Oh. Sorry. God, I'm incredibly obvious." I cover my face. "Sorry. I'm here. How's Callum? Did you invite him?"

"No, no. He's with his parents this weekend. Also, you're fine. One of the reasons I like you is because you're okay hanging out in silence."

"Yes, I am. My dad always says it's because I'm 'thoughtful.'"

David smiles. "Not a bad thing. Have you talked to him recently? Or your mom?"

"I talk to my mom every Sunday. I've texted my dad a bit, but not much. That's normal, though."

This past Sunday, I think I spent a little too much of our conversation talking about Isla because my mom asked, "This woman is *just* a friend?" I could tell she didn't believe me when I denied any romantic entanglement, despite it being the truth.

In that instant, the door to the pub opens and Isla enters, guitar case strapped to her back. I catch the second she spots me. Her eyes go wide, lighting up, and I can't help the flutter in my stomach. I give a small wave, and David turns to see Isla as well. I watch as she leans over the bar and says something to the bartender, before heading over to us.

"Hiya?" she says curiously. "Did you know I was going to be here?"

David nods. "Ben mentioned it."

She wrinkles her nose. "That rat." She offers a smile just for me as she absently adjusts the gold necklace around my neck. "This is pretty." She takes her hand away as she seems to recognize what she's doing, clearing her throat. "Well, good to see you both. I best go set up."

She walks toward the designated stage at the back of the bar. I watch as she adjusts the oversized button-up she has layered over a typical cropped tank. With the light shining on her, I spy her piercings through her shirt. I let myself stare for another beat before I move my eyes back to her face. It's not cool to stare at your friend's nipples. No matter how often you fantasize about putting them in your mouth.

Isla sets up in a chair in front of the microphone.

"Hello," she says, putting on a deep and sultry voice that makes me squirm.

Fuck me. For no reason other than the music of her voice, it occurs to me that I have no idea what she tastes like, and now all I can think about is how exactly I can make that discovery. I want my head buried in between her legs, fingers digging into her strong thighs, tongue lapping her up.

These thoughts need to *stop*.

"I promise I will start singing, but I'm trying to work out a song in my head, so we're going to listen to a melody real quick."

I cross my legs tightly.

She starts strumming on her guitar, putting together a song I haven't heard before.

I whisper to David, "Is this hers? Did she write this?"

He whispers back, "Wouldn't shock me. She was planning to study music before she switched to business."

"Huh." I didn't know that.

She hums the words to a song that remains in her head, but it's beautiful. Once she finishes, receiving a smattering of claps throughout the pub, she starts to sing a song I recognize, her voice as beautiful as I remember.

My eyes are glued to her for the entire set. She is majestic up there, her silhouette backlit by a light shining on her. I could watch her all evening.

I nearly do but then I feel a buzzing in my bag. I pull my phone out to see three missed calls from Nick. "That's weird," I mutter.

I excuse myself from the table, stepping out into a surprisingly chilly night to call him back.

When he answers, his voice is husky and quiet. "Rach, hey."

Alarm bells go off in my head. I order, "What's wrong? Is Piper okay?"

"Piper's fine. Um, Dad…Dad was in a car accident on his way to work today."

The words are said so simply that I almost have to ask, "What?" even though I perfectly understood him. I swallow hard.

"You there, Rach?"

"Yeah," I say quietly. "Yeah. Is he…I mean, he's not…?"

"He's alive," Nick says quickly. "Sorry, I should have led with that. He's at the hospital now, doing alright. He hit his head pretty hard in the accident but he just woke up."

"Just woke up? He was unconscious? How long was he unconscious?"

Nick pauses for a beat. "Six or seven hours."

"Six or seven *hours*? And you're just now calling me? How long have you known about the accident, Nick?" My voice slices across his name. Oh god, I don't even know when the last time I spoke to Dad was. How could I let this happen? I repeat, "How long?"

"Since this morning. Rach, we didn't want to call you when there was no news to report. There's nothing you can do but worry from that far away."

That feels like a punch to the gut, even though I know Nick didn't mean it that way. "You're right," I say. "I should come home. I need to come home." I search around like a cab is magically going to pull up and whisk me off to the airport.

"No," Nick says swiftly. "You do not need to come home. He'll be fine. I'll let you know if that changes, but he's fine. They want to keep him overnight for observation, but as long as all looks well tomorrow, they'll let him come home."

"Are you sure?" I demand.

"Yes, I am sure."

Why do I live so far away? Why did I do this to myself? "Okay," I whisper.

"Okay. Do you need to talk longer? I can stay on the phone for as long as you need. We can keep talking about Dad, who is going to be fine, or we can talk about something else. Tell me about microplastics."

"No," I mumble. "That's okay. I'm fine."

"Are you sure? I have nothing to do but talk to you. Or I can have Piper call if you'd rather her."

"I'm sure. Thanks, Nick. Give Piper a hug from me." My voice sounds so flat.

I hang up the phone, but cannot go back inside. I lean back against the side of the pub wall and find that I'm crying. No, no. I'm not crying. I'm sobbing, my body convulsing as I fold into myself. Soon enough, David is there and his arms are around me.

"Shhh," he says, hand gently rubbing my back. "Silly question first: Are you okay?"

"No," I sob. No other words can make it out of me. Why did I choose to live so far from my family?

Then, for some reason David is pushing me away, and when I realize the reason he is doing so is because he's pushing me into Isla's arms, I cry harder.

She strokes my hair, holding me tight. "Oh, my love." She doesn't say anything else, just continues to hold me for as long as I need. And I need to be held for a while. With David beside us, we sit on the sidewalk outside the pub, my head in the crook of Isla's neck, snot and tears everywhere. I should blow my nose and get away from her because this is gross. But I can't move, and she doesn't seem to mind. I cling to her even as the tears stop flowing because I can't see the need to escape from her arms.

Eventually, I find my voice enough to whisper, "My dad was in a bad car accident."

"Oh, fuck," Isla says into my hair, pressing a kiss to my head. I am a magnet to her touch. "Is he…?"

"He's alive," I say, still unable to speak at a normal volume. "I…I feel so powerless. So far away. I can't…I hate that I can't be there. I can't be at his side."

"Shit," David mutters. "I'm sorry, Rach."

Isla holds me tighter. "I'm sorry, love. I'm so sorry."

And that's all I need. I don't need them to tell me it'll be okay. I don't need them to offer me a solution to my problem. I just need David beside me and Isla's arms around me. My friends are all I need.

They are a reminder that I have family here as well.

…

I text Nick for updates to the point where he has to tell me to stop. I know Dad is going to be fine, but what if he's not? What if he falls unconscious again? People take turns for the worse all the time with no word, no warning. Who's to say he won't do just that?

Piper checks in as well, reemphasizing that my dad is okay. I appreciate that, but for once, her words don't set me at ease.

Isla comes back to my apartment with me after we bid David goodnight. I didn't ask her to, but she knows I need her.

When I thank her, she says, "There's nowhere else I can think to be."

We don't talk much when we get to my place. She tells me to take a shower and get cozy. We're swapping places from the other night. I love taking care of her, but god, do I love when she is taking care of me. When I come out of the shower, she's exiting my kitchen with two mugs of tea in her hands, head inclining toward the couch. I nod, finding words more difficult than normal. I sit down and let her hand one mug to me. I take a sip. I like the British mindset of tea fixing all problems. A cup of tea always makes me feel better, filling me with warmth from the inside out.

Isla sits beside me. Too far away. I scoot closer so my leg is pressed against hers. She takes this as a sign of permission and snakes one arm around my shoulder, pulling me into her. I welcome the contact from her, like I always do. Now, I have two things warming me from the inside out. She is fire in the hearth of my heart.

We sit there as we finish our tea, not talking, breathing in sync. After a while, my eyes grow heavy.

Isla notices, taking the empty mug from my hands and pulling away from me. "Go to bed, love. You need it."

"You too," is all I can say.

"Okay," she nods. "I'll sleep on the couch, yeah?"

I'd actually prefer her in the bed with me, but I am certain that is the vulnerability talking. The couch is best. Right?

I shuffle out of the living room, but before I close my bedroom door, I say, "I have coffee if you want it in the morning. You'll have to dig out the French press, but I do have it."

She narrows her eyes. "But you don't like coffee."

Simply, I say, "You do."

I close my bedroom door and climb in bed. Lying in the dark, staring at the ceiling, I am unable to focus on anything other than Isla on the other side of the wall.

...

I stumble out in the morning to the kettle on but Isla nowhere to be found. Stuck to the kettle, there is a note.

Had a tour this morning but wanted to let you sleep. I'll text when I'm through.

P.S. Still no kitchen table?

—I

I crumple the note and toss it in the trash. I don't need a kitchen table. I've managed to function fine without it so far, I don't see the need to rush into one.

Then I pull the note out of the trash and stick it in my pocket. I like her handwriting, messy and quick. I'd get a tattoo of anything in her handwriting, even if just her grocery list.

I check my phone anxiously. It's too early for Nick to be awake, but I text him anyway.

Morning. Dad still okay?

He'll get back to me when he wakes up. It's a Saturday so I have no idea what to do with myself. I take a long shower, letting my mind go blank. I stand under the water for so long that my fingers and toes prune. When the water goes cold, I crank it off, stepping out of the shower and pulling a towel around myself. I check my phone for messages even though I know it is still too early for Nick to have texted me back.

I do have a text from Isla, however.

> Hey, love. Tour's done. Want me to come over?

I lean my hip against the counter as I type a response.

> No, but can I meet you somewhere?

> How about here?

She sends me the location of a park. I heart the message, then catch a bus to meet her. After walking through a passageway I'm not sure I'm supposed to be cutting through, I locate Dunbar's Close Garden. Inside the gates and past rows and rows of flowers and greenery, I find her with her legs pulled up to her chest on a bench, typing something on her phone. The garden is empty beyond us. I take the seat next to her.

She nudges me with an elbow. "You know, while this garden wasn't built until the 70s, its design is inspired by gardens from the 17th century. On top of that, it was built to homage Patrick Geddes, a Scotsman of the 19th century. He wanted Old Town to be revamped by what he called 'pocket gardens.' By 1911, he had nine of these so-called pocket gardens built."

"Huh," I say, leaning into her. I love when she gives me fun facts about Scotland. "That's interesting."

"Any word from your brother?"

I check my phone again. "No. But it's like 5 a.m. there."

"Is there anything you want to do?"

"Not really. Do you mind if we just sit? I brought my e-reader. I needed to be out of my apartment and I figured it'd be nice to be out of my apartment with my friend."

She smiles. "Works for me."

We spend the afternoon on the bench. Isla runs to get lunch from a Tesco Express, coming back with a wrap, chips, and drinks for both of us. We eat in silence, my mind swimming and swirling until Nick finally texts me back.

> He's fine, Rach. Heading home today. Mom took the whole week off to take care of him, but he looks like he'll be alright. Pip and I are heading over there later to see him, but we won't stay long so he has a chance to rest

> He's okay

Relief swarms my chest. They said he was okay last night, but to hear it again drills it in my head.

"He's okay," I whisper.

Isla loops an arm around my shoulders, giving a light squeeze. "Good." I nestle into her so she keeps the arm around me.

Once the hour gets a little later, I head home, exhausted. Alone, I sit on the couch to watch TV. I'm on my laptop the entire time making a PowerPoint. I've been researching recovery from head injuries. I had my mom send me the advice from Dad's doctors and incorporated it in a nice, easy-to-read, and colorful manner.

Now, I've done something to help.

I email the slides to my family and close the laptop, prepared to go to bed and probably spend the entire next day asleep.

...

When I walk out of the labs at the end of the day on Monday, I'm surprised to see Isla waiting for me. She's parked in front of the building, leaning against her car, staring at her phone. As I approach, she doesn't see me until I say, "Hi?"

She looks up sharply, but quickly throws me that signature crooked grin of hers. "Hiya."

"What are you doing here?"

"Picking you up, of course."

"Don't say that like this was a previously agreed upon arrangement."

Her shoulders sag. "Get in the car, love. I've something to show you."

...

"What you wanted to show me was an IKEA?"

Isla grins as she gets out of the car and gestures for me to follow her. I do so and she locks the car as soon as my door closes, like she's thwarting any attempt of mine to get back in. "Yes, love, IKEA."

"Why are we at IKEA? I've been to an IKEA before. They have one in St. Louis." I trail behind her. "It's right by this big food hall called the Foundry, which is by an Alamo Drafthouse. Which is a movie theater with food. Like, advanced food that they'll bring straight to your seat." She doesn't answer so I keep talking. "Are we here for the meatballs? I'm not actually a meatball kind of person."

"I've never been a huge fan of balls either," she responds. When we walk past garden chairs and under an awning, she spins around, opening her arms wide in a grand gesture as the automatic doors slide open behind her. "We, my darling, darling Rachel, are here to buy you"—she pauses for effect—"your very own, definitely the furthest thing from one of a kind, kitchen table!"

My jaw drops. "What?"

"A kitchen table. You've lived here for, what, two and a half months? You still don't have a table."

"Tables are expensive," I argue.

"I'm happy to chip in."

"I don't need you to chip in."

"Then you can afford it. Great." She walks into the store.

I have no choice but to trail behind her.

"I don't need a table," I protest.

"You eat all of your meals either standing at your kitchen counter or sat on your couch."

I scoff. "So?"

She sighs and pulls me aside into a child's bedroom. "I don't understand."

"Understand what?"

"Your resistance. This is about more than your budget. What's the big deal about buying a table? You have all of your other furniture. You're just missing a kitchen table."

I cross my arms and admit quietly, "Tables are permanent."

She cocks her head, confused. "And beds aren't?"

I huff a sigh through my nose. "Not in the same way. It's hard to explain."

"Can you try?"

I roll my head, mulling over my thoughts. She's patient while I put my words together. "When you rent a hotel room, there is always a bed in the room, but not a kitchen table. Kitchen tables are in homes. And I know dining tables are in places other than homes, but there's a difference between a table and a kitchen table. Lives are lived at kitchen tables. Meals are eaten, homework is done, glitter is spilled, toes are stubbed. Does that make sense?"

Isla gives me a slow assessment. "Actually, yes." She takes a seat on the twin bed behind us and pats the spot beside her for me to take. "But what I don't understand is your resistance to permanence. What's wrong with having a kitchen table?"

I take my place at her side, considering the question. "On the surface level, nothing. Permanence is comfortable. But the thing is, so many things aren't permanent. What if I buy a kitchen table, but then I receive an offer somewhere else? Back in America, maybe, or like, New Zealand. I don't know. Then I'd have to give up my kitchen table."

"Do you have to?"

"Well, they're kind of expensive to ship."

She chuckles lightly. "No, love. I mean, if you are offered an opportunity in New Zealand, do you *have* to go?"

"I…I guess I don't have to."

"Do you want to move to New Zealand?"

"New Zealand was a hypothetical. I applied to a program in New Zealand but didn't get in."

"Okay. Do you want to move away from Edinburgh?"

"No," I answer honestly.

"Then why are you assuming you will? Why are you so afraid of staying?"

"I…I don't know." I shake my head. "I don't know. Okay, but what if it's not another program or job offer? What if my dad isn't okay and I have to move back home?"

She gives me a small smile. "He's okay. You know that."

I counter, "But things change."

"They do. You're right. But as of now, he's okay and it looks like he's going to stay okay." She squeezes my hand. "Since you want to stay, let's buy you a table. And hell, if need be, I'll take the table off your hands." She stands up. "Though, I'd rather keep you here and not the table."

CHAPTER TWENTY-TWO
Isla

Once she stops fighting me on it, Rachel is excited about buying a table. And to be in IKEA in general. Everyone loves a good wander about IKEA. She locks in on four different tables and then spends an extraordinarily long time comparing and contrasting them all in terms of size, color, and durability.

Once she decides, we find the warehouse and load the box onto a trolley (which, by the way, watching a woman that tiny handle a box that big is both hilarious and astoundingly erotic). After the table is purchased, we shove the box into the boot of my car—it does not fit. Luckily, I did think ahead, so I have bungees available to secure it. When that's done, I drive us back to her flat and we haul it up the stairs.

We carefully lay the box down where it will live once assembled. Before taking on this task, I pull out the takeaway containers for the Indian food we picked up on our way back. We eat first, then once we're both done, I clap once and say, "Okay! Let's assemble a table."

Rachel grabs scissors from her kitchen, then kneels next to the box so she can cut it open. Piece by piece she removes the table from the box until it's empty. I tow the butchered box out of the way.

With Rachel leading and me acting as her second set of hands, we assemble the table in no time flat. Once it's set up evenly on all four feet, Rachel gazes at it, hands clasped under her chin and hearts in her eyes.

"I have a kitchen table," she whispers.

I match her whisper. "You do."

She surprises me by throwing her arms around me. I laugh as I squeeze her back, only for a brief moment, before she pulls away. "Sorry," she says, blushing in that adorable way as her hands wring together.

"You don't have to apologize," I insist, brushing a loose strand of golden hair behind her ear, my thumb tracing her jaw as she angles her chin upward. Closer to me. "I always welcome a hug. Though, I must say, you tend to launch yourself at me."

Her focus travels up. "What do you mean?"

"When you hug me, take my hand…kiss me, it's like you need a running start. Like you're scared if you don't do it immediately, you won't do it."

"I didn't realize I was doing that." She shakes her head. "You're right, though. That kind of thing makes me nervous, so once I decide I want to make a move, I have to make it. But…" She regards me carefully, pupils dilating. "Maybe tonight I can attempt a more constrained approach?" Gently, she closes the gap between us.

The relief of this contact sinks into me like water quenching a desperate thirst. My mouth moves on hers, kissing desperately. God, I wish my lips could live on hers as she kisses so sweetly, yet so hungrily.

Into my lips, she says, "Are we considering this a special

occasion?"

I falter. Of course, that's all this is—an enactment of the benefit clause in our friendship. I can't help the ping in my chest, but what I say is, "A very special occasion. You own a kitchen table."

Then my lips are on hers again and she is pushing me back into the table, hands clinging to my waist as her tongue roams my mouth. I find the hem of her shirt and when she lifts her arms, I remove it from her, revealing a properly devious bra. It's a simple navy blue with a thin trim of lace along the cups, performing a job I am extremely jealous of.

In this mandatory separation of our lips, she says, "We should break in the table."

My lips find hers again. "Hmm?" I manage to get out as I revel in the taste of her, sweet and refreshing.

She clears her throat and backs up a fraction to say, "You heard me. I want you naked on the table so I can do very, very dirty things to you with my mouth. Understood?"

I raise my eyebrows at her directness. I was fully planning on making her a priority tonight, but she spoke with such determination that I would be an arsehole to say no. And, really, would I say no to this beautiful woman offering to lick me into oblivion? Of course not. "Understood."

Her fingers find the waistband of my trousers, locating the button. "I'm going to take off your pants," she says.

My teeth sink into my lower lip. "Do as you wish."

She unbuttons my trousers and draws them down my legs, tossing them to a corner of the room near her discarded shirt.

"Shirt next." She pulls the tank from me before I can even move to do so myself. Her eyes instantly go to my exposed breasts, mouth practically watering.

I hoist myself onto the table, now just in my pants. Her hungry eyes stay on me as she takes a step forward, securing her position between my parted legs. Her hands stroke up my sides slowly, moving for my breasts. She's taking her time getting to know my body as her thumbs trace over taut nipples, lightly touching the rods that pierce through them.

"You like those?" I ask, eyes flashing down to my nipple piercings.

"Very much," she grounds out. "Does it hurt if I touch them?"

"Not in a bad way."

Her pressure on my hard nipple increases so I hum in approval. Keeping one hand on my breast, her lips find my ear, teeth tugging lightly on one of the hoops, causing my back to arch at the good pinch of pain. Her mouth travels down my neck, kissing over the vine tattoo that reaches a spot under my collarbone. She moves her kisses to my aching breasts, tongue landing on the nipple her fingers are not caressing. I draw in a sharp gasp, adding a, "Yes, love," so she knows I like that. Her lips close over a nipple, sucking lightly, tongue tracing over the piercing, sparking a whimper.

Her kisses explore down my body, finding the tattoo on my right hip—a treble clef line drawing with Forget-Me-Nots woven in, similar to the guitar tattoo.

"It's taken you way too long to show me this," she murmurs as she settles herself on her knees before me. She looks up at me with a silent question. I nod, my legs spreading wider with her gazing at me like that. Her mouth kisses over my knickers, tongue darting out to scrape lightly against the thin fabric.

"You're already so wet," she comments, sounding impressed.

I laugh lightly. "You're doing your job, love. Very well."

"Lay back," she whispers. I do as she asks, my bare back

meeting the cool wood of the table. My eyes close in anticipation of her touch. Her thumbs hook under the sides of my underwear and draw them down over my legs and off. A moment passes so I open my eyes to look at her.

She's just staring. "Look at that pretty pussy," she says, more to herself than me. She moves forward cautiously—scientifically. Her lips meet my thighs, kissing up toward the middle, but stopping before she arrives. She moves to the other side, kisses turning into light sucking. She's taking her time. And she's driving me mad.

Just when I'm about to explode from the anticipation, her open mouth meets my clit and I suck in a sharp gasp. Mouth not leaving my pussy, she looks up at me and raises an eyebrow.

"Shut up," I whine.

Her tongue glides over me as one hand moves to splay over my stomach, the other hooking around my leg, holding me open to her. She takes her time tasting every inch of me, tongue sliding over my sex in an unexpectedly skilled way considering she has never done this before. She's been studying up, I presume. Soon, as if she can't hold back, her mouth hastens, burrowing in.

"Fuck, love." I have nothing to grab onto, my fingers clenching against the wood of the table. Searching for some form of grounding, my hand laces in her soft hair, tugging lightly. As her tongue moves faster, more intensely, the pleasure builds in my core. My stomach hardens beneath her hand, muscles getting ready to explode.

Her tongue swipes over my clit lightly, startling an orgasm out of me. I cry out, my back arching in pleasure as my whole body buzzes. She's not done. Her tongue keeps working, focusing on that perfect spot, the pleasure building again.

"Rachel," I choke out, tugging her hair.

Her eyes meet mine and I give her a barely perceptible nod to keep going. Her gaze stays on mine, her mouth continuing to move on me.

"Fuck."

She hums in satisfaction against me, making my toes curl. Her fingers trace along my edges, asking permission before entering.

"Please," I choke out.

One delicate finger dips inside of me, followed soon by another, curving as she works, fast and hard. The sound of her mouth on me and fingers pumping inside of me is properly pornographic. A moan emanates from deep in my chest as I find my second release.

After she carefully draws her fingers out, she moves her mouth away, kissing at my thighs as I ride through the orgasm. My chest is heaving as she pushes herself to her feet. I should move, but I can't. I am stuck splayed on this table like a finished meal. She skips to the head of the table and dips down with her long hair curtaining us, pressing a moist kiss to my lips. I lean upwards, not letting her pull away as my mouth moves hungrily on hers, tasting myself on her lips. Finally, I let her go.

"Not that I'm fishing for compliments..." she mutters as she hovers over me.

I choke out a surprised laugh. "If you couldn't tell I enjoyed that, you're the daftest Ph.D. candidate I know."

I catch a satisfied smile as she moves to kiss me again. When I can manage, I pull away slightly to say, "Love, once I get my breath back, it's your turn."

"You don't have to."

"If I walk away tonight without making you come, I will not be able to sleep. I can assure you of that. And you love it when I manage a full night's sleep."

Her eyes roll as she confirms, "That's true."

I force myself up and twist on the table so I can pull her body between my spread legs. Her arms loop themselves around my neck. "I have an idea," I say, heartbeat remaining a steady pound. My fingers trail below the band of her bra, tracing over the hourglass tattoo she has on her ribs before my hands move lower to cup her jeans-clad ass. "You can say no, but I will admit this particular thought has been doing a lot for me lately."

She cocks her head. "What idea?"

"Touch yourself for me."

She reels back slightly, confused but open. "Touch myself for you?"

My mouth quirks upward, taking in her swollen lips and hair mused by my hand. I feel selfish even asking for this, but sometimes I need to allow myself a moment of selfishness. "Yeah. You said you're still exploring different ways to make yourself come. I want to watch." I kiss her again before I add, "I need to make sure you're doing it right."

She laughs incredulously, leaning closer to me. "Are you serious?"

"Deadly," I murmur.

She bites her lower lip and nods softly. "Are you telling me that you think about me when you touch *your*self?"

"I have." *Exclusively you, since we met.*

Quietly, she admits, "Me too. With you." Her gaze travels down and over my naked body with appreciation. "Okay."

"Okay." My hands squeeze her ass, taking generous handfuls. "Do you prefer to use your hands or do you own any toys?"

"I have a rabbit," she says, wriggling under my hands. "But it kind of freaks me out."

My hands continue to move over her, finding bare skin under

the waist of her jeans. "Why?"

She looks at me seriously. "It gets really intense."

"That's what gets you there."

Her lips press into a line. "Right. Well, maybe I get in my head too much."

"That's why we're doing this. To get you out of your head."

Her face moves closer to mine so I can feel her breath on my lips as she asks in a low voice, "Is that the only reason?"

I brush my lips over hers, unable to let them be this close without contact. "No. I also *really* want to watch you touch yourself. Want to give it a go for me?"

"Yes."

She pulls out of my arms and goes to her bedroom. I consider pulling on my tank or pants but decide I'd rather have Rachel on equal footing with me as she returns a short while later holding a teal device with three buttons at the base. I hop off the table and meet her in the middle of the living room. Watching her, I undo the button of her jeans, then move downward with them as she lifts one leg, then another to take them off, leaving her only in a bra and underwear.

"Sit down against the couch," I direct, taking the rabbit from her. "I'll give this to you when you're ready."

She takes a seat against the couch, feet flat on the ground and knees angled upward, legs held open.

I fight very hard the urge I have to forget this whole thing and make her come with my own hands. I swallow that need as I kneel in front of her and say, "Touch yourself over your underwear first."

She bites her lip, keeping her eyes on mine as a finger slowly traces up her navy-blue cotton underwear. Her fingers swirl over a soft spot in the middle as she asks, "Like this?"

I gulp. "Good girl. Exactly like that."

She continues to touch herself as she watches me, eyes trailing over me, fingers moving in delicate circles. Once I determine she has done so for long enough, I direct, "Take off your knickers now and keep touching yourself."

She slowly draws the panties down her legs, tossing them to the side. Her fingers connect with her clit and she lets out a small gasp that makes me squeeze my thighs together.

"Feel how wet you are," I request.

Her fingers move lower and her eyes flutter closed when she reaches her entrance. "Hard not to be this wet when the most beautiful woman in the world is naked and watching me touch myself. Your taste is still on my lips, Isles."

I smirk. "She's full of compliments tonight." My fingers twitch with the need to touch her. Why am I torturing myself like this, again? My nipples pinch around my piercings as I watch her fingers continue to move on herself. "You're ready," I murmur, turning the rabbit on the lowest setting and handing it over. "Put this inside of yourself and watch me while you do it."

She takes the device from me, eyes staying locked on mine as she slides it home easily, slick with arousal. She gasps as she moves it slowly in and out, never losing my gaze.

"Now turn on the clit vibration."

Her fingers press that button. "Fuck," she says as soon as the tremor starts. She squirms under it, toes curling into the rug. She turns the rabbit off. "It's too intense." Her chest heaves.

I nod. "Keep going with the base on, then you can turn the ears on again. Make sure to start gentle, then increase intensity as you go. Ease into it."

"Okay." She turns the vibrator back on, moving it in and out, the shining slickness of her coating it. "Fuck," she says again, thumb clicking the button to turn the ears back on. "Fuck, fuck, fuck." She pauses, as she takes her time to adjust.

"Spread your legs a little wider," I quietly direct.

She does as I request, body twitching and freezing again as the vibration hits and her eyes squeeze shut.

"Too much?" I ask.

She nods, slowly starting to move again. She reaches for me with her free hand and I take hold. Her hand squeezes mine so tightly I fear a few bones may be crushed, but that pain is quickly forgotten as she moans loudly. Her eyes shoot open. I see the instant the orgasm hits. She cries out, breath labored as her gaze finds mine, full of satisfaction. I expect her to be finished, but she keeps moving the toy, pausing again when it grows too intense.

"You're doing so well. Let me help?" I practically beg. Her hand is exchanged for mine as I take hold of the device, moving it deeper, letting the ears settle on her.

"Yes," she says, nodding her head quickly with my movements. "Yes, Isles. Yes." She's panting as she says, "Come here. Come closer." I straddle one of her legs, my breasts near her mouth. Her lips close around my nipple, tongue flicking against the piercing as I work the rabbit inside of her. As I continue to fuck her with the toy, her hand grabs my hip and pushes me down, urging me to grind my pussy against her thigh. God, I am already so close again. She whines, "Isla," as she comes again under my hand. That's enough for me to find my release with her, my back arching in pleasure.

"More?" I rasp.

She shakes her head, breathing heavily. I remove the toy, a trail of wetness following it. I know orgasms knock any intelligible words out of her so I don't try to request them as I set the toy aside to be cleaned later.

I lean down, my hand finding her cheek as I press a kiss to her lips. "That was a good experiment, yeah?"

"Very good. Many findings. Holy shit."

CHAPTER TWENTY-THREE
Rachel

I have been staring at this slide for twenty minutes. Every blot looks the same. I cannot stare a second longer. I remove my eye from the eyepiece of the microscope, blinking a few times to refocus in the brightness of the lab.

My forehead meets the cool surface of the counter before me, a long sigh escaping my nose. Of course, not every day is a breakthrough day. Most days aren't. But for whatever reason, today I am in desperate need of a breakthrough I will not get. My head should remain here. I feel like I'm getting more done here than I was staring at that slide. I stay where I am, dozing.

When my advisor Professor Zgheib says, "Hello," I nearly jump out of my skin, knocking my slides to the floor.

I pick my head up. "Good morning," I say back as I bend in my chair to snatch the now-contaminated slides from the ground. This, oh this, is the reason we make sure to take more than plenty of every sample we can find. When the scientist is being careless and knocks all her samples onto the floor.

Professor Zgheib just watches me pick everything up. She then takes a seat beside me and slides my handwritten notes toward herself to take a peek at what I'm working on. She nods but doesn't comment. I hope that's a good sign. I know it is. She would tell me if she thought something in my findings was completely off-base.

"Are you planning to attend the gala? I don't think I've received your RSVP."

Oh my god. I forgot about the gala. "When is it, again?"

"Next weekend."

"Oh," I say. "That's soon." I don't have anything remotely nice enough to wear to this and that is not a lot of time to find something.

"It is. So, will you be attending?"

I have to. Of course I have to. "Yes, I'll be there."

"With a date? You can bring a friend if you don't have a romantic partner to ask."

An image of Isla and me dancing flashes across my mind. Her holding me close. Me breathing her in.

I can ask her, right? As a friend? I would ask her even if we hadn't had sex the other night, so it's not like I'm disobeying our casual rule. If anything, I'm maintaining our friendship first rule.

"Can I let you know?"

"Sure." Professor Zgheib gets up, her work here done. Before she leaves, she says, "You're making great progress here. I cannot wait to see what you discover." Then, she leaves me to it.

I text David as soon as she is out of sight.

Gala

Yes?

I forgot about the gala

Oh. Well, there's a gala next weekend

Yes, thank you

You and I talk almost every day.
How could you not bring this up?

I also forgot, tbh. It's boring as hell

Are you going?

Of course. So, I suppose you being
there will make it slightly less boring

Ah, a great compliment. Slightly less
boring

Haha. You need a dress

Indeed

...

I ask Isla to pick me up in the afternoon. Before the car door is closed, I say, "You can say no."

She cocks her head. "To what, love?"

"Going to a gala with me."

"A gala? What are you talking about?"

"Sorry. I'm doing this in the wrong order. The school hosts a gala each year at the start of term and we're allowed to bring a...we're allowed to bring someone. I figure since David will have Callum there and I don't want to be third-wheeling all night, it would be fun to bring you. I mean, it would be fun to bring you even if David *wasn't* bringing Callum. If you'd like to come."

Isla smiles. "Like, as your date?"

"Technically."

Her smile grows. "Sure. Any excuse to dress up is an instant yes from me. When is it?"

"Next weekend."

Her eyebrows lift. "That's soon."

"It is. I completely forgot about it."

"Have you anything to wear?"

"Not a thing."

"Not saying I would mind you wearing not a thing, but do you want to go shopping today?"

My shoulders sag in relief. "Yeah, that would be great. I don't even know where to start looking. David sent me a few photos from last year so I could gauge the general attire, though." I pull out my phone and show her the photos.

She nods once. "I know where to go." We drive off.

About fifteen minutes later, we pull up to a resale store. Isla puts the car in park and I follow her into the shop. "They always have the best gems in here."

She leads me straight to the back where dozens upon dozens of formal dresses are hung in a line. My eyes instantly go to a navy-blue floor-length gown. I love this color and Piper always says it's the best color on me. Isla seems to spot it at the same moment I do. Her eyes light up as she yanks it off the rack and chucks it at me.

"Try it on!"

I take the dress with a laugh and pull the curtain for the tiny dressing room at the back of the store closed. In the tight space, I struggle to remove my jeans without knocking my head into the wall, but once I manage that, I slip the dress on, pulling the thin straps over my shoulders. I reach around behind myself to pull at the zipper and get it about halfway, but then it gets stuck. I yank on the zipper a few times to no avail. I groan loud enough for Isla to hear, so she calls through the curtain, "Something wrong? Does it not fit?"

"That's not it," I say. It seems like it's a perfect fit, actually. "The zipper is snagged." I swallow. "Can you help?"

She doesn't answer, but a moment later, she slips through the curtain. The tiny dressing room suddenly feels so much smaller. I gather my hair up, moving it away so she has clear access to the back of the dress. My heart skips a beat when I feel her breath on the back of my neck as she grips the zipper between her fingers, giving it a swift tug and guiding it to the top.

"There we are," she says quietly.

"Thanks," I exhale. I turn around to find myself face-to-face with her, staring into her dark eyes. "What do you think?"

She doesn't even look down at the dress as she says, "You're beautiful."

My face burns. "You like the dress?"

"I like everything on and off of you."

"Isla…"

"Just being honest." She steps back, pulling the curtain with her as she finally studies me in the dress. "It looks great on you. Come have a look in the mirror."

I step out, lifting the skirt as it is a little long. I'll wear heels and suffer the consequences of my feet hating me for a few days. I look in the mirror and…wow. Okay. Yeah. Wow. I love this dress. I remove the scrunchie from my hair so I can see what it looks like down with the dress, handing it to Isla. She takes the scrunchie and slips it around her wrist. I turn back around, fixing my hair and admiring myself for a moment before I find her in the mirror.

"You like it, then?" she confirms.

"Yeah. Yeah, I do."

"Let's test it out."

She holds out a hand, letting me take it. She unexpectedly twirls me and I almost lose my footing. I giggle…*giggle* as I grasp tighter to her hand to stay on my feet.

"I think it works," I say, my delight making me practically float. "Though if you pull a move like that again and I re-sprain my ankle, I may have to take you up on your many offers to carry me around town."

"Gladly," she says, unapologetically scanning me up and down.

"Do you need something to wear, or do you have something?"

"I have something that'll be perfect."

We stand there for a moment longer looking at one another before I realize that we are just standing there looking at each other. And the only reason I realize that is because someone clears their throat. There's a woman with a mound of clothing in her hands glaring at us.

"Are you almost finished with that changing room?"

"Oh," I say. "Yeah. Sorry. I'm done. Just let me change." I pull the curtain closed, but I can't get the zipper back down. I call for Isla to help and I hear the waiting woman audibly sigh.

Isla whispers in my ear, her breath warm, "I have an idea or two on how we could make her wait even longer." Her fingers linger on the zipper drawn down to the base of my back.

I gulp, her suggestion causing an ache between my legs. "I'm not in the mood to piss her off further," I say, throat tight at the memory of my head buried in her thighs.

"Up to you, love." She slips out of the dressing room.

I quickly change, gathering the dress in my arms as I exit and give the woman a tight smile that she does not return. I pay for the dress at the front.

Isla then takes me back to my place. After I get out of the car, I ask through the open window, "Do you have a tour tonight?"

"Aye. I better get going so I'm not late."

"I'd ask to come along, but I much prefer our private tours. I like having you to myself."

Her eyes flash. "Can't argue you there."

"I'll see you next weekend?"

"I'll see you sooner," she responds. "Come 'round mine tomorrow. We can have a telly night. I'll have snacks and cocktails." Before I can even say yes, she pulls away.

...

It's dark out as I'm heading home from a night at Isla's place on Friday. I was not the only one invited to the movie night. Which is fine. Obviously. Corrine was also there, with her girlfriend Madison. Aileen made an appearance, sans boyfriend. It was nice to hang out with a group. Isla and I have one-on-one time all the time. But I am self-aware enough to admit that I was disappointed.

Around the corner from my place, I pass by a man crouched on the ground, back pressed up against the wall of a building, head in his hands. I give him a glance but keep going to let him have his moment. Then, once my brain catches up to who I just saw, I backtrack and take a seat on the ground in front of him.

"Ben," I say, poking his arm.

A tear-stained face lifts from his hands, blinking in confusion before realizing who I am. He clears his throat. "Rachel. Hi."

"What's going on?"

"Not much," he responds blandly. "And you? Lovely night."

I purse my lips. I don't know Ben well, but what I do know is he means a lot to two of my best friends. "Yes, lovely night for a cry in the middle of the street."

"I'm not in the middle of the street," he mumbles, eyes losing mine.

My head tilts. "You don't have to tell me what's going on. I just want to make sure you're okay."

He's quiet for a while, forehead pressing back into his hands. I'll sit here as long as I need to. Finally, his head picks back up. "I'm not," he says matter-of-factly. "I'm frustrated. Frustrated with myself. With my life. With everything. I'm just so bloody frustrated." His ass falls to the ground as he leaves his crouch for a seat.

"I'm sorry," I offer. "Do you want to talk about it?"

"Absolutely not," he says. "No offense."

"None taken." I scoot myself so I'm beside him, leaning against the wall. "Want a hug or something?"

He lets out a surprised laugh. "Isla said you don't like physical touch."

A weird, warm twitch hits my gut from knowing that Isla and Ben have spoken about me without me present. "I don't like when strangers touch me. I can get overwhelmed by too much of it even from people I love. I have trouble initiating it. But I'm not against it."

"A side hug would be fine," he mumbles.

I stretch my arm around his shoulders and let him lean into me. His tears stopped when he saw me, but his breath is still labored. It calms the longer we sit.

"Please don't tell Isla about this," he whispers. "Or David."

"Ben…"

He sits up, pulling out of my grip. "I'm not asking you to lie. Just…don't bring it up. If they ask specifically what you did on your walk home tonight, you can tell them. But…just, please."

I don't like the idea of keeping this from Isla. She's already worried about him and I know what is happening is further fuel for worry, but he looks panicked at the idea of her or David finding out. "Okay. I won't tell."

He nods in thanks. I figure I'll sit with him until he's ready to get up. I don't expect him to say, "Don't let her convince you she doesn't care."

"Who?"

"Isla. She's terrible at saying what she wants and feels—she likes to say what she *thinks* people want to hear. She cares about you. As more than a good mate. Don't let her convince you that's all she wants."

I pick at my nails, trying to process this change in subject. "All *I* want to be is friends. We agreed on that."

"I don't believe you."

I correct myself because he's right. "All I *can* be is friends. At least right now. I don't know if I can give her everything she needs. I don't want her to wait for me. I don't want her to expect me to be here next year when I don't know if I will be. She deserves someone who can stay."

He looks at me for a long moment, searching my face like he's surveying for any mistruth in my unfortunately truthful statement. He finally settles on saying, "I'm sorry to hear that." He clears his throat. "Want to come to a flashy club and get pissed and snog random people with me?"

I snort. "That is so not my scene. But I'll go if you need someone."

His eyes grow distant. "Naw. I best be heading home." He stands and pulls me up with him. "See you soon, yeah?"

I nod. "Yeah. Get home safe."

When I make it home, I take a seat on my couch, turning on an episode of *Criminal Minds*. I have to be honest, it was one of the shows that made me realize I was bi. I would wonder who I was more into, Derek Morgan or Spencer Reid. But soon enough, Emily Prentiss was in the mix, and wow. Yeah. So, basically, I'm into every single character on this show and I stand by that. As I'm watching, I see an email that makes me sit up stark straight in my seat.

I read the email that came in three hours ago three times to make sure what I'm reading is correct. The Victoria University of Wellington in New Zealand has emailed me, offering me a spot in their Ph.D. program. This was my dream choice. I didn't get accepted originally. But the person who had originally taken the spot dropped out. They want me. They want me to start in January. *Oh my god.* I could move to New Zealand and—

Wait. No. I can't say yes to this. I'm already in a Ph.D. program. One I love. In a city I have come to love as well. I can't just pick up and leave in the middle of the research I have already begun.

But maybe I can. This is a great opportunity. I could start fresh. I could—

No. I don't need a fresh start. The life I'm building is great.

But what if the life I can build in Wellington is better? What if I say no to this amazing opportunity and regret it for the rest of my life?

What if I leave Scotland and regret it for the rest of my life?

I should call Piper. I pull out my phone to dial her but stop myself. She and Nick are having a date night. She's probably getting ready for that. I can't call her right now. I'll call her later. Except if I do, I know what she'll tell me. *No.* She'll be supportive of whatever I decide, but at the same time, she will be actively against me moving all the way to New Zealand.

It's my choice. Not hers. It's a choice I will make on my own.

CHAPTER TWENTY-FOUR
Isla

"I'm sure you're wondering why I called you here today," Ben says as I take a seat across from him in the pub.

"I asked you to meet me, you fucking tyrant," I say, sipping the beer I ordered when I walked in.

"I've always wanted to say that to a group of random people in a lift."

"I too saw that Tumblr post. Ben, I need to talk to you about something serious."

His eyes widen. "Rachel?"

"No. The café."

"What café?"

"*The* café. *Our* café. I want it. I want to open it. I can't wait for you any longer. I've filled out a loan application to open it myself, but I haven't submitted it yet. I want to open this place with you, but I'm at the point now where if you won't commit, I will do it without you. For real, this time."

Ben takes a slow sip from his beer, nodding as he does so. "Okay," he says. And that's it.

I was expecting something more from him. It took me two

weeks to buck up the courage for this conversation, and that's all he has to say? This was our dream and he's willing to just hand it over to me to carry on alone. I was ready for this. I planned for this. But I didn't expect him to actually give up.

I take another sip of my beer before I stand. "Okay. I guess I'll turn in the loan application."

"Don't you want me to look it over first?"

"No." I turn on my heel.

"I'll need to make sure you spelt my name right."

I spin back around slowly. "Come again?"

"On the application. When you were wee, you used to spell Bennett with either one N or one T, when there's two of both. I don't trust you to spell it right."

"Wait…are you saying you're in?"

"Aye. Of course I'm in. Let's do it."

I sit back down, my eyes wide. "You've been unwilling to commit for years. What changed?"

"You gave me an ultimatum. I love an ultimatum."

"Ben."

He shrugs. "I'm moving to Edinburgh. I decided. I found a readily available flat a couple of weeks ago. I quit my job at Laggan Wolftrax, so now I can focus all my energy on our café. That way you can keep working as much as you need to. If I need income, I can keep selling feet pics."

I understand the words he is saying, but they still make no sense. "Excuse me?"

"I'm joking."

"I don't believe you. I don't believe *this*."

"You've seen my feet. Who would want pictures of them? Use your head, Islington."

"No, Ben. Not your fecking feet. I don't believe you're moving here. Just like that?"

"No, I've been thinking about it for a while. All of my mates are here. You. David." He swallows. "Molly and I broke up. What's to hold me in Newtonmore?"

I'm finally starting to believe him. He's being sincere. Something rare for him, but he's actually being sincere. "You really found a flat?"

"Yeah. I move in the Monday after next."

I squeal and hop up to throw my arms around him, squeezing tightly. He squeezes me back. "We're opening the café!" I yell.

"We're opening the café," he confirms.

...

I have to leave Ben to give a tour, but once I'm done, we submit the small business loan application with both of our names. I'm not sure how long it will take to hear back, but I hope not too long. My business plan is solid and having Josie on as an investor gives us additional financial backing, which looks good.

Because we have Josie, I've already contacted the leasing agent for the space we've had our eye on. I am waiting to hear back from her as well. Once everyone gets back to us, we can start sorting the logistics of everything else.

I am in disbelief that it's happening. This is actually happening!

I call Rachel without even thinking about it.

"Hello?" she answers cautiously.

"Ben and I are opening the café," I say as a greeting. "Officially. Like for real. We submitted the loan application."

"Oh my god! That's amazing. Congrats, Isles."

"Thanks, love. Do you want to get a pint tonight? To celebrate?" There's silence on the other end of the line. "You there?"

"Oh, sorry. I can't. Sorry."

My shoulders sag. "That's okay. Doing something with David?"

"Uh, yeah. David and I are doing something."

"Alright. Well, sorry for the unprompted call. I'll see you soon?"

"Yeah. Soon." We hang up.

That was weird, right? Or am I reading too much into it? I'm sure I'm reading too much into it. It's Rachel. I'm sure she just feels guilty for having to say no. That's very Rachel of her. But now I don't know what to do. I'm not working tonight. The music shop is closed so I can't go bug Josie. I have no outlet for my joy. Ben had to head back home so I can't celebrate with him. The only other person I can think to text is Corrine. We never do anything one-on-one anymore, but I suppose there is no reason for that.

However, that's also a no-go. I ask Corrine to meet up, but she informs me that she is in Glasgow for the weekend, but we can get together on Wednesday. I tell her it's a plan.

I can go get a drink by myself, but I hate to celebrate by my lonesome. My hands find my pockets as I walk down the street. When I pass a pub I sing at sometimes, I immediately head inside to find the owner behind the bar.

"Isla," Bonnie says, smiling at me. "What'll you have?"

"Nothing, now," I say. "You need a singer tonight?"

She shrugs. "Sure. Why not?"

"Perfect. I'll fetch my guitar and be back."

...

I strum my guitar as I finish one of the standard songs in my set to a smattering of applause. With a glance down at the blue scrunchie around my wrist—Rachel's scrunchie that she handed over at the resale shop—I make a decision. The audience seems rapt enough, but not enough to deter me from doing what I'm doing next.

"I wanted to try something new out tonight. My own song. You all will have to tell me if it's awful." I get a gentle titter and that's all I need. Once I double-check the words I have drafted in my notes app, I start playing a melody that has become very familiar to me since I met a certain blonde woman. Then I start singing.

She's looking at me again
And again, I can't breathe
Because those eyes are full of wonder
And that heart is full of hope
And those legs can't stop running,
Searching to find a home

Love, come home
Just come home with me
I'll be your home
Just come home with me
I'll be your home

She's holding my hand again
And again, I can't speak
Because she leads me to that spot
And her lips taste like gin
And my legs have stopped running
As home settles in

Love, come home
Just come home with me
I'll be your home
Just come home with me
I'll be your home

Stay with me
Stay with me

I'll be your home
Just stay home with me
I'll be your home

I finish to more claps from the pub patrons. No whooping, but that's okay. I'm happy with it. I survey the crowd and spot a familiar face smiling at me. David. *Oh no.* If David is here, Rachel must be too. I don't see her, but maybe she's in the toilet? My heart rate increases. *Oh god.* What if she heard the song and hated it and is now in the loo to avoid me?

I say into the mic as calmly as I can manage, "I'm going to take a quick break, but don't worry. I'll be back."

I rush up to David. "That song—" he starts, but I cut him off. "Where's Rachel?"

He cocks his head, confused. "I don't know. Home, probably."

Now it's my turn to be confused. "She's not here?"

"No. Should she be?"

"She said she was with you tonight."

His eyes widen. "Oh. Yeah. Well, she was. Earlier."

He's lying. I can tell he's lying. He said that too fast. And if he's lying, that means Rachel lied to me. Why did she lie to me?

"Oh," I say. "Alright."

He regards me curiously. "Was that song about her?"

"Yeah," I admit.

"She should hear it."

I click my tongue. "I'm not sure she wants to."

He gives me a sympathetic look. "Can't know unless you sing it to her."

···

Come Wednesday, I have yet to see Rachel again. Don't get me wrong. I try. She keeps giving excuses that I can't decipher if are real. They're valid if they are real. Busy with school. I mean, yeah. Understandable. Earning one's Ph.D. is time-consuming. But I can't help but feel that she is lying. The problem is, I have no idea why.

Unless she somehow heard the song and got spooked. But I think she was lying about being with David that night, so it had to be something before then. We had a nice little moment in the dressing room and I was flirting my arse off, but that's nothing new. I consistently flirt my arse off every time I speak to her and she either one, seems interested and somewhat thrilled by the flirting, or two, ignores it. Maybe she's upset Friday night wasn't just her and me? It was a last-minute, nerve-induced choice to invite the others as motivation to keep my hands off of her. Is she angry because I stole her scrunchie? I like carrying something of hers with me. What if she needs to pull her hair back one day and doesn't have one of her own to use?

I'm trying not to let it bother me, but it bothers the bloody hell out of me because I miss her. Simple. I miss her and I want to see her. I could show up to pick her up at the end of the day or even to take her to campus in the morning. I've done it before. But I can't rid the feeling that she is avoiding me and if she is, a random appearance by myself would be rather unwelcome.

However, the whole situation has me on edge. So much so that when I walk into the pub on Wednesday to meet up with Corrine, she clocks it immediately.

"What's got you in a tizzy?" she asks as I slide into my seat.

"I'm not in a tizzy. I'm a little antsy, that's all."

"Why?"

I decide to be honest. "I haven't seen Rachel in a few days and I would like to. I'm afraid she's avoiding me."

"Why would she be avoiding you? You didn't say something to put her off again, did you?"

"Not that I'm aware of." I may have sung something to put her off, but you know. "I'm sure it's nothing."

"What's the big deal, anyway? I thought you were friends."

"We are friends."

"You want to be more," she says matter-of-factly. "Last Friday, you watched approximately two minutes of the film because you spent the entire night staring at her."

I don't bother to dispute that fact. "I fancy her, yeah. But it could never work. I'm not a relationship person." Corrine makes a face so I ask, "What?"

"You've said that before. To me."

I shift uncomfortably in my seat. "Yeah, well it was true then too. I'm better for casual."

"What about Micky?"

I sigh. "I called Micky my girlfriend, but that was more of a her thing than me. She wanted someone there without question, not me specifically. She introduced me as her girlfriend after a few dates and I figured I would give it a shot. But that relationship lasted only three months. I gave it a shot and it didn't work."

"I know. I was there, remember?" She quietly scolds, "Did you even catch what you said?"

"No?"

"Better *for* casual. Not at. Isla, I knew Kenna fucked you up but I don't think I understood how badly." I open my mouth to interject but Corrine cuts me off. "She convinced you that everyone you've ever had a relationship with is using you for something. An education, sex, an unconditional person, whatever."

"I...I don't think that."

"You do. You think I was using you for sex."

I snort. "I think we used each other."

"Isla, I wanted more. I told you I wanted more but you convinced yourself that I didn't—that I was just saying that to play along."

My mouth gaps, but I can't come up with a single thing to say, so she keeps talking.

"And now, you've found someone who you really, really care about and you've once again convinced yourself that she doesn't want you." She shakes her head. "I've seen the way she looks at you, Isla. She cares about you so much. More than anyone else, I'd wager."

I feel inclined to disagree. "Then why does she keep insisting we're better off as friends?"

"Maybe because you keep insisting the same thing. One of you has to be brave and tell the other person how you feel. Why can't it be you?"

She's right. Bollocks. She is so right. How thickheaded am I?

Well, if there is as good a time as any to confess my feelings, it's at the gala. If there is any night I'll be able to make Rachel fall for me, it's that night. If it doesn't happen then, when we're both dressed up, I'm continuing to flirt my arse off, and twirling her around the dance floor, it is not going to happen for us.

CHAPTER TWENTY-FIVE
Rachel

A knock sounds on my door as I'm pushing pin after pin into my hair, praying it will hold. *Isla.* She's early. I'm not surprised.

"Coming!" I yell, shoving one last pin in and dousing my hair with hairspray before I pick up the skirt of my dress and hurry to the door. I haven't seen Isla in a week. My doing. I just…I wanted to have made a decision about New Zealand before I saw her. However, I still haven't and here we are. I'm going to try my hardest not to think about it tonight.

I open the door and…*oh.* Isla is mesmerizing. Her curly hair is pulled back on one side, leaving the other side loose and big. Her lips are painted my favorite lip color, her burgundy eyeliner matching. Both matching her dress. The dress has thin straps so her arm tattoo is shown off. I love it when I'm allowed to see the entire work of art.

She scans me up and down. "Wow," she says aloud, eyes still combing over me. "Just, wow."

My cheeks burn at her reaction. I haven't done anything extreme. She's seen me in this dress before, but now my hair is done in a simple updo and I've donned on a light coat of mascara and a teeny bit of blush.

"You're sparkling," she breathes. "Actually, in my opinion, you are always sparkling. But in this getup… god, don't tell me you can't see it."

I smile, face still blushing that frustrating dark red. My eyes slip from hers as I ask, "You think?"

"I think."

I look up at her through my lashes. "You look pretty wow yourself."

Isla does a little twirl in the hallway. "I do, don't I?"

"I like the dress. I wasn't sure you'd wear one."

"Felt like a good night for it." She gives me another long and very obvious assessment, making her approval clear once again. "Plus, this color looks good with your dress."

"It does." My hands wring together. "You ready to go?"

"Yeah."

I lock my door and she leads us down the stairs so she can open the car door for me. Then we drive to campus and I direct her to the building where they are holding the gala, not the normal building I go to. Obviously. It would be very silly to host a gala in a bunch of labs and classrooms.

We park and enter the building with a line of nicely dressed people. The building is lit up brightly, with white panels of curtains draped around the walls, likely covering academic posters and volunteer sign-ups that would normally deck the halls. Immediately we spot David and Callum. I wave at them across the room and they come up to us.

David looks at me joyfully. "Permission to hug the most beautiful woman in the room?" He glances at Isla "No offense, Isla. You also look amazing."

"Can't be offended if I agree," she says.

I laugh, doing my best to let the compliment slide by, and say, "Permission granted."

David takes no time to wrap his arms tightly around me. He whispers, "I'm glad you're here with Isla tonight," in my ear, only for me to hear. I squeeze him tighter because I'm glad as well.

Once he releases me, I take him in. He's wearing a maroon suit with a white button-up shirt beneath. "I like the suit. A little tight," I add jokingly.

Callum says, "Could be tighter," as David retakes his hand.

The corner of David's mouth perks. "We're going to find drinks. You guys want anything?"

I shake my head. "I need to find Dr. Andonov and Professor Zgheib first. But Isla?"

She nods at David and Callum. "Yeah, I'll go with you."

We split off. I locate my advisor and professor deep in conversation with other faculty members. I poke in to say a quick hello, both offering me huge smiles and introducing me around.

"We're so excited to have Rachel here with us," Dr. Andonov says.

A wave of guilt crashes into me. No, no. I am not going to let anyone else decide this for me. I will choose the best path for me. But I don't want to make enemies, academically, where I should be making friends. This is absurd. Why am I even considering New Zealand? Except, if it shouldn't be an option, why can't I rid it from my head?

I smile through the conversation, answer a few questions about my research and how I am assisting Dr. Andonov with theirs, then excuse myself as soon as I deem it polite to do so, desperate to have Isla by my side again. The amount of people in here is overwhelming. It's not nearly as tightly contained as that club we went to, but the tightness I feel and the visceral overreaction I have to someone brushing my arm as they pass by makes me want to run away and hide.

I find my friends a moment later, feeling like I can breathe again. Isla hands me a glass of wine with a smile. I zero in on the blue scrunchie around her wrist, my heart fluttering.

"Is that mine?"

She freezes. "Do you want it back?"

"No." I inch closer, needing to consume the same air as her.

We drink our wine standing in a circle with David and Callum. Though, it doesn't take long for David to get distracted by someone he knows, gesturing them over to introduce to me and saying something along the lines of, "She'll be with us for three years!"

That guilt thrashes in my chest, attacking the walls I have built in an attempt to contain it this evening. God, no. I cannot move to New Zealand. I already spent all this money to move here that, at this point, I will never get back. But the opportunity is calling to me. How the hell am I supposed to pass this up?

However, that was the same thing I thought about Scotland. And now I'm abandoning it. Or considering abandoning it. I haven't decided yet.

To prove how much this decision is weighing on me, Isla says, "Love?" bringing me back to reality. Everyone in our little circle is staring at me.

My face goes red involuntarily, but Isla's hand rests on my lower back, putting me at ease. "Sorry," I mumble. I clear my throat and say a little louder. "Sorry. I'm distracted. I've been busy with microbiology…and things." My face goes even redder because that was a ridiculous thing to say. But Isla's hand is still firmly on the small of my back, breathing life into me.

David explains to one of his friends, "Rachel's program is all year round, so she's been roaming an empty campus since June."

His friend nods. "Oh, so will you be happy or a little disappointed to have the campus full come start of term?"

I laugh, rejoining the conversation, "A bit of both, if I'm being honest. I'm excited to meet some new people, but I work well in the quiet."

"I understand that."

We keep chatting until it is time for dinner to be served. Isla, David, Callum, and I make it to our white tableclothed table and take our seats. Dinner is placed before us, as well as new glasses of wine, and we eat, drink, and make merry through the meal. Once dinner is over, the dancing begins. There is a large designated section in the middle of all the tables. I'm a little hesitant, but Isla pulls me onto the floor and instantly puts me at ease when her arms wrap around me.

"This okay?" she asks in my ear.

"Of course," I answer, confused. "Why wouldn't it be?"

"I know you're not big on physical touch."

"I told you I don't mind it from you."

"And..." she starts, but trails off.

"And what?"

Her mouth makes a thin line. "And you've been avoiding me for a week."

"I've been busy."

"That's what you keep saying."

"Because it's true." It's not.

Her eyes fall, filling with hurt. "Okay. Sorry. I've missed you."

My heart drops as my hands tighten on her. "I missed you too."

"Good." She twirls me, causing me to release a sharp laugh. Then she pulls me close enough that a whiff of cinnamon hits my nose. She swings me around and I giggle the entire time.

"Isla," I say through my gasps.

"Yes, love?"

"This is fun."

Her eyes crinkle as she brings me in closer, her hands closing around my hips as the song slows and we sway together. I wrap my arms around her shoulders and take the time to look in her eyes. I don't think I do that often enough. Look at her. No, well, I spent an inordinate amount of time looking at her. What I don't do often enough is look into her. What I mean is…I take so much time to look at her, yet not nearly enough to see her. Once I see her, I can't stop because all I want to see is her. And I can't see her if I move to New Zealand.

Shit.

I need to stop thinking about this. I need to think about something else. As a way to change the subject in my mind, I say, "You look beautiful. I don't know if I said that aloud."

Her mouth quirks. "You've said something along the lines. But even if you didn't, it would be okay. We don't need to be hurling compliments back and forth all night."

I find a curl at the back of her head and loop it around my finger. "Some things need to be said aloud so I can make it clear how lucky I am to have met you."

The tempo of the song speeds up and Isla dips me, causing a sharp cackle to release from my mouth. She pulls me back up so we're face to face. She glances down at my lips and I strain my eyes to keep from looking at hers.

Then she kisses me. Lightly at first as though she's being cautious. Then deeper as I lean into her, letting her part my lips with her tongue. And—

No.

I pull away, startling us both.

"What's wrong?" Isla asks quietly. We've stopped dancing, but the crowd continues to move around us, our static bodies feeling immensely in the way.

"We shouldn't."

Isla gives one sharp nod. "Right, sorry. I shouldn't be kissing you in front of your professors."

"It's not that," I sigh.

"Then what?"

"You shouldn't be kissing me."

"Why? Am I embarrassing you?"

My hands tighten on her. "What? No. Isles. Of course not. We shouldn't…we're friends. Just friends. Friends don't kiss."

She scoffs. "Then why am I here, Rachel?"

"What?"

"Why did you ask me here? Why are we all dressed up? Dancing together. You telling me how lucky you are to have met me. Telling me I'm beautiful. Playing with my hair. *Looking* at me like that. Why? I don't get it."

"Because I want to be here with you."

"But why don't you want me to kiss you? I don't understand."

"Because I'm leaving!" I don't mean to shout it, but it comes out so loudly that a few of the people dancing around us pause to glance our way.

"Leaving?" Her voice cracks with the word.

My shoulders sag. "I might be. I got offered a position in New Zealand and—"

She cuts me off. "You can't be serious."

"I am. My research would focus on the function and resilience of biogenic shellfish—"

She cuts me off again. "But that's different than what you're doing now. I thought you liked learning more about micro-plastics. The way you talk about it, it's the most interesting thing in the world."

"This is interesting too."

"More interesting?"

"Equally."

Isla finally lets me go, ice engulfing me. This entire time we have been standing with our arms wrapped around each other. I've finally gotten her to the point where she does not want to touch me.

Crossing her arms, she accuses, "You're running."

"I am not."

"You are."

"Toward an opportunity, then. There's nothing wrong with that. I need to take on opportunities when they're offered to me."

She huffs. "Whatever. Excuse me." She storms away.

I am left standing alone, freezing. She's walking away from me again. Leaving me *again*. But this time, I can only blame myself.

This can't happen again. I follow her.

She pushes into the bathroom and I push in moments after her, watching as she slams into a stall. I stand outside the stall, hand on the door, unsure of what to do. Then I hear her. I hear her breathe in and out, loud and rapid but like she's trying to control it.

She's having a panic attack.

"Isla," I say through the door. "I'm here."

She doesn't respond. I stand there, leaning against the door, listening to her shallow breath, and noting that it does not regulate. If this were a standard American bathroom, I'd be able to see her through a gap in the stall. Or crawl under to get to her. But these stalls are completely private and I cannot reach her.

Then the door unlatches.

It swings open to her sitting on the edge of the toilet in her dress, hands braced on either side of the stall as tears run down her face and she hyperventilates. She doesn't look at me as I step inside the stall, closing it behind me. I crouch in front of her, hands on her knees.

I start to count. "One, two, three, four, five, six, seven," I say evenly. "Now out. One, two, three, four, five, six, seven. And in." I keep counting and eventually, her breaths start to match my pacing. In for seven, out for seven.

She starts to breathe normally, but the tears still fall. I pull toilet paper from the roll on the wall and hand it to her. She blows, then drops it in the gap behind her into the toilet. I hand her more.

"I shouldn't have told you here."

"Yeah," she confirms.

"I'm sorry. A better friend would have waited until we were alone."

"We're not friends," she struggles out. "I don't want to be your *friend*. I don't want you to leave."

"Isles…"

She snatches another wad of toilet paper to blow her nose. "I accept that this is your decision to make, but I don't understand it. I want you to stay. Please stay. Or at least tell me why you want to leave."

I sigh. I suppose I owe her an explanation. No one has ever asked before. Not Nick or Piper. No one understands my desire to keep moving, keep going, to take every opportunity. Except my mother.

"My mom," I say as though that is an actual explanation. Then I expand. "She went straight from her parent's house to the sorority house to her husband's house. And she regrets it." I swallow. "I mean, she loves my dad. My parents are sort of disgustingly in love, despite how busy they both are. But she's told me herself how much she wishes she had done more. How she wished she had lived alone. Taken an opportunity to go to law school in California instead of St. Louis. The only reason she went to St. Louis is because of my dad. They got married right out of college and went to law school together. She always feels like she never got the opportunity to be her own person. All she wants for me is opportunities."

Isla nods slowly. "You think you'll disappoint her if you don't take any and every opportunity offered to you?"

"No. I'll disappoint my future self."

Isla nods again, pursing her lips. "What if your future self isn't disappointed with you for missing opportunities but for leaving them?"

"I…" I don't know what to say. "I don't think so."

She stands abruptly, eyes still wet. I stand as well as she pushes past me and out of the stall. "I can't do this tonight. We can talk more tomorrow. Can you get a ride home from David?"

She doesn't wait for my response before she pushes out of the bathroom, leaving me standing alone under the harsh fluorescent lights, wondering what I have just done.

Not knowing what to do, I wander back out into the main room and find myself in the middle of the dance floor. Alone. Though, I am not alone for long. David swoops in, taking me in his arms and moving me into a dance.

"What the hell was that?" he asks.

"I…I told Isla I might move to New Zealand. She didn't take it well."

He cocks his head. "New Zealand? When?"

"Term starts in January."

David almost drops my arms but maintains his composure and keeps us moving. "You got into that school in Wellington?"

"Yeah."

He sighs sharply. "Why are you even considering it?"

I huff. "Because it's a great opportunity. I don't know why everyone is fighting me on this."

He stops dancing. "Because you're running."

Isla said the same thing. I pull away from him. "I am not."

"You're happy here, but you wonder if you could be happier. I get it. But if you move to fucking New Zealand, you are running away from the chance to be happier *here*."

"I am chasing a really cool opportunity. There's nothing wrong with that."

"Edinburgh is a really cool opportunity."

My shoulders drop. "You don't get it."

"I don't. I don't get it, Rach. You think you're chasing happiness, but all you're doing is running away from it."

I shake my head. He doesn't get it. No one gets it. No one gets why I need to keep moving. I can't miss out on things. I have to take every opportunity because I will never be able to live with myself if I have any regrets for missing out on something like this. My eyes fill with tears as I march away. I'll find my own way home.

...

Once I enter my flat, my phone starts buzzing in my bag before I even have a chance to take off my shoes. I pull it out, both expecting and hoping for it to be Isla. It's not. It's David.

I answer with a cautious, "Hello?"

"Hey, Rach. I'm sorry about earlier."

I purse my lips together. I am so sick of talking tonight. "It's fine. I didn't mean to spring it on you like that."

"Yeah, that wasn't the best time for that conversation. I just am enjoying having you in my life and I would hate to lose you to the Kiwis."

My heart is in my throat. "Yeah. I'd miss you too."

"Isla would miss you as well."

That's a knife to my chest. "I know. She told me."

"Would you miss her?"

"Of course, I'd miss her. I—" I cut myself off before I can finish that sentence, scolding my wine-loosened tongue.

"You love her," he finishes for me.

I sigh. "David…"

"She loves you."

She told me she didn't want me to leave, but she'll be fine without me. She's so good at making friends. This is her home. I was just a temporary part of it.

I say, "She likes to flirt."

"She does. With you." He sighs. "I have something to send you. A video. I…I wasn't going to send it because it really is not my business, but I'm going to be aggressively selfish because I do not want you to move to fucking New Zealand. Just, before you make any kind of official decision, watch this video. Please."

I lament, "Okay. I'll watch it. And I'll talk to you tomorrow? I'm really tired."

"You got it. 'Night, Rach."

I finally take the chance to kick off my heels and limp over to my couch, my feet both thanking me for removing the heels and screaming at me for putting them on in the first place. I sink into my couch, letting the cushions comfortably consume me before I open the video David sent.

I perk up when I realize it's Isla. It's Isla singing. I turn up the volume so I can hear her better. I love her voice so much.

I don't recognize this song. However, I know that melody. She hums it all the time; I don't even think she notices she's humming it sometimes. But I haven't heard these words before. Then I really start to listen to them.

> *She's holding my hand again*
> *And again, I can't speak*
> *Because she leads me to that spot*
> *And her lips taste like gin*
> *And my legs have stopped running*
> *As home settles in*

Oh my god. She's talking about me. That first night. Holy shit. I spring up from the couch, rushing toward the door, not even knowing where I intend to go. I turn back around. What the hell am I doing?

She loves me. That song…*Shit*. She loves me. I didn't…I mean, I know she's into me. She's attracted to me. She enjoys being around me but…in love with me? No one's ever been in love with me before. *I've* never been in love with anyone before. Logically, it was bound to happen eventually, but I did think I would be more aware of it. On both ends. Mine and hers. I thought I'd be able to tell. Is love less obvious when you're in the middle of it, or have I been deliberately ignoring it?

Oh my god. I was deliberately ignoring it because I was afraid I was going to miss out on an opportunity which is the most absurd thing in the world because this…*fuck*. Being in love with Isla is the greatest opportunity I have ever been given. I am not going to mess it up. Not anymore. Not any further. *Dammit*. I need to go. I need to find her. I need…I need…

I need speakers.

CHAPTER TWENTY-SIX
Isla

I'm lying on my made bed still in my dress with my eyes wide open because *bloody hell.* She's moving. Even if she doesn't go to New Zealand, she'll get offered another great opportunity she has to jump at, and once again, she will have no hesitation to chase after it, not caring who she's leaving behind. I have no idea how to convince her to stay. I have no idea if I even can.

I am halfway into motivating myself to get up so I can take a shower and wash my makeup and my pain away, when I hear loud music coming from outside my window. Och, I'm sure it'll stop by the time I get out of the shower. I force myself to my feet, fingers finding the zipper on the side of my dress, when I hear which song is playing.

Wait a damn minute.

That's *my* song.

I rush to my bedroom window and shove it open, leaning my head out to find the source of the noise. There I spot Rachel standing in the middle of the road, still in her dress from the gala, a portable speaker held above her head, playing the song I wrote about her.

We lock eyes and she offers me a small smile.

"Hi!" she calls.

I did not expect that to be her opening line to whatever the hell is happening right now, so I am flummoxed by my response of, "Hiya." She does not say anything as she holds the speaker over her head, so I ask, "What are you doing?"

"Annoying your neighbors, probably." The song ends so she brings the speaker down, holding it to her chest. She takes a deep breath. "David sent me the song."

I lean my forearms on the ledge of the window, still peering down at her. "He shouldn't have done that."

"He acknowledged that when he did it, if that makes you feel better."

"Eh." I toy with the scrunchie on my wrist and ask, "What'd you think?"

"It's beautiful. I...It's so beautiful." She laughs lightly to herself. "You popped out of the window and I got flustered. I swear I had a plan when I decided to do this. Um, sorry."

My throat is tight as I say, "It's okay, love. Take your time."

"Thank you." Her hands tighten around the speaker. "So, when I heard this song, it helped me come up with a unplausible hypothesis. Except, that hypothesis stopped seeming so un-plausible when I gathered more evidence to support it. When I started doing that, I realized there is an abundance of evidence."

"What hypothesis is that?"

"You love me."

I don't say anything. Of course, I love her. I've loved her since I removed that eyelash from her cheek.

She smiles as though she can tell what I'm thinking. She continues, "I also gathered evidence for an additional hypothesis that I have successfully proven as of this evening. Though, the data to support this has been staring me in the face for a while."

"And that hypothesis is?" I ask, willing my voice to stay steady.

"I love you as well." Her eyes tear up. "I am so ridiculously in love with you. And I am so thankful that you…that you—" Her voice cracks and she sniffs loudly, willing her tears to stay in place. "Sorry. I *hate* crying."

A dam breaks in my chest. She loves me, too. I grip the window ledge to steady myself. "Oh, my love. Come inside."

She shakes her head. "Give me one second. Let me finish this." She takes another deep breath, her voice straining to force its way out through the tears. "I am so thankful that you didn't give up on me. Because if you did…I wouldn't have fallen in love with you and my life would *suck*. I would probably be moving to New Zealand. Which I won't be doing, by the way. That was ridiculous—I shouldn't have even considered it. I don't want to move there. I love it here. I want to stay here with my program, and David, and you. Isles, you are my home. I finally found it, with you. I want to spend every day with you. I want to wake up every morning with you and go to sleep at your side every night. I want to sit together at *our* kitchen table and watch movies and eat Indian food and tour the city and kiss you senselessly."

"I want that too. I want that so much." Tears spring from my eyes, streaming down my cheeks. "*Come inside*, my love."

She sniffles. "Okay."

She picks up her skirt as she walks, and I notice her lack of shoes.

"Hang on," I say, voice thick.

Halting, she looks up at me, eyes wide.

"Are you not wearing shoes?"

Her face burns. "No. I didn't want to put my heels back on because they hurt and I wanted to run here and I knew if I tried to run here in heels I would trip and fall and probably sprain my ankle again. My only thought was 'speaker' when I left so I came barefoot. Except, since my brain is a little less one track now, I am realizing I could have put on other shoes."

I tip my head back with a chuckle. "I love you, you mad woman."

"Good," she says joining my laugh.

She knocks on my door moments later. I hurl it open and pull her to my lips. "We should clean your feet," I say into her mouth.

"Is this your way of telling me you have a foot fetish?" she murmurs.

"I have a Rachel fetish. And I'm not letting those dirty feet in my bed."

She giggles and lets me pull her into the bathroom where I sit her on the edge of the bathtub as I run the water to ankle level. She begins to pluck pins from her hair, one by one, setting them on the counter. As she continues to remove pins, I clean the bottom of her feet with a washcloth. The skirt of my dress brushes the water but I can't find it in me to care. I don't plan on wearing this frock for much longer. "I can't believe you ran here without shoes."

"It was urgent. What's the risk of tetanus in the face of a love confession?"

I shake my head with a chuckle, reaching over her to pull the stopper from the tub, draining the water. I take her hand in mine, placing a kiss on her palm. I move my mouth up her arm until I reach that tattoo just above the crook of her elbow—the one she got on the day we met. Here, now, I finally let myself press my lips to it. I remember why she said she got the tattoo: for courage.

It takes all the courage I have to ask the question I do. "This isn't one of those courageous decisions you make that you immediately regret, right?" I look up at her with timid eyes.

"Of course not," she says instantly. "This, like moving to Scotland, is a courageous choice that I will never regret." She stands and pulls me up with her. "I'm in love with you," she says like a reminder.

With that one remaining worry I had now washed away like the street grime off her feet, I say seriously, "I'm going to need you naked so you can prove that."

I kiss her again, my fingers finding the zipper at the back of her dress. I undo the zipper, slide the straps off her shoulders, and let the dress pool at her feet. She kicks out of it. Beneath the dress, she wears a nude strapless bra and nude underwear. Quickly, she removes her bra, letting it fall to the ground with her dress.

"Strapless bras are the worst," she moans, her lips finding mine again.

With a hum of agreement, I pull back to admire her. Hair curled from the updo curves around her chest. My mouth practically watering, I realize that this is the first time I have seen her breasts. "Fuck," I swear. They're round and pert with sinful, pink nipples, standing tight and at attention.

Her hands are moving around my back, trying to locate my zipper. "What?"

"You have perfect tits." I use my fingers to gently trace around them before taking their slight weight in my hands.

"*You* have perfect tits," she argues back, making a small whine of frustration when she can't find my zipper.

"Naw, I have great tits, but yours, my love, actual perfection." I run a thumb over each of those rosy buds, letting Rachel suck in a sharp gasp. "Though, if you want to spend time comparing, I'm not wearing a bra under this dress."

"I am trying my hardest," she says before she finally locates the zipper on the side of my dress. I let it fall to the floor beside hers, stepping out. She eyes my bare chest hungrily. My mouth curves upward. "You want to put your mouth on these?"

"Yeah." Her tongue darts out to wet her lips.

"Patience." I pull her forward, pressing her flush against me, my tongue finding the inside of her mouth again. When I can manage a breath separate from hers, I drag her into the bedroom with me, unable to not note that while we have had sex twice before, neither time has been in a bed. Because of that, this feels…well, powerful. Real. All I've wanted with Rachel since we met was real, even if I couldn't admit it to myself. We're finally here. It's finally real.

Rachel pushes me down onto the bed with a gleam in her eyes. I prop myself up on my elbows. "I said I need you naked, love." She shakes her head with a laugh and bends over to remove her knickers so she is now completely bare before me.

"Happy?"

"Desperately," I answer, meaning it more than I ever thought I would. More than I ever thought I *could.*

She gets her fingers under the waistband of my underwear to pull them off, then climbs onto the bed and straddles my legs. "This is as patient as I can manage," she murmurs. "May I?"

Still propped up on my elbows, I say, "You can do anything you want to me."

Her hands find my breasts in an instant, thumbs brushing over both hard nipples before her hand chooses one to focus on. Her fingers pinch lightly below the piercing before twisting slightly to offer a wee bite of pain, my skin pebbling around her touch. With her loose hair pooling on my chest, she dips down, her mouth meeting my aching breast, tongue passing over the point. She sucks lightly, pulling a gasp from my lips, remembering how I liked this before.

I stroke her hair away from her forehead and make a request. "Sit on my face."

She freezes, her mouth floating over my chest as she looks up at me. "I've never been asked to do that before. How…how close do I sit?"

I grin, gently guiding her up my body. "I need you to suffocate me, love."

"Okay." She gets into position, pussy hovering over me, filling my nose with her sinful scent.

"Good girl," I mutter before grabbing her by the thighs to pull her fully down on my face, tongue taking its time to taste every sweet inch of her. I suck her clit into my mouth, tongue working over it as her wetness soaks my chin. She grinds on top of me, letting out soft whimpers I can barely hear with her thighs earmuffing me. As her legs start to tremble, I dig my fingers deeper into her skin, pulling her even nearer because I can tell she is close. I offer a featherlight scrape of my teeth to take her over the edge. She releases a cry, body still moving above me as she rides it out.

I'd be content to stay right here for the rest of the night—or my life, rather—but she struggles out, "Isla. Isla, I can't see you. I want to see you."

I offer one final stroke of my tongue in an attempt to lap her up before I let her quivering thighs set me free. She backs down my body with labored breath as her fingers trace over my face, still drowned in her arousal.

With her legs now on either side of my waist, she kisses me, tasting herself in my mouth. As her mouth stays on mine, her hand slides down my stomach, moving in between both our legs to find my clit. I gasp as her fingers press into me.

My own hand finds the center of her legs, still so satisfyingly wet for me, and it's not long before a deep whimper emanates from her against my mouth. She pulls away and we sit up together, moving to our knees. My lips find hers again while my hand stays in between her legs and her hand stays in between mine. I slip one finger inside her, soon following it with another. She mirrors my action. I *really* like this game.

My fingers press inside of her, deeper, palm working her clit. She follows suit. We moan into each other's mouths, sharing our gratification. Her inner walls clench around my fingers.

"Are you going to come for me again, my love?" I ask, my fingers curving inside.

She nods, unable to say anything. But her hand is speaking enough as she traces my g-spot and I beat her to it. I cry out in pleasure, soaking her fingers as she keeps her movement steady inside of me. I pull out of her and focus on her clit, finally pulling a gasp from her as she comes, head thrown back in bliss. When she's back on earth, she leans her head into my neck, breathing heavily.

"I need you," Rachel murmurs, grinding on my hand. "I need you."

"You have me, my love. You have me." I move on her hand, so close again already.

She pleads, "I need more of you. I feel like I can't get enough. I need to touch you. All of you. I need everything."

"I know what you need." I remove my hand to a whine of protest from Rachel.

I adjust myself so I am now sat on the bed, legs spread. I grab Rachel by the hips and position her in between my legs, then I have her swing one leg over my thigh, winding her other leg under my own so that we are fully interlocked. I stretch forward to kiss her on the lips. "Move with me."

The slick excitement between us makes the movements quick and fluid, sliding against one another. This is closer than we have ever been before, but I understand her desire to be closer and closer. I want to spend the rest of my days tangled up with her like this. My love. Finally, my love and I are here together on the same page, running at the same pace. I'm so glad I took my time with her because we are finally here. Finally home.

I keep one hand on Rachel's hip as we move. Her hand finds its way back to my aching breast, thumb circling the taut point. I bring her in for a quick kiss that is cut off by a moan. We move faster, building off one another, heat growing between us. Her pleasure pulses as she lets out a deep whimper, everything coming to surface. My release arrives quickly after hers as we lean into each other, bodies still interlocked and pressing close as we exchange hot, heavy breaths.

"I love you," I whisper.

"I love you," she says back.

...

I am awoken in the morning by lips on my cheek. I smile before I open my eyes to see Rachel hovering over me. As soon as my eyes are open, she presses a kiss to my lips and murmurs, "Morning."

"Morning," I say back, covering my mouth. "I haven't brushed my teeth yet."

"Well, I didn't expect you to brush them in your sleep," Rachel says, handing me a hot cup of coffee from off my nightstand.

"You on the other hand smell minty fresh. Did you steal my toothbrush, my love?"

"Gross, no," she says, taking a sip of tea as she still stands hovering over me. "Your flatmate gave me one of the extra, new ones you keep under your sink."

My eyebrows raise. "Aileen is here?"

"Yeah, she came in this morning while I was poking around your kitchen trying to find coffee. I am very glad I grabbed one of your T-shirts to put on because I almost went out there naked."

I grab my glasses from off the nightstand so I can better appreciate her wearing my shirt, the hem hitting just below her hips. Her legs are bare and surprisingly long for her short stature. I want to ask her to turn around because I know the base of her arse is poking out the bottom of that T-shirt, but I refrain from completely drooling over her. My voice thick with what I can only describe as lust, I ask, "Can we make a new rule?"

"Rule?"

"Yeah." I scan her again. "If you absolutely have to be wearing clothing, it better be mine."

A huge smile grows on her face. "Okay."

She's still standing over me, holding her mug with both hands, bouncing back and forth lightly between her feet.

"Why are you hovering, love? Get back in bed."

"Can't. I'm waiting for—" A ding goes off in the kitchen, interrupting her. "That." She sets her mug back down on my nightstand and pivots to leave my room, saying, "Be right back." I finally get that shot of her arse I was longing for.

Moments later, she comes in supporting two plates of toast, eggs, and sausages. She hands me one, then loops around the bed to sit beside me with her own plate.

I look down at the plate and then back up at her a few times before she asks, "What? I only know how to do scrambled. Every time I try to fry an egg, it ends up all rubbery and gross. And don't get me started on when I've tried to poach an egg."

"That's not it," I say quietly.

Her tone gentle, she asks, "Then what?"

"No one's ever made me breakfast in bed before."

"Really? I mean, me neither. Well, no. I guess my mom has. But that's different."

"A tad. I've been brought a cuppa or coffee before, but breakfast? Naw. Not even cereal or beans on toast."

"Beans on toast."

"Have you tried it yet?"

"I don't plan to."

"Why? It's so good."

"I'm not a beans person."

"Ugh. Americans," I say playfully. "But seriously. This is lovely. Thank you."

She shrugs like it was nothing. "I prefer it when you're nourished. Also, if vigorous sex is what it takes to get you to sleep for six or more hours, I am willing to keep that up." She takes a bite of her eggs. "Have you noticed that whenever someone in movies or books makes someone they've been romantically involved with breakfast in bed, it's always just for that person? Like, I need to eat too. Or are we supposed to assume they ate while cooking? Because that seems rude."

"It does seem rude."

I take a few bites. Damn, this is good. Then I lean over the side of the bed to set my plate on the floor. Rachel cocks her head, confused. She grows more confused when I take her plate as well. The confusion fades when I pounce, tackling her into the bed.

She giggles into my lips, saying, "The food will get cold."

"That's a risk I'm willing to take."

"Me too."

CHAPTER TWENTY-SEVEN
Rachel

Isla and I spend the rest of the day tangled up in each other. The rest of the weekend, to be more specific. Aileen only came back in the morning for clean clothes to bring back to her boyfriend's and was gone pretty quickly, so we had the place to ourselves. We could have gone back to my flat, I suppose, but even the ten-minute walk between our places seemed too long to be separated.

As is proven when she does eventually walk me back to my flat on Sunday evening and we have to pull over more than once, far too distracted by each other's lips to keep walking. We finally arrive at my door, meaning I should separate us, but our hands stay firmly interlocked.

"Are you sure you don't want to spend the night?" I ask, giving her my best puppy dog eyes.

She kisses me slowly, pressing me against the door before pulling away and saying, "Of course I want to spend the night, my love. But I need to meet Ben early in the morning to help with the move. And you need to sleep so your brain is at full strength tomorrow. If I stay the night, we will not be sleeping. Those microplastics aren't going to be researched on their own."

I puff out my lower lip. "I can control myself, you know."

"Aye, but I can't control myself around you." She gives me another kiss. "I'll see you in the afternoon, though. I'll pick you up from campus."

I sigh dramatically. "Fine. I'll miss you though."

"I'll miss you too."

I finally push my key into the door, but twist around to look at her before I turn the lock. "Isla?"

"Yes, my love?"

"Can I call you my girlfriend?"

She smiles softly. "Is that what you want to call me?"

"Very much so. I just…you said something once about breaking things off with one of your exes when it got too serious and I didn't know if you thought it was too soon to use the word 'girlfriend.'"

She takes my hands away from the door handle, holding them tightly. "Too soon? Far, far from too soon, my love. You can call me your girlfriend because I finally get to call you mine."

"Okay. Good."

"Good." She kisses me again before we separate, much to my dismay. I make it up to my flat alone. I miss her. Oh my god. If I knew that this is what being in love feels like, I might not have teased Nick and Piper so much.

No. I'll be honest. I would have teased them just as much. But I understand all the gooey words and feelings and looks and wow. I'm just as gooey as they are.

I am far too wired to sleep. In an attempt to ease my mind, I take a shower. While I am always a fan of a nice shower, my last two showers involved another person so this is boring.

As I apply lotion to my face after I get out, a thought occurs to me that makes me grin like a fool. I get to call Piper and tell her *everything*. I haven't talked to her or Nick all weekend. Though, while I wished I wouldn't have, I did check my phone often enough to make sure there were no urgent messages or calls from either of them. I did briefly speak to my mother this morning, as I always do on Sundays. When I let it slip that I had been at Isla's since Friday, she quickly let me go with a teasing laugh and the comment, "I *knew* she wasn't just a friend."

Being this far from my family, I don't think I'll ever be able to take a break from my phone for more than a couple of hours. It's okay. I'd rather know what's going on with them, good and bad, at all times.

I slip the shirt I took from Isla's place back on and take a seat at my table. Nick answers my FaceTime to Piper. "Hey. Piper's in the shower. We had somewhat of a jam mishap on our way home from the farmer's market and it got in her hair."

I'm happy to see my brother, but I can hardly hide my disappointment that my best friend isn't immediately available to talk to me. Knowing Piper, she would make a comment about how cute it was that we were showering at the same time across continents. I chuckle. "God, you two and your jam."

Nick grins, then squints. "You're smiley. What's up?"

"Nothing. Well, something. But I'd rather wait for Piper to get out of the shower. Though, I will tell you that I'm not moving to New Zealand."

His brow furrows. "Were you planning on moving? I know you applied to that program, but you didn't get in. Right?"

"I didn't, but then I was put on a waitlist. They told me I got in officially last week. But I decided against it. I'm happy here."

"I'm proud of you." With a serious look, he says, "You found a reason to stay somewhere, Rach. That's amazing."

"I've always had reasons to stay places, Nicky. You and Piper were a reason to stay in St. Louis."

He shakes his head. "Yeah, but staying in St. Louis would have been bad for you, just like leaving Edinburgh would be bad. I know you considered it though. What changed?"

My fingers move over the wood of my table. "I own a kitchen table here."

"A kitchen table?"

"Yeah."

He nods with understanding and says quietly, "Rachel and Isla sitting in a tree…"

"K-I-S-S-I-N-G!" Piper shouts from a distance. "We're singing! Rachel!" She pushes into frame, towel on her head and body wrapped in a dark green robe. "You were at Isla's place all weekend. I was tracking you."

"Of course you were. Yes, I was at my girlfriend's place all weekend."

Piper squeals so loudly that Nick rears back from the camera with a hearty chuckle.

"Girlfriend! You have a girlfriend! Oh my god! Do you love her? You love her!"

Nick comes back into the frame, pressing a kiss to Piper's temple. She beams wildly at him then looks back to me, wiggling in her seat as she waits for me to confirm.

"Yeah, yeah. I love her. She loves me. The whole shebang."

She squeals again. "Yay! This is so exciting. Nick, we have to go back to Edinburgh so we can meet Isla in person!"

"Okay, sweetheart."

She's still grinning widely. "Are you happy?"

I laugh. "Yeah, babe. I am so, so happy."

Now she's crying. Oh my god.

Through sniffles she says, "I'm so happy you're happy. I want to hug you. Can you give me Isla's number? Or David's?"

"Why?"

"So that whenever I want to hug you, they can do it for me."

"Piper, you are ridiculous in the best way, as always," I say with a light laugh.

"How else am I supposed to react to such a great life update?!" She settles back into the couch, handing the phone to Nick to hold. He leans back next to her.

"Speaking of updates," Nick says, "Dad is still doing fine. Has a check-up tomorrow and yes, I will let you know how it goes."

Relief fills my chest because I didn't have to ask. "Thanks," I say genuinely.

Piper snatches the phone back and says, "Nick, I love you, but go away. I need to ask Rachel questions she won't want to answer in front of you."

"I have a feeling I won't want to know the answer to those questions." He kisses Piper on the temple again, and says, "Bye, Rach."

I laugh out a, "Bye," watching Piper as she waits for Nick to be out of the vicinity.

She turns back to me and says, "I was serious about wanting Isla's number. I need it for hug requests and to send vaguely threatening texts."

"You are not allowed to threaten my girlfriend."

She holds her thumb and pointer finger a centimeter apart in front of the screen. "Only little threats, I swear. Standard 'take care of her or you'll have me to deal with' stuff."

"Uh-huh." I look at her seriously. "She wants you to like her. You make her nervous."

She bounces in her seat. "Do I?"

"Yes."

She bites the corner of her lip. "I like her. Really. Especially because I can tell how much she loves you, even from our minuscule virtual interactions."

"Good."

"So, how many fingers did she put inside of you?"

I cover my face. "Oh, good lord."

"What?! It's an important question!" She cackles as she continues to ask extremely inappropriate things.

We keep talking until I yawn one too many times and Piper tells me to go to bed. I protest for a bit, but I really am so tired. We hang up, exchanging I love yous and promises to talk tomorrows, and soon I am crawling into my bed, feeling lonely without my girlfriend on the pillow beside me. However, that feeling doesn't last for long because I soon rush into a much-needed sleep.

•••

In the morning, Dr. Andonov and I go to a local beach to collect samples. Now that it is nearing the start of term, I'll have some actual courses to take, so we both feel the need to get as many samples as we can now so I can continue to focus on my research as well as coursework that will inevitably be overwhelming.

On a boat in the middle of the lake, using a device to collect sand from the bottom, Dr. Andonov asks casually, "Forgive me for prying, but the woman you took to the gala, is she a friend, or…?"

I beam as I focus on pulling the device up, now filled with sand. "She's my girlfriend."

Dr. Andonov smiles. "That's nice to hear. I'm glad you grew your circle outside of me and Professor Zgheib."

I laugh. "Well, Isla wouldn't give me the choice not to. I'm grateful for her. Immensely." I gnaw my lip and admit, "Though, my initial reservations about getting into a relationship are still lingering in the back of my mind. I love her, but I know my coursework is going to keep me so busy. I'm afraid I won't be able to offer her the time and attention she deserves." I cringe. "Sorry, that's too personal. You don't care."

Dr. Andonov shakes their head. "I disagree. I do very much care, Rachel." They purse their lips. "I understand your reservations, but I believe if you make an active effort to have space for your girlfriend and your studies, you'll be alright. Getting your Ph.D. is a full-time job, but many people manage to have both demanding full-time careers and healthy relationships." They gather up some sand on their end. "I met my now husband during my second year of my Ph.D. studies. It was tough sometimes, but that is the nature of an adult relationship."

I nod, taking their words to heart. "Thanks. Yeah. I needed to hear that."

"If you ever find yourself getting overwhelmed with work, that is what both me and Zgheib are here for—even if you just need to talk something through."

"I appreciate that." I laugh, mostly to myself. Dr. Andonov doesn't question it. It's unbelievable how quickly I have managed to build a community here. It came upon me suddenly, even though it has surrounded me practically since I arrived in Edinburgh. Perhaps my gut feeling wasn't wrong after all. Perhaps it was perfectly correct.

Gut feelings seem to be working out for me lately. Heriot-Watt. Edinburgh. Isla. I knew they were all right for me, but I let doubt consume me and get in the way, tricking me into believing my gut feelings were wrong. They were right. Gut feelings for the win.

CHAPTER TWENTY-EIGHT

Isla

I pull into a spot in front of Ben's flat in Newtonmore and turn off my car. As I unbuckle my seatbelt, I glance down at my phone to see Rachel has responded to my good morning text with one of her own and a heart. My chest lurches at the sight of her name on my phone, feeling in perfect bliss with her.

I go to open the door of my car but pause when I spot a very familiar vehicle in the car park. I text Ben.

Is mum here??

No??

I huff a sigh of relief.

There's a car parked outside your flat that looks just like hers

I shake my head, feeling ridiculous. I'm so paranoid about my mum—it's sad, really. I exit my car, aiming to walk up the pathway to Ben's flat when I hear my name called. My shoulders slump. Not so paranoid after all.

I turn around to see my mum rushing up to me, holding a drink tray with three cups of coffee in her hands like a tribute.

"Isla," she says again, as though I may not have heard her the first time.

"Mum," I say back, body going stiff.

As she stops a few feet from me, I cross my arms, involuntarily angling myself back and away from her. She holds out the tray of coffee, indicating for me to take one of the cups.

My arms stay crossed. "What are you doing here?" I ask.

She pulls the tray back, holding it close to her chest. "Ben mentioned you were helping him move. I…I was hoping to see you"—she swallows—"to apologize for the last time we saw each other."

I raise an eyebrow but don't say anything. Saying you want to apologize is not the same as an apology. She needs to say it.

She gets the message, because as the heavy silence between us thickens, she says, "I'm sorry. I'm sorry for the way I spoke to you and I am sorry for not respecting your identity. Your sexuality. But in my defense, your generation seems to be attracted to everyone, so I genuinely thought you may be interested in the man I brought up."

I resist the urge to roll my eyes. She was so close, but had to add that last sentence. "I'm a lesbian, Mum. I only like women."

"I know, darling. I'm sorry. I know and I accept that."

"And it's not that my generation is attracted to 'everyone,' it's that my generation gets to live in a more accepting society. We feel more able to accept ourselves, so queer people are freer to be open with who they love. My generation is not queerer than yours, we just have the ability to be more open about it."

"You're right. I'm sorry." She holds out the coffee again and this time I take one of the cups. It'll get cold if I don't take it. "I'm also sorry for overstepping with the café. I…I truly want to help. Not in exchange for anything in return. I don't need to offer money if you won't take it. I'm happy to offer assistance even in blind support."

I blink slowly at her, waiting for her to say something to ruin what she just said. She always does. But this time, she doesn't.

"Thanks," I say finally. I squint at her then, asking something I've been wondering since she called my name. "Why now? I don't get why you're apologizing. What happened at breakfast has happened before. Many times."

Her head hangs and she has the grace to look ashamed. "Josie called me. Really had a go at me. Called me a terrible mother."

I feel guiltily giddy. "She called you a terrible mother? To your face?"

"Not in those exact words, but I heard what she meant. She was right. I get so caught up in what other people think and…and how I feel that I forget that what other people think doesn't matter and how I feel shouldn't matter as long as my children are happy."

Huh. "Well, I appreciate that. Though I have to say, it's fucked up that Josie had to be the one to get that in your head. Ben and I have expressed similar sentiments over the years."

She still looks ashamed. Good. "Ben also said something to me."

My eyebrows raise. "He did?"

She nods. "At the café. After you left. He had a go at me as well. He said…he said that it's my fault you think no one can love you without cause."

My throat is tight all of a sudden. I manage to get out, "He's right." I shake my head. "It's not all your fault. Other people…Kenna…It's something I need to work on. Something I have been working on." I add in my head, *something Rachel has been helping me work on.* Her loving me the way she does isn't a cure-all, but it doesn't hurt.

She nods. "You are completely worthy of love. Both of you are. I'm sorry for ever making you feel different. I'll be better."

I don't believe her, but I'm open to giving her the chance to prove me wrong. "Thanks," I say again. Then in an effort to extend an olive branch, I say, "Speaking of me being a lesbian, I have a girlfriend."

Mum's eyes brighten. "Do you? What's her name?"

I smile because I can't help it. "Rachel. She's a Ph.D. candidate at Heriot-Watt."

"Ah, so she's a genius then. Good for you." She purses her lips. "Can I see a picture?"

I nod. "Sure." I pull out my phone, catching a text from Ben that I missed.

Be cautious. That may be Mum then

Too late for that. I go to my photos to find one that David took of Rachel and me at the gala, and hand my phone to Mum.

She smiles down at the photo. "You look beautiful. She's gorgeous as well." She hands the phone back to me. "I hope I can meet her someday."

There's a small twitch in my heart. "I hope you can too."

At that moment, Ben exits the front door of his flat and says, "I can smell the coffee you're letting turn cold." He walks up to us and snatches one of the cups still in Mum's tray. Twisting around, he says, "Now that you're here, Mum, you may as well offer a hand."

As a family, eventually including my dad, we spend the next few hours packing up the last of Ben's things and loading them into the van he rented. Once the van is loaded up, Ben slides into the driver's seat and I follow him in my car back to Edinburgh.

He'll retrieve his car later in the week. Mum and Dad do not come with us to Edinburgh, but that's okay. Mum tried today and hopefully that means she'll keep trying.

David is waiting for us when we get to Ben's new flat two hours later. Ben practically leaps into his arms as he gets out of the van saying, "Thanks for helping."

David hugs him back. "Of course, man. What are friends for?"

As we unload the boxes, we chat about the café. We applied to let the space and are still waiting on approval, but the agent expressed that there should be no problem securing it. Ben has made a long list of suppliers and has already contacted a few. I hate to say that I'm surprised by how into this he's getting. Once he decided he was in, he went all in. I've already spoken to vendors about a sign for our café and have been looking into purchasing tables, chairs, and whatever other furniture we might need. We have a meeting with the bank tomorrow about our loan.

It's happening. I can't believe it's all happening.

With only a short break for a late lunch, we spend the rest of the day helping Ben unpack. A bit before five o'clock, I say, "I've got to go pick up my girlfriend. But I'll see you tonight?"

"Girlfriend?" Ben calls after me as I rush to my car.

I cackle wildly but don't bother to respond.

...

Hi! It's Piper Greenway (Rachel's friend). She gave me your number. I hope that's okay. I wanted to say thank you. Thank you for being there when I can't be. Thank you for helping her build a home. Thank you for loving her

Also, her birthday is in November so I'm here if you want to brainstorm ideas

I wanted to fly to Scotland to surprise her but Nick said that was excessive since she'll be home at Christmas (with you???). I haven't decided if I agree or not

Well, there you have it: Piper likes me well enough. A weight I didn't know was on me lifts. After I reply, I stand in the doorway of my bedroom, gazing down upon my beautiful, naked girlfriend lying in the sheets we tangled up together as she watches videos on her phone.

"You're staring at me," she says without looking up.

"Damn right," I respond. I push myself off the door frame and begrudgingly pull on clothes, hating that I need to get dressed at all, but I have a gig tonight. "You want to come?"

She tosses her phone to the side. "Yes, please."

We both finish getting dressed, then walk together to the pub hand in hand. The way it's supposed to be. Ben and David are at the pub when we get there.

Ben looks pointedly at my and Rachel's still linked hands. "There's been some development, I see."

I pull Rachel's hand to my mouth and kiss it. "Lots of sexy ones. Ben, this is my girlfriend, Rachel."

Ben rolls his eyes but smiles. "How do you do?"

Rachel beams back. "Very good." She unlinks our hands, kisses me on the cheek, and says, "Go on! I want to hear you sing," before she takes a seat at the table with Ben and David.

From behind the microphone, I say, "Hello, hello. I'll be starting my set with a song I wrote myself. It's dedicated to my muse, who would hate to be singled out, but she is somewhere in this room."

Her face goes red, but her eyes never leave mine. They stay with me as I strum my guitar in that familiar melody and sing her song to her, as I should have the first time I sang it.

Afterward, I launch into my regular set, watching my girlfriend the entire time. She's watching me too. She's engaging with David and Ben, but when she speaks to them she hardly glances their way. When I finish up my set, I retrieve my always-promised free drink from the bar, then join them at the table.

"That was beautiful," Rachel whispers in my ear after I sit.

In thanks, I kiss her. I take her hand in mine, my thumb tracing lightly over hers. My tongue slips into her mouth, almost involuntarily. I pull away, but only a fraction as my eyes stay on hers and we continue to share our space.

Ben elbows David and loudly proclaims, "I think we should leave them alone."

David laughs. "Yeah, perhaps we should." He swallows the last of his drink. "I've got to get to Callum's anyway."

Ben's expression droops a bit before he picks it back up. "Do you?"

David nods, standing up and pulling on his jacket. "Yeah, but I'll come over tomorrow morning to help you unpack some more if you want."

"Thanks. Uh, can I talk to you before we split off?"

David's face softens. "Of course."

"'Night, guys," David says to Rachel and me.

"Yeah, 'night," Ben says, hardly looking at us.

We both watch them leave.

Rachel's hand squeezes mine. "That was weird, right?"

"Yeah. That was weird."

I can see David and Ben through the warped window of the pub. Rachel and I watch them in silence as they talk, saying words we can't hear. Ben grabs David by the shoulders as he says something emphatically. David stands there, still for a moment, before he says something with a slight shake of his head. Ben's hands drop. He nods once, and then walks away.

Rachel and I look at each other before our focus goes back to David. He stands there, dumbstruck, as he watches Ben depart.

Rachel sucks in a sharp breath. "Should we…?"

"Yeah," I say.

We get up and exit the pub. As we approach David, and Ben shifts into a spec in the distance, I text Ben asking if he's alright. Rachel puts a hand on David's arm and he jumps, surprised by our sudden presence.

"Are you okay?" she asks.

"Yeah," he says. He clears his throat. "Yeah. Sorry. Uh, Ben and I…had an argument. Or, well, no. Not an argument. A disagreement."

"A disagreement?"

"Yeah. Yeah." He shakes his head like he's trying to shake himself back to reality. "I have to go. I have to get to Callum's."

"Okay," Rachel says. "Call or text if you need me."

"Of course." He stretches down to hug her. He offers me one next. Then he walks away.

Rachel and I head back into the pub, sliding back into our seats at the table. "What kind of disagreement do you think they had?" she asks.

Ben has not responded to my text. "Who knows? Ben can be dramatic. I'm sure it was nothing. We once got into a huge argument about a cheese toasty. Like our mum was making them and he wanted his first, but she gave it to me. He stormed away then too. He was twenty-one when this happened, by the way."

She chews her lip. "Yeah, I'm sure they're fine then. They

don't seem like they fight a lot."

"As far as I'm aware, they never do."

"And, well, he asked me not to tell you but…no, sorry. I promised I wouldn't say anything."

"Come on, love. You can't lead me on like that."

A sigh escapes her nose. "A little over a week ago I found Ben sitting on the ground on a random side street. He was upset. Frustrated, he said, but wouldn't tell me why. He asked me not to tell you or David, but now this has happened and I'm worried."

That is odd. I have to ask, "Was he drunk?"

"Maybe a little."

"He's a sad drunk. I'm sure that's all." I make a mental note to check in with him more. Something else has to be going on.

Ben finally responds to my text.

> I'm fine. No biggie. I was being dramatic. You know me, I love a grand exit

I show the message to Rachel. "See, there we are." I'm still worried about him, but if that's all he's going to offer me tonight, this is all I can do.

"Good. You were right." Her eyes find focus in mine. "I love it when you sing."

"I'll sing to you whenever you want."

"I'll hold you to that."

We keep drinking our drinks and chatting, hands staying interlocked the entire time. When I finish my drink, I say, "I have an experiment to propose."

"An experiment? Do tell."

"Yes, I think we should head back to yours and conduct an in-depth experiment of whose bed is better."

Her teeth sink into her lower lip. "Oh yeah? I assume that experiment will take many trials." She weighs her head. "We may have to test some other locations so we can establish a baseline."

"I believe we can succeed in that."

She kisses me softly. "Then let the trials begin."

Rachel

I knock twice on the glass-pained front door of Isla's café, Somewhere Special. Through the window, I watch her jog over to unlock it. She pulls me through the open door and presses a hard kiss to my mouth before saying, "Doctor Moreau, it's lovely to see you."

I laugh. "I still have another year before you can call me that." She pouts. "But I love calling you that. Not sure I can wait until it's official."

"Fine, but you're only allowed to call me that when we're alone. You take your meds this morning?" She likes it when I remind her because she is awful about remembering her anxiety medication.

"Shite, no. Thank you." She heads back behind the counter to dig them out of her bag, tossing them in her mouth and taking a gulp of water. Then she starts messing with the register. "I'll be done in a tick."

"Take your time," I say, turning around to examine myself in the reflection of the window to see if she got any lipstick on me.

She did, but just a bit on my lips, so I'll let it stay. I pull a chair off one table, then take a seat.

It's about six o'clock in the morning, the café set to open in an hour. Isla and Ben have both been here since 5 a.m.

Speaking of Ben, he bursts through the door to the kitchen, full of typical dramatics. "Ah, Rachel. Just the bisexual I was looking for. I have a question."

Isla hands me a takeaway cup of tea as I ask, "What?"

"Now, the ring thing, is that a requirement?"

I narrow my eyes. "Well, women who identified as lesbians would wear thumb rings as a signal, historically. Now, I know a lot of queer people do wear a lot of rings, and some do use it as a signal of sorts. But no, it's far from a 'requirement.' The only requirement of queerness is identifying as such." I set my tea on the table and hold up my hands to show him my naked fingers. "I don't wear rings."

He sighs. "I know. Not even one, which I find appalling." He throws his eyes toward Isla and says, "Hint. Hint."

She throws a balled-up napkin at him. "Go back to the kitchen, you tyrant."

He cackles as he pushes back through the kitchen door. I take a sip of my tea to hide my smile. Isla and I have discussed marriage, especially after Nick and Piper's wedding (and because it may be the only legal way to keep me in the country), but both agree it would be best to wait until I have my Ph.D. and her café is earning a profit. It'll happen one day, no need to rush it. We can take our time.

Isla yells after him, "Are you sure you'll be fine without me today?"

"Yes! Please, leave!" he yells back.

Isla and I have plans today so Ben will be running the café on his own. It's not the first time he has done so, so Isla does know it'll be fine. Isla pours a cup of coffee, then directs her attention back to me. "Ready, my love?"

"Ready," I confirm.

I follow her out the door and interlace my fingers with hers as we walk down the street. "So, rings."

Isla's hand tightens in mine. "What about them?"

"Well, I know we talked about the finger kind already, but you know what kind we haven't talked about?"

Isla regards me with a furrowed brow. "Neither of us has the appendage for that kind of ring."

I snicker. "No! God, no. I meant key rings."

"Key rings?"

"Yeah. Key rings. For a flat. A flat that we both live in."

"As flatmates?" She smiles.

"The kind who are in love with each other, yes."

Her thumb traces over mine. "Are you asking me to move in with you?"

"Yes, I am."

She stops us in the street and throws her arms around me, a little coffee splashing out of her cup. "Yes! Oh, my love, yes, I would love to move in with you!"

I laugh as I hug her back, more careful with my drink. "Yay! I can't wait." I really can't. The idea of waking up with her in my bed every single day is more than I could ever ask for.

"I can start bringing bags to yours tonight."

"Like half of your stuff isn't already at my place."

We start walking again, hands finding each other as they should. "Well, now all of it will be at your place."

"*Our* place."

We finally make it to our destination, Isla's car.

"Can I drive?" I ask, knowing the answer.

"You don't know the way," she says, opening the passenger door for me. I slide in as she runs around to the driver's side, hopping in the seat.

"I never get to drive," I whine. "I love driving."

"You can drive on the way back."

I smile, satisfied. "Yay, okay."

"Now, fasten your seatbelt, my love. We're in for an adventure."

Isla

As we near Glencoe, I start to get antsy. I've been talking this place up for two years now, so I hope it'll live up to expectations. I find the car park and secure a spot. We're here early enough that it has yet to overcrowd, but this particular location has found its fame on the internet, so it won't be long before it's overrun.

I'm taking Rachel to the Fairy Bridge of Glen Creran. It's a spot I first mentioned on the drive we did through the Highlands, just a couple weeks into our friendship that was always meant to be more. And now it is more. We're going to be flatmates. *Roommates*, as the historians will say.

She is my best friend, my greatest love, and my forever person. I couldn't ask for even an ounce more in this life.

We get out of the car and I lace my fingers through hers, leading her down the path toward the bridge. The grass is tall and the air is full of midges, so we both have on long pants and long sleeves, lucky the morning has a deep chill so we don't overheat. This is Scotland, after all.

Finally, we come to the spot and Rachel stops in her tracks.

"It's beautiful," she whispers. The bridge is made of stones, piled together to create an archway (or a doorway) over the clear, rocky stream. Bright green moss grows in the gaps and lush greenery and flowers find their place at the top and on the sides.

"It is," I agree. I look around, finding that we are somehow alone in this spot, even if it won't last for long. The universe is on my side consistently, isn't she? "To earn our blessing, we need to cross over the bridge, but it is kind to say hello to the wee folk before tromping about atop it."

Rachel glances at me before bowing her head and saying in all seriousness, "Hello. Thank you for allowing us to visit you. We're going to cross your bridge today."

The wee folk don't respond. Though, perhaps they do. Their voices can be made out in the small waterfall creating the flowing stream, the powerful gusts in the trees, or even the swarming midges.

"Hiya," I add artfully.

Hand in hand, we cross the bridge. On the other side, Rachel looks longingly at the water.

I squeeze her hand. "Do you want to take a sample?"

"Am I allowed to?"

"Yes, you are. Visitors normally take the water for medicinal benefits, but there's nothing wrong with taking it for research."

Together, we awkwardly make our way to the water level, ensuring to be careful and not slip on the wet rocks. Rachel squats down by the water, pulling a couple of test tubes from her backpack.

Softly, she says, "I'm going to take some water and test it for microplastics." At first, I think she's talking to me, but as she says the next bit, I realize she is speaking to the fairies. "Hopefully I don't find much. I want you guys to have clean water."

She always puts her whole heart into things. It's one of the things I love most about her, though that is a very long list.

She takes her samples then secures them in her bag and stands up straight. I stick a hand in the water just to say that I've touched it. Also, I got a papercut this morning I'm hoping it'll heal. Then, I stand with her. I slip my arm around her waist and stare at the mystical bridge with her at my side.

"You sure do know how to show a girl a good time," she says. "You should be a tour guide."

"Don't know about that," I say. "Though, I do have the whole day-long date thing down to a science. Maybe I should keep doing that. This'll be a you-exclusive deal, of course."

"My own private tour guide? I'll take it. She's pretty hot."

I laugh. "You're not too bad yourself, my love."

"Hmm," she muses. "'Not too bad.'"

"Most beautiful, gorgeous, smartest, funniest, kindest woman in the entire world," I correct.

"Much better."

She angles her head up to kiss me. I meet her mouth with mine and thank the universe for sending me her over and over again.

ACKNOWLEDGMENTS

Writing the acknowledgments section of my books is always so wild to me because for whatever reason, here is where I feel like the biggest imposter. Who am I to act like a real author and write this little letter at the end of my book that my mother and a few friends will read, and other readers may take a glance at? (If you are a reader who found this book and decided to read this section, hello! Happy to have you here and thank you for giving *Down to a Science* a chance, whether it was a 5-star or 1-star book for you. I truly, madly, deeply appreciate it.)

This is the section where a trad author would thank their agent, their in-house editor, perhaps the marketing team, the publicity team, the art team, maybe even the production team. But alas, that is not something I can do. I don't have a huge team of people to thank, which is why I always start off feeling silly when I go to write this.

Of course, you know this so I suppose I should know it as well: this is my second book. I *am* a real author. I am an indie author who, obviously, did not get here alone. I may not have a *huge* team behind me, but I do still have a team. So, let's get to it, shall we?

Also, fun fact, this is *my* acknowledgments section, so I can do whatever I want.

It has been less than a year since my first book came out, yet so much in my life has changed, much of it not for the better. I used to live with two roommates and two cats, but now I am down to one roommate and no cats. My best friend no longer lives in the same city as me. My grandfather passed away in November. I now live in a new (overpriced) apartment and have a new office (with a window), but I am unsure of how long either of those will last because I am still struggling to solidify my place in this city and in my own life. This, of course, has nothing to do with writing, but I felt the need to add it, because, with all these stresses added to my life, I still wrote the damn book.

I wrote the damn book where half of it is supposed to be in a Scottish accent. How did that come through? Okay? Cringy? I don't want to know. I tried to have the voices of Merida, Karen Gillan, and a random Scottish tiktoker in my head while writing and editing, but I'm sure my overt American-ness is still there. Eh, I tried. (Also, that song? I was hoping my beta readers would tell me it was awful, but they did not, so maybe it's not too bad. No matter what, I like the meaning of it.)

And now to the part where I actually start to thank people.

First of all, I'll start with the simple and obvious. I would like to extend a thank you to my cover designer Katie Pridige. Once again, you have created an absolutely beautiful cover and I am so thrilled to have this one on the first go around for this book! I am excited to work with you again on the cover for the yet-to-be-named book three.

Well, book three is named, but no one knows that yet. I'll throw in a teaser for the hell of it. Who is reading this? The initials are SIAT (unless I get a wild whim and change it).

Next, I would like to extend the biggest thank you to my beta readers. I had reached out to four (4) people and unfortunately only one of those original four got back to me (Melisa, thank you, thank you. You were the one I had no doubts about, so thank you for proving me right). Two others did eventually reach out after my requested due date to tell me they would not be finishing the book, and a third ghosted me entirely. Now, to be clear, this is not me complaining about that because everyone has things come up in their life that they can't control, and not every book is for every person. I get it.

My point in bringing this up is that this experience made me think this book was terrible. I knew it needed work, but that's *why* we use beta readers: to learn what can be done to help our stories. I sent it to four people, and it was so horribly unreadable (my words) that three of my beta readers were unable to complete it? I felt like a failure who should just pack it up and give up. It made me feel so low and so crushed.

Thus, the panic set in. I posted to Instagram close friends' stories about it because I was so stressed and unsure of what to do, and the indie author community had my back, through and through. So, this thank you is to everyone who offered to beta read for me after my panic post (because so many of you did!). And thank you to Yasmin, Paige, and Layna for reading so quickly and offering feedback. Layna especially, you gave me so much to think about and this story would not be where it is today without your helpful and insightful comments.

And, moving on from that sob story.

Next thank you is to my mother, always for your support and for being the person I can come to with any complaints or stresses, joys or excitements. You are my number one fan (even if Molly, Melissa, Renee, and Aunt Lori's book club are trying to beat you at that). Again, I warned you off the spicy chapters (17, 22, 26), but I know you read them anyway. I love you and am so thankful for you every day.

Of course, I cannot write this without thanking my roommate, Mikaela. Thank you for reading my book. You are the friend I can count on to read my writing without prodding. I promise I will always read yours.

My next thank you goes to my ARC readers. It amazed me with *Bumps in the Road* and it amazes me this time that people want to read my book. You all give me confidence and so much joy. I am ever thankful for you and hope you keep an eye out for sign-ups for book three (SIAT), so we can all find out what the hell happened between Ben and David (I mean, I know, but you don't, and I figure you want to? IDK. I have a feeling this book may not go the way some people are expecting).

I also want to throw in a thank you to the people who work at the facilities printing my books. I know digital/POD printing is not quite as hands-on as offset printing is, but there are still people behind it, so thank you!

Lastly, this feels extremely self-centered, but I want to thank myself. I am not going to sit here and rave about how talented I am or whatever, but I do want to give myself a pat on the back. I wrote [another] book. I edited another book. And proofread it! I've read this book about seven thousand times and am still not sick of it, so that has to say something about its enjoyability, right? I also formatted both the paperback and the e-book. (Though I am glad I gave myself the break of designing the cover this time. I mean, I did have a cover ready to go, but we all know that Katie's covers are better than the silly little ones I make in Canva.)

Publishing a book is so much work. I am so tired (because I am also marketing the hell out of it while having a full-time job and trying to live off a single income in New York City. And maintain something close to a social life). But it's all worth it because, by the end of this process, I came out with something I am so immensely proud of. Something I hope will give other people at least a fraction of the joy it brings me.

So, thank you to my readers. Thank you to my supporters. Thank you to my friends. Thank you to my family. Thank you to my parents' entire neighborhood and random family friends who have now read probably their first spicy sapphic romcom. You're welcome. You should read more spicy sapphic romcoms.

It's rough out there, y'all, so have a drink (coffee, tea, wine, beer, hard liquor) on me (figuratively. You're actually the ones paying me by reading this book). I hope to see you soon.

ABOUT THE AUTHOR

Kat Paige is a writer of romance books with humor, heart, and a touch of spice. She lives in New York City with a roommate who is more like family and an abundance of personified succulents. When she's not writing, she's probably reading, baking, going to Broadway musicals, or watching TV shows she will inevitably get too emotionally invested in.

RACHEL & ISLA'S PLAYLIST

Cloud 9 - *BEACH BUNNY*
Talk too Much - *RENEÉ RAPP*
A Night to Remember - *GIRL IN RED*
Big Love Ahead - *MON ROVÎA*
She's Pretty - *BETH MCCARTHY*
Stuck in the Middle With You - *STEALERS WHEEL*
LUNCH - *BILLIE EILISH*
IDK How To Talk To Girls - *BETH MCCARTHY*
Edge of the Earth - *THE BEACHES*
I'm Gonna Be (500 Miles) - *THE PROCLAIMERS*
Blondie - *TALON*
Red Wine Supernova - *CHAPPELL ROAN*
Girl - *76TH STREET*
Perfume - *PALE WAVES*
You Are so Gentle with Me - *ELLA LUNA*
ink - *JULIA CAMPBELL*
Home - *EDWARD SHARP & THE MAGNETIC ZEROS*
Human - *DODIE, TOM WALKER*
Come On Eileen - *DEXYS MIDNIGHT RUNNERS*
Lady Lady - *MOLLY GRACE*
Morning Pages - *THE JAPANESE HOUSE, MUNA*
Swim Until You Can't See Land - *FRIGHTENED RABBIT*
Touch The Sky - *JULIE FOWLIS*
space girl - *FRANCIS FOREVER*
There She Goes - *THE LA'S*
Cheerleader - *LIZA ANNE*
Disco - *SURF CURSE*
Slow It Down - *AMY MACDONALD*